The
Perfect
Son

a novel by

FREIDA MCFADDEN

The Perfect Son

ISBN: 9798635011362

To Libby and Melanie (as always)

Chapter 1

Transcript of police interview with Erika Cass:

"Can you please tell us what happened, Mrs. Cass?"

"Am I under arrest?"

"Why do you ask that?"

"I know what you found. I know what you must be thinking."

"What do you think we found, Mrs. Cass?"

"A... a dead body."

"And can you explain how this happened?"

"I..."

"Mrs. Cass?"

"Am I under arrest? Please just tell me."

"At this time, no, you are not under arrest. But obviously, we need to know what happened."

"He was... stabbed to death."

"And who did it?"

"..."

"Mrs. Cass?"

"*I* did it. I killed him, Detective. And I would do it again."

Chapter 2

About one week earlier

ERIKA

You're not supposed to have a favorite child.

If you ask most mothers, they'll say something along the lines of "Sammy is really smart, but Nicole has a great heart." They refuse to choose. And some of them are sincere. Some mothers genuinely love both their children equally.

Others, like me, are lying through their teeth.

"Good morning!" I say as my fourteen-year-old daughter Hannah pads into the kitchen. She's in her bare feet and an old pair of gym shorts, and her reddish brown hair in disarray around her face. She's supposed to be dressed and ready for school, but clearly she's not. She always waits until the last possible second to get ready. She likes to keep me in suspense over whether or not she's going to make the school bus. But I've learned from experience that nagging her doesn't help at all—in fact, it only seems to slow her down—so I turn back to the eggs I'm scrambling in a frying pan.

"Mom!" Hannah can't seem to say that word anymore without the whiny edge to her voice that draws the word out for at least two syllables. *Mo-om.* I remember how happy I was the first time she said "mama." I shake my head at my old naïve self. "Why do you have to say it like that?"

"Say it like what? I just said 'Good morning.'"

"Right." Hannah groans. "Like that."

"Like what?"

"Like… oh my God, you know what I mean."

"I really don't, Hannah."

"You say it like… I don't know. Just don't say it like that."

I'm not sure how to respond, so I focus my attention back on the eggs. I pride myself in making really fantastic eggs. It's one of my superpowers. My eggs are so good that when one of Hannah's friends ate them on the morning after a sleepover, she said that I should be the lunch lady at their school. It was the highest compliment.

Hannah yawns loudly and scratches at the rat's nest on her head. "What's for breakfast?"

I ignore the irony: if I asked Hannah what she was

making for breakfast while she was very clearly in the middle of cooking eggs, she would have a meltdown. "I'm making eggs."

"*Eggs*? I *hate* eggs."

"What are you talking about? I thought eggs are your favorite breakfast."

"Yeah. When I was, like, eight years old."

I put down the spatula I've been using to slowly stir the eggs. That's the trick to making good eggs. Cook them low and slow. "I made them for you this weekend and you ate them up."

"Yeah, but that doesn't mean they're my *favorite*. God, Mom."

I don't know what to say to that. It seems like lately, every conversation I have with my daughter is an exercise in trying not to say something really mean back to her. I close my eyes and repeat my mantra to myself: *I am the adult. This is just a phase.*

After fourteen years, it's harder to convince myself it's all just a phase.

"What else is for breakfast?" Hannah asks, even though she is two feet away from the refrigerator and three feet away from the pantry.

"Frozen waffles?"

"Yuck." She sticks out her tongue. "What else?"

"You can make yourself some cold cereal."

"What kind of cereal do we have?"

I sigh. "I don't know, Hannah. Go look in the pantry."

She lets out a grunt as she stands up that would make you think she is ninety years old rather than a high school freshman. She limps over to the pantry and studies the boxes of cereal intently.

While Hannah contemplates the cereal selection, my son, Liam, joins us in the kitchen. Unlike his sister, Liam is fully dressed in what is a surprisingly nice blue button-down shirt and khaki slacks. I bought a new wardrobe for him over the summer when he shot up four inches and all his old clothes looked comically short. He recently turned sixteen, which means he went to the DMV last month with my husband to get his learner's permit to drive. I had thought my son getting his learner's permit would fill me with terror, but I'm oddly calm about the whole thing. Liam will be a good driver. He'll be careful, he'll pay close attention to the road, and he'll never drink and drive. I'm certain of that much.

That's not why I'm worried about him driving.

"Eggs. I love eggs. Thanks, mom!"

Liam's lips spread into an appreciative smile. He was always an attractive kid, but in the last couple of years, he's grown downright handsome. We were out at a restaurant as a family last weekend, and I caught a woman who was in her twenties giving him a second look. A full grown adult was checking him out! There is something about his thick dark hair and chocolate-colored eyes that almost twinkle when he smiles. Unlike Hannah, Liam never needed braces, and his smile reveals a row of perfectly straight, white teeth.

According to my mother, Liam looks very much the way my father did when he was young. My father died when I was a child and I barely remember him, but I've seen pictures, and I agree the resemblance is uncanny. I keep one of those photos in a drawer by my bed, and lately, every time I look at it, I get a pang in my chest. It was hard enough knowing my dad never got to see me grow up, and it's another sting to know he'll never meet the grandson who looks just like him.

Hannah pulls a box of Cheerios out of the pantry and studies the label, her nose crinkling.

"What's in Cheerios?" she asks me.

"Poison."

"Mom!" That was at least four syllables right there. *M-o-o-om*. "You *know* I'm trying to lose weight and be healthy. Don't you want me to be healthy?"

Hannah has always been a little on the chubby side. I think she looks cute, but in the last year, she's been obsessed with losing ten pounds, although she has not done anything to lose it. In fact, when I brought home a bag of chips that I had been planning to pair with guacamole to bring to a mom's night out last month, Hannah demolished it before I made it out the door. I ended up bringing some sliced up apples. They haven't invited me back.

"Of course I want you to be healthy," I say.

She rolls her eyes. Hannah has mastered the eye roll. It's her favorite facial expression. It can be used when I've asked her to do something she doesn't want to do. Or when I've said something so terribly lame, she just can't bear it. Or best of all, when I express any sort of love or affection.

"Eggs in two minutes," I say to Liam.

"No rush. I'm gonna have some orange juice." Liam goes for the fridge, but he's not quick enough. Hannah shoves him aside to get to the quart of milk. He raises his eyebrows, but he lets his sister get away with it without commenting.

"What are you all dressed up for, Liam?" I ask as I turn off the heat on the stove. Usually my son wears jeans and a T-shirt, regardless of the weather. I'm just happy when they're clean.

"Debate." He finally gets his turn and grabs the orange juice from the fridge. He pours himself a heaping glass, so full that the juice is licking the edges, threatening to spill over. Like every other teenage boy in the world, Liam has a huge appetite even though his build is lanky and athletic. "We're competing against Lincoln High after school."

"Can I come to watch?"

Hannah rolls her eyes. "*Seriously*? Liam's debates are mega boring."

Liam smiles crookedly and takes a swig from his orange juice. "She's right. It won't be fun for you."

I scrape the eggs onto a plate for him, giving him his portion in addition to the eggs I made for Hannah. I'll make more for my husband later if he wants it—Jason should be back from his run before long. "It will be fun if you're up there."

"Okay, sure." Liam digs into the plate of eggs. For some reason, I get a lot of satisfaction out of watching my children eat. It dates all the way back to when I was breast-feeding. (Hannah says it's super weird.) "These eggs are great, Mom."

"Why, thank you."

"What's your secret ingredient?"

I wink at him. "Love."

Hannah lets out the longest sigh I've ever heard. It lasts for at least five full seconds—which is a long time for a sigh. "Oh my *God*, the secret ingredient is Parmesan cheese. Mom *always* put Parmesan cheese in the eggs. You know that, Liam. God, you're such a…"

He lifts an eyebrow. "I'm such a what, Hannah."

"You know what."

For a moment, the two of them stare at each other, and it's so quiet in the room that I could hear the coffee machine humming. But then Liam snorts loudly and goes back to his eggs. I envy his ability to ignore his sister's irritability. If eggs are my superpower, ignoring Hannah is Liam's. Nothing she says ever gets to him. And the truth is, despite their sparring, Hannah adores Liam. The minute she started walking, she was following him around. These days, he's probably her favorite person in the house. I suspect I come in fourth, after Jason and probably her phone.

"Well, I think the eggs taste especially good today," Liam says. And he smiles, blinking up at me with those eyelashes that Hannah complains are unfairly long. "Thanks, Mom. You're the best."

And Hannah rolls her eyes.

I love Hannah. I really do. I love her more than I love my own life. She's my daughter. She's my little girl.

But Liam is my favorite. I can't help it. From the moment he was born and I became a mother, I knew no matter how many other children I had, he would be my favorite. Nobody else had a chance. Even if Hannah liked my eggs better and didn't roll her eyes, it wouldn't matter. Liam would still be my favorite.

He's my favorite, even knowing what he's capable of.

And I will protect him with every fiber of my being.

Chapter 3

ERIKA

Just as Hannah and Liam are finishing up their breakfast, the back door slams shut. It's Jason, back from his jog.

About a year ago, I purchased a scale for our master bathroom. The first time my husband stepped on it, he was horrified. "Did I really get that fat, Erika?" he asked me about twenty times over the next several days. Followed by, "How could you let me get that fat?" By the end of the week, he made a solemn oath that he was going to get back in shape. He was going to eat right and exercise and get back to the weight he was when we got married. (To be fair, he was at least ten pounds overweight when we got married.)

At the time I laughed. But then he actually did it. He jogs every morning now. He doesn't buy giant jugs of M&Ms. He switched from regular Coca-Cola to diet. (Or Coke Zero, which he says tastes much better than diet, although I am skeptical.) I don't know much about what the numbers should be on the scale, but it's obvious that at age forty-five, Jason is in the best shape of his life. I never noticed that he had been getting a gut until it vanished. And recently, when we got together with some other couples, another wife made a comment about my husband being "hot." I was oddly proud. Although it made me feel like I need to start taking kickboxing or Zumba or something to firm up some of those soft, saggy areas on my middle-aged body.

"Erika!" Jason limps over to the stove to join me, his T-shirt damp with sweat. His knee has been acting up for the last few weeks, but he's trying to push through it. "Are you making eggs? I'm starving."

I crack an egg into the sizzling pan. "You got it."

He leans in to kiss me on the neck, which is nice, despite how sweaty he is. "Egg-cellent."

Hannah groans. "Oh my God, Dad. Please."

"What's wrong?" Jason blinks at her. "I'm just egg-cited about your mom's cooking."

Liam laughs. We're all used to Jason's puns. The general rule is that they're always terrible, but sometimes they're so terrible that it's funny.

"Please stop, Dad." Hannah shakes her head at him. "You're being so cringe-y right now."

Cringe-y is the word Hannah frequently uses to describe basically everything that Jason or I do. I hate that it bothers me on some level, although Jason seems to find amusing. His reasoning is that he was never cool, so why would it bother him that his teenage daughter doesn't think he's cool?

"Don't you have to get ready for school, Hannah?" Jason says. "Don't you have an egg-xam today?"

Even I laugh this time, although it's more because of the look on Hannah's face.

Hannah dashes upstairs to get dressed and hopefully brush her hair so I don't get accused of child neglect, while Liam wanders into the living room because he gets a sense of when we want privacy. I continue to stir Jason's eggs. Low and slow.

"You know I've been eating your eggs for twenty years?" Jason muses as he runs a hand along the back of my neck. "Twenty years of Erika's eggs."

"Aren't you sick of them?" I say it as a joke, but there's a tiny part of me that's serious. After all, Jason spent the last year getting in great shape. He's gotten a lot hotter. All he needs is a shiny new car and contacts to replace his wire rimmed glasses, and he'll be in full on middle-age crisis mode.

"Hell no." He pulls me to him and presses his lips against mine, which totally interrupts the egg cooking process, but I don't mind. He hasn't shaved yet and his chin tickles mine. "I hope I get to eat your eggs for another twenty years."

"Gag!" Hannah coming down the stairs interrupts what *had* been a very nice little moment between me and Jason. She's dressed in blue jeans and an oversized T-shirt with her hair pulled back into a messy ponytail. She's probably going for stylishly messy, but it's just messy. "You two need to get a room."

"Um, this is *our* house." Jason raises his eyebrows at her. "If you want to start paying rent, then you can tell me when I'm allowed to kiss my sexy wife."

Hannah just rolls her eyes.

"All right, Hannah," I say. "You've got to get a move on. The school bus is going to be at the corner in…" I look down at my watch. One minute ago. "Damn it."

"Oh no. I guess you have to drive us."

"Gosh, funny how that worked out…"

Hannah hates the school bus with a passion. From the moment she wakes up every weekday, she's plotting a way for me to drive her to school. We've already agreed that when Liam gets his license, he can drive the two of them to school every morning. Of course, he'll be in college in less than two years. And the thought of Hannah being behind the wheel is nothing short of terrifying.

I finish cooking Jason's eggs and reluctantly pile Hannah and Liam into my green Toyota 4Runner. I never thought I'd be the sort of mom who drove an SUV, especially one so freaking big. I held onto my little Honda Civic even after we had Liam. But then Jason pointed out how hard it was going to be to strap two car seats into the backseat of the Civic, and I knew it was time to upgrade. So we got the SUV. I know this sounds melodramatic, but the first time I saw it parked in my garage, I almost burst into tears. But now I'm used to it. It makes me feel safe, which is important when you've got your kids in the car. That's why when Jason took Liam out for a driving lesson last week, he used the 4Runner.

Hannah has called shotgun, which is unfortunate, because it means that she's going to be controlling the music in the car. She's very much partial to music from young men who don't look like they're capable of growing facial hair yet.

"Can we *please* listen to something different?" Liam complains about two minutes into the drive. I have to agree. "*Anything* else?"

"You know," Hannah says, "Justin Bieber is an incredibly talented singer."

"Oh, is he?"

"Yes, he is!" She adjusts her messy ponytail. "He has a phenomenal vocal range."

Liam smirks. "Sure. That's what you like about him. His vocal range."

"So I think he's cute. So what? It's not like you're

interested in *Olivia* for her intelligence."

Olivia? Who is *Olivia*? I glance in the rearview mirror just in time to see Liam's entire face turn red. He has become incredibly skilled at masking his reactions to things, but he couldn't hide it this time. But when I look away for a moment and check the mirror again, he's regained his composure.

The car skids to a halt at a red light. "Who is Olivia?" I say as casually as I can manage.

Liam looks out the window. "Nobody. Just a girl."

But thank God Hannah is in the car with us. "*Just a girl*?" She snorts. "Liam is totally in love with her."

He laughs. "No, I'm not."

"Oh my God, you *so* are. Don't even deny it." Hannah gives me a look, like I'm her new confidante. "You should see the way he looks at her. He's *totally* into her."

"Whatever."

I glance in the rearview mirror one more time to look at my son. Liam is the most composed sixteen-year-old kid I've ever known. That's why he's so good at debate, in addition to his natural intelligence and his diligent preparation. He *never* loses his cool. He never lets anyone know what he's thinking. But I've known him long enough that I can usually tell. Usually.

I'm really glad I'm going to this debate after school. I wanted to see Liam perform. That was the reason I told him I wanted to come. And I meant it. But now I've got a new, more important reason for going.

I've got to figure out who Olivia is.

And I've got to keep something terrible from happening to her.

Chapter 4

Transcript of police interview with Sharon Anderson:

"Can you tell me how you know Liam Cass?"

"He attended kindergarten at the school where I work as principal."

"For how long did he attend?"

"About four months."

"And this was eleven years ago?"

"That's correct."

"So you still remember a child who attended your school for four months over a decade ago?"

"Yes. I remember Liam. Very well."

"And what was your impression of him?"

"At first? He seemed like a great kid. Real cute. Smart—certainly the smartest kid in the grade. I remember he got up during assembly and gave this long speech he memorized. I couldn't believe a kindergartner could remember all that. I was impressed."

"How come he only attended the school for four months? Isn't the school year nine months long?"

"Liam was… expelled."

"A kindergartner was expelled?"

"It's unusual. But the circumstances called for it."

"I see. And why was that?"

"There was an incident."

"Can you describe the incident to me?"

"Yes…"

"Will you please describe the incident, Mrs. Anderson?"

"It was… there was a girl…"

"Yes…?"

"Well, she and Liam were friends. They often played together at recess, or so his teacher told me later. And then one day during recess, the girl… disappeared."

"I see. And did they find her?"

"Yes. They did. And she was… fine."

"Where did they find her?"

"Does this have to do with that girl from the high school? The one who…?"

"I'm afraid we can't discuss it at this time."

"Yes. Yes, of course. But do you think Liam is the one who…?"

"Once again, Mrs. Anderson, this is not something I

can discuss."

"Of course. I'm sorry."

"Now can you tell me where they found this girl?"

"So… the story I was told is that Liam and the little girl were playing janitor. They sneaked away and went to the custodial closet during recess. It seems she was quite infatuated with Liam and he talked her into it."

"And what happened in the custodial closet?"

"They found a roll of duct tape. And they were playing with it."

"How were they playing with it?"

"…"

"Mrs. Anderson?"

"I'm sorry. It was just… so shocking. I still can't get over it. That a kindergartner would…"

"Would what?"

"He convinced her to let him bind her wrists with the duct tape. Then he put tape over her mouth. And then…"

"Yes…?"

"Well, we're not sure what he did next. The one thing we know for sure is he locked her in the closet and walked away. And even when she was noticed to be missing and teachers were looking for her, he didn't tell anyone where she was. It was several hours later when we finally found her—she was bound on the floor of the closet and refused to speak to anyone. For days, actually."

"What do *you* think he did?"

"I don't know. He was just a little boy. It's hard to imagine he could have done anything that bad, but the look in that girl's eyes when we found her…"

"I see."

"Of course, her parents were hysterical. And given everything that happened, we had no choice but to expel Liam from the school."

"When you confronted him about what he did, how did he react?"

"He apologized. Of course he did. He claimed it was all just a fun game and she had agreed to it. He even cried. But…"

"But what?"

"But I never believed him. Even when he was sobbing in my office, it seemed incredibly fake. I don't think he was sorry at all. Not even a little bit. The only thing I think he was sorry about was that we found her."

Chapter 5

ERIKA

I make it to the school about sixty seconds after the school bus arrives.

Hannah says a quick goodbye and then darts out of the car. I remember when she was in preschool, how she used to cling to my leg with both arms when I tried to drop her off in the morning. When I would try to leave, she would shriek at the top of her lungs like somebody was trying to murder her. Now if I attempt to even give her a kiss goodbye, she's mortified beyond all belief.

Liam is the opposite. When he was younger, he never had any trouble at all separating from me when I dropped him off. He would kiss me goodbye and then run off to play without a second thought. And now, he leans forward from the backseat and kisses me on the cheek, oblivious to anyone who might witness this show of affection.

"Bye, Mom." He opens the back door. "I love you."

I smile. Liam has an incredible knack for saying the

exact right thing. "I love you too, sweetheart."

He swings his backpack onto his shoulder and hurries towards the front door before the bell rings. I watch him, looking out for any girl who might be Olivia. Anything that will make my job easier. And this isn't an easy job. It's just going to get harder as he gets older.

"Is that Erika Cass in there?"

I jerk my head up. Jessica Martinson is standing outside my car, peering through my cracked open window. I don't know where she came from, because her car is nowhere in sight. She must have been meeting with somebody within the school, which is not unusual for Jessica, who is head of the PTA. Jessica and I used to be close, years ago, when Liam and her son Tyler used to be friends.

Jessica and I only became close because of Liam and Tyler's friendship, and we've grown apart since the boys stopped spending time together. I have to admit, it concerned me when they stopped being friends. I asked Liam why he didn't have Tyler Martinson over anymore, and he just shrugged. If it had been Hannah, that question would have sparked an hour-long monologue about everything Tyler had done wrong. But Liam isn't like that. He doesn't talk about things the way his sister does.

Kids grow apart. Both of them are older, and they don't share any clubs or interests in common. Tyler is more popular than Liam, and they run in different circles. Tyler plays football, and Liam does track and debate. Also, Liam doesn't have any close friends—he doesn't seem interested in having the sort of tight friendships that other kids have. But I always worried about what caused their friendship to fracture. Growing apart—that's fine. But it scares me that Liam might have done something to accelerate the demise of their friendship.

It certainly wouldn't be the first time.

"Actually," Jessica says, "I'm so glad I saw you, Erika. There's something I need to speak with you about. It's urgent."

Urgent? A knot tightens in my stomach. What's Liam done this time? "Oh…"

She tucks a strand of her golden blonde hair behind one ear. She has a messy ponytail, like Hannah, but unlike Hannah's, hers is painfully stylish. "Can we grab some coffee? Do you have time?"

I have a long list of errands to take care of this morning, but I can't say no. "Sure."

"Great! How about Charlie's?"

Charlie's is a diner about five minutes away from here. Good for a quick cup of coffee in the morning. Jessica and I have met up there dozens of times over the years. "I'll drive right there."

She winks at me. "See you in five."

As Jessica hurries away to her own monster SUV, I look down at my hands gripping the steering wheel. They're shaking. What does Jessica want to talk to me about? It can't be that bad, could it? She seems friendly enough. But that's the thing with Jessica. She could tell you something horrible right to your face with a smile on her lips. I've seen her do it before.

I throw my car back into drive and make my way to Charlie's.

Chapter 6

OLIVIA

Thanks to Liam Cass, I'm failing math class.

No, I probably won't fail, but things aren't looking good for me. I'm good at math—I've always gotten A's, if not an A+. But this semester, I'll be lucky to swing a C. And it's all because of Liam. It's because from the moment I step into the classroom at ten-thirty to when the bell rings forty minutes later, all I can focus on is the boy sitting in front of me.

I've never been boy crazy. I can't say the same for my best friend Madison, who thinks about boys nonstop. Madison has *definitely* failed classes before because of a cute guy sitting in front of her. She has blown off studying for tests to hang out with the boys she liked. It's sort of her *thing*. And I always made fun of her. Like, how could you prioritize a *boy* over your education? I mean, boys my age are all pretty idiotic and not even that attractive—they mostly have greasy faces and scraggly little beards.

I want to get into a good college—that's my priority. How could you jeopardize your entire future for a cute guy? That's *so* lame.

Then on the first day of school this year, Liam sat down in front of me in math class, turned his head to flash me a smile, and I was gone. He didn't have a greasy face or patchy facial hair—he was *gorgeous*. I hate myself for it, but I can't help ogling him. Every time he smiles at me, my heart speeds up. He has a *great* smile. And *really* beautiful brown eyes. His eyes are like creamy, endless pools of milk chocolate. I could write bad poetry about this guy. In another month, I'll be etching our initials in a heart scratched into the wood of my desk—that's how bad it is.

We had a test a few days ago, and it was a bona fide disaster. I can't focus when I'm studying, because the second I crack open the textbook and see sines and cosines, my mind goes to Liam. And of course, I couldn't focus when I was actually *taking* the test—not with him sitting right in front of me. I passed by the skin of my teeth—a seventy-two. Liam, who obviously isn't having any problem at all focusing with little old me behind him, got a ninety-eight.

I've got to stop thinking about this boy. He's just a boy. My education is much more important. I've got to focus.

Focus, Olivia.

Except when Liam comes into the classroom today, he's not wearing his usual jeans and a T-shirt. He's dressed in nice khaki slacks and a dress shirt. And a tie. Oh my God, he's wearing a *tie*. Usually, he's cute, but in dress clothes, he's upped his game. It's like a sneak peek into how handsome he'll look when he's an adult. Against my will, my stomach starts doing cartwheels.

Focus, Olivia!

As Liam slides into his seat in front of me, he flashes me that grin that makes my legs weak. "Hey," he says.

"Hey," I say back. I search my brain, trying to think of something clever or funny to say. I spend most of math class trying to do that. "You're all dressed up."

Good one, Olivia.

"We have a debate today," he explains. "It's sort of a big deal. We're competing against another school."

"Wow. Are you nervous?"

"A little." He laughs, although there's a bit of a tremor in his voice that makes me think he's more nervous than he lets on. "If we win, we get to go to the state competition up in Albany. That's pretty cool."

"What do you do during a debate anyway?"

He scratches at his dark brown hair. "Argue, mostly. It's sort of fun." He raises his eyebrows at me. "Do you, um... do you want to come watch?"

"Me?" I say in an embarrassingly squeaky voice.

Oh my God, that was *such* a stupid thing to say. *Obviously* he's inviting me. Who else would he be inviting?

And what does this *mean*?

"Uh…" His smile slips slightly. "I mean, if you want. It'd probably be pretty boring for you. You probably don't want to go."

Oh no, he's taking it back. "No, it sounds like it could be fun. I don't have anything else I'm doing."

That's an outright lie. I'm supposed to be at chorus practice after school today. But the truth is, I've soured on chorus since I didn't get the last two solos I tried out for. And even if I had, I can't say no to Liam. This is the first time he's ever invited me somewhere.

His eyes light up. "That would be great. I mean, if you can come. But if something else comes up, that's cool too. No big deal."

I can't believe it. He actually seems really happy that I'm coming. Oh God, there's no *way* I'm going to be able to focus in class now. I'm going to get a terrible grade in math this semester. And the scariest part is, at this moment, I couldn't care less.

CHAPTER 7

ERIKA

As soon as I walk into Charlie's, I blink my eyes to adjust to the neon lights overhead. Those lights have been flickering for as long as I can remember, but it's part of the diner's charm. Just like the plastic tables and ripped bench covers. Charlie's been around forever and makes no effort to hide that fact.

Jessica has already got a table and is sipping on a cup of coffee. I watch her for a moment before approaching the table. I know she's my age, but she looks fantastic. She's got the same laugh lines that I do on her face, but somehow she makes them look sexy. She has mastered the casual stay at home mom look, with her T-shirt that boosts the high school football team and the fitted yoga pants, paired with ballet flats. I threw on the first thing my fingers touched when I got into the bedroom to hurriedly get dressed so Hannah and Liam would get to school on time. Mom jeans and a sweater, as it turns out. What can I say—

mom jeans are comfortable.

Jessica and I are both essentially stay at home moms, like a lot of other parents out here. You could almost say it's epidemic. When I met Jason, I was working as a journalist at a newspaper in Manhattan. I was getting paid practically nothing, but there was a lot of upward mobility at the paper, and if I had stayed on, I'd probably have a pretty good job there by now. Maybe I would've moved on to a better paper. Maybe I'd be an editor-in-chief. But after I got pregnant, Jason convinced me to move out to the island. I agreed because I was sick of our tiny Manhattan apartment, but once we got to the island, the commute was insane. He pointed out that I didn't earn even close to the amount we would be paying in child care, and that his income could easily support us.

So I quit. Temporarily.

I had every intention of going back to work after Liam started preschool. But then Hannah came along two years later. And between the two of them, there was always some emergency popping up. Hannah got ear infections every other week, and on the weeks she didn't get ear infections, she got conjunctivitis. And then there with the whole mess with Liam.

Right now, I work for a local newspaper called the *Nassau Nutshell*. You can tell by the name that they do a lot of hard-hitting journalism—not. They put out one paper per week, and I contribute a couple of articles, mostly on local events or parenting advice. Last week, I wrote an article featuring three meals you could cook for the whole family in twenty minutes or less. What they pay me each month didn't even cover the price of the groceries I bought to cook those three meals, but it stimulates my brain and I could write the articles from home. Jason always makes a big fuss when the paper comes out and reads all my articles, and it's fun to see my byline in print. No, it's not *The New York Times*. But it's something. For now.

Jessica, on the other hand, has absolutely embraced the stay at home mom lifestyle. She is the most visible parent at the high school, and her kids are involved in every sport and extracurricular activity you can imagine. In my more optimistic moments, I hope that's why Tyler and Liam aren't friends anymore. Because Tyler is just too damn busy.

"Erika!" Jessica flashes me a bright smile as I slide into the booth across from her. "It's so good to spend a little time with you. It's been ages, hasn't it?"

Can we dispense with the small talk and you just tell me what urgent thing you need to tell me? I force a smile. "Yes. It really has."

"We should do this more often, shouldn't we?"

I nod. "Definitely."

We won't. I used to be friends with several of the parents at the school, but I've got my reasons for keeping my distance now.

I flag down a waitress to place my order for a cup of coffee. Whatever she's got to say will be easier to take after a shot of caffeine. "How is your mother?" Jessica asks once the waiter has left.

Jessica Martinson should be a politician. She is fantastic at remembering little details about everyone she knows. Even though I know it's all an act, I feel oddly touched that she remembered to ask about my mother. And the truth is, my mother has been on my mind a lot lately. She is nearly eighty and living all alone in a small house in New Jersey. But she's tough—my father died when I was very young, and she's been doing it alone ever since.

"She's hanging in there," I say. "I'd love for her to move closer, but she's really stubborn. She'll never leave her house."

"I know what you mean." Jessica takes a sip of her coffee. She has poured so much cream into it, it looks like chocolate milk. "My mother is the same way. We've got a room for her in our house, but she won't budge."

"I suppose I understand. She's got all her friends out in Jersey."

Jessica crinkles her nose. "But it's *Jersey*."

We both laugh, and I remember why I used to be friends with Jessica. She's so good at talking to people, whether she likes them or not. In that sense, she's not unlike Liam.

But she's not really like him. Not at all. Nobody is.

I clear my throat. "So what did you want to talk to me about, Jessica?"

I hold my breath, waiting for her to take another sip from her coffee. "Oh, right," she says. "I need your help, Erika. Movie night is turning into a disaster. Would you take over the reins?"

I let out the breath. I should have known that's what Jessica wanted to talk to me about. Movie night takes place at the high school once a year. They put up a big screen in the football field and charge people three dollars each for entry. They sell pizza at two dollars a slice. It's a big fundraiser for the PTA, and therefore, it's on Jessica's shoulders to get it organized.

"Rachel was in charge of it," Jessica says. "But her husband—you know Rob?—he had a minor heart attack. He's okay, but her head isn't in the game. The thing is in two weeks, and nothing is organized yet. Is there any chance you could take over? Pretty please?"

"Of course," I agree. Unlike Jessica, I could never stomach the PTA. When she and I were close, I used to go to meetings, but they were always oppressively boring. It made me feel guilty that all I wanted to do during the meetings was take out my phone and play Candy Crush. But I try to volunteer for things at the school as much as I can.

"You are a star, Erika!" She reaches out to take my hand across the table and I resist the urge to pull away. One thing I have in common with Liam is casual physical affection makes me uncomfortable. "Thank you so much. You'll come to the PTA meeting this week to help organize then?"

I'd rather eat dirt. "Um, sure."

The waitress arrives with my coffee, which gives me an excuse to yank my hand back. I don't pour in any milk or sugar. I like it bitter and black.

"We should all get together again," Jessica says. "Your family and mine. It's sad the boys don't hang out much anymore. And Hannah and Emma never really got along."

"Yes." I absently stir my coffee with a spoon, even though I'm drinking it black. This get-together will never happen. Tyler and Liam aren't friends anymore, and Hannah actively dislikes Jessica's younger daughter.

"Of course…" Jessica shrugs. "Tyler spends most of his free time these days with girls. You must know how that is. I'll bet Liam has a million girlfriends."

My mouth feels dry. Olivia. I've got to find her. "Actually, he hasn't really been dating yet."

"No?" She raises her eyebrows. "That's surprising. Liam is… Well, I've always noticed how much girls like him. I've even heard Emma and her friends talking about him. She had the biggest crush on him for a while."

"Yes…" It makes me sick just to talk about it. Knowing deep down that I can't really stop this. It's like a freight train barreling down a track. You could throw a few big rocks on the track to possibly slow it down, but it's going to get through eventually. I look down at my coffee, and a wave of nausea overwhelms me. "I'm sorry, Jessica, but I just realized I've got an appointment to get to."

"Oh." She blinks her pretty blue eyes. I wonder what kind of eyes Olivia has. "Well, it was good seeing you again, Erika."

"You too." But I've already gotten up from the table and I'm hurrying out the door.

Chapter 8

OLIVIA

I've never had a boyfriend.

I've never even kissed a boy. Well, that's not true. During a game of Truth or Dare in middle school, I exchanged a few kisses on the cheek. But I don't count those. They weren't real kisses. Not like the kind Madison has had.

Madison has had two boyfriends already. Right now, she's dating a guy named Aidan, and the two of them are *always* making out. It's like I can't do anything with Madison anymore without Aidan coming out and kissing her in this gross, slobbery way. It doesn't even look like a good kiss. If that's what kissing is, I can wait.

But I have a feeling Liam Cass won't kiss like that.

I think a lot about what Liam's kisses will be like. Not just during math class, but all the time.

Madison is prettier than me, but not by a lot. On a scale of one to ten, she's probably a seven and I'm probably a six. My hair is mousy brown, and people tell me I have pretty eyes, but I know I have way too many freckles. I had a lot of freckles on my face when I was a kid and I read they're supposed to fade when you get older. But my stupid freckles won't do what they're supposed to. Yes, they're lighter than they were, but I *still* have these tiny little spots all over my face. Even though I smear sunscreen all over myself whenever I go out and I have this giant hat with a brim that my little brother makes fun of me for wearing.

That's why I don't have a boyfriend. All my stupid freckles.

Not that I haven't been asked out before. This one guy asked me out earlier in the year and he was kind of a jerk about it when I said no, but I didn't really like him. I don't want to go out with just anyone so I can have a boyfriend. I want to go out with a guy I actually *like*.

"There he is." I nudge Madison as we sit in the audience of the giant high school auditorium. I convinced her to come with me to the debate today, and she agreed only because Aidan has football practice so she has to wait around anyway. A smattering of students and parents came to watch, but the audience is pretty sparse. I've never seen a debate before, so today will be my first. Maybe I'll learn something about…

Well, whatever it is they're debating.

Madison follows my gaze to the stage, where our

school debate team is assembled. And *he's* up there. Liam. Oh my God, he looks *so* handsome in that nice blue button-down shirt. Once again, my heart does this weird thing in my chest. If I didn't know better, I'd think I should go see a doctor.

"He is *so* hot," I murmur as I lean back in my seat.

Madison crinkles her nose, which is totally free of freckles. Madison doesn't have one freckle, but she always complains about her double chin. "I don't know, Liv. I don't like him."

"You are so weird. What don't you like about him? He's, like, perfect and gorgeous."

"He's…" Madison's gaze travels back to the stage. "I don't know. He just seems really… Like, when he talks, he seems so fake."

"What does that even mean?"

"It's hard to explain. I feel like everyone else is real, like they're really living life. But Liam is, like, this actor who is being paid to hang out with us."

I stare at her. "What the hell are you talking about, Mad?"

"I'm just saying. I feel like I don't trust him entirely. He's a phony. You know?"

I'm not going to point out to her that between Aidan and Liam, it's clear who is more trustworthy. Liam is a straight-A student, and he's a star on both the debate team and the track team. Whereas Aidan is built like a bull, he's failing two classes, and he almost got expelled last year for getting into a fistfight in the hallway at school. If anyone makes me uneasy, it's Aidan.

Liam catches my eye, and maybe it's my imagination, but his whole face seems to light up when he sees me and he waves enthusiastically. Is it possible he likes me as much as I like him? I mean, he invited me to come today. So maybe he does. The thought of it is enough to make my heart start beating faster again. Liam Cass. God, he's *so* cute.

But then he starts talking to another girl, who is on stage with them. That's Olivia Reynolds. She and I share the same first name, but that's where the similarities end. She's on the debate team, like Liam, and she's *really* gorgeous. She has silky blonde hair that looks professionally styled, and she's totally stacked. *Unfairly* stacked, given how skinny she is. When she's talking to Liam, the two of them look like a really attractive couple. Between the two of us Olivias, she's clearly the superior one.

How could Liam like me when she's around?

I try not to think about it.

By the way, Liam is totally brilliant during the debate. I don't even entirely understand what they're debating. Something about transportation between different states.

It's all really boring, honestly. But Liam is *such* a good speaker. He should become a politician or something. Whenever he talks, everybody is paying such close attention to him. Even Madison looks up from her phone for, like, two seconds.

The judges deliberate at the end, and our home team wins the debate. I applaud as loudly as I can. Madison just rolls her eyes. She isn't into extracurricular activities, and to be honest, neither am I.

"So are you going to go talk to him now?" she asks me.

"What?" My eyes fly up to the front of the room, where Liam is now talking to Olivia Reynolds. *Again.* God, she's really pretty. It's so unfair. "*Now?*"

Madison huffs. "You made me sit through that whole stupid boring debate and you're not even going to go talk to him? Seriously, Olivia?"

"He's busy."

"So? Interrupt him."

"I can't just talk to him out of nowhere."

"Why not?"

"It would be weird."

"Seriously, Liv." She holds up a hand. "I can't even."

Maybe if Liam weren't talking to Olivia Reynolds, I could go up to him. But I'm not wrong. It would be weird if I went up there now. I mean, he's going to think I'm some total stalker or something.

I start to explain that to Madison, but she's not listening anymore because Aidan has burst into the auditorium to find her. He's still wearing his outfit from football practice, and he stinks of sweat. God, couldn't he have taken a shower or something before coming here? The first thing he does is plant his lips on Madison's and they kiss for like five minutes straight. It's so gross. I try not to look. They probably wouldn't even notice if I left right now.

"Hey, Aidan." Madison separates from Aidan for a split second, probably because she needs to breathe. "Tell Olivia she should go talk to Liam."

My face burns. I'm not surprised Madison told her boyfriend that I liked Liam, but I still hate that she did it. Can't Madison and I have any secrets anymore? Plus Aidan is like the worst person to know. He has a big mouth and he'll tell everyone.

"Liam Cass?" Aidan makes a face. "I hate that guy. He's such an asshole."

"Why is he an asshole?" I say. "He's really nice."

Aidan snorts. "Yeah. Nice to *you*. Anyway, you could do better, Olivia."

"That's what *I* said," Madison chips in.

"Whatever," I mumble.

"Anyway." Madison grabs her backpack off her seat.

"Aidan and I are heading out. Want a ride home?"

I absolutely do *not* want to sit in the backseat while Aidan drives erratically because he has to make out with Madison and touch her legs while they're driving. I'd rather walk the two miles home.

Aidan and Madison take off through the back exit while I sit back down in my seat. I really must be a stalker, because I'm still looking at Liam. He looks so good dressed up. Part of me wants to snap a picture with my phone so I can look at it later. I'm totally staring. It's awful. But I can't stop. This is why I'm failing math.

Liam goes up to talk to the debate teacher, Mrs. Randall, and then he talks to an attractive woman in her forties that has the same dark hair and eyes that he has and also a similar nose. I think it's his mother. He looks a lot like her. He seems to be really polite to her, which is good. I read online that it's a really good thing when boys are nice to their mothers. I don't know what Madison was talking about. How could she say she doesn't trust him?

It isn't until most of the people in the auditorium have a filtered out that Liam looks into the audience and our eyes meet. He gets that smile on his face again, and I feel this warm tingle in my whole body. I'm sure Liam doesn't give slobbery kisses like Aidan. I bet he kisses really well.

Oh my God, he's coming over to me.

I stumble to my feet, trying to temper the dopey smile on my lips. How do normal people smile? It's like I forgot how. God, he's going to think I'm *such* a loser.

"Hey, Olivia," he says.

"Hey," I say.

That sounded good. Casual. My voice didn't squeak and I didn't spit when I talked. Score.

Liam rubs at the back of his neck. When he was up there on that stage, he looked so confident. I'm terrified of public speaking, but he didn't look even the slightest bit nervous. But now he keeps rubbing his neck and shuffling his feet. "So, um, you saw it?"

"Uh huh." I squeeze my fists together. They seem abnormally clammy, like I've got a fever. "You did a really good job. I mean, I think so. I've never seen a debate before."

"Thanks." He coughs and smiles. "It went really well. We won."

"I know."

"Oh."

And now we're both just standing there. I wrack my brain, trying to think of something interesting to say before he walks away. "Did you get to your math homework yet?"

That'll do.

He shakes his head. "No. I've been busy with the

debate since school ended."

"Oh. Right." Duh. Obviously. God, why do I sound like such a moron? "Well, I did it, and it wasn't too bad."

Actually, that's a total lie. There was no way I could focus on math homework when I knew I'd be seeing Liam shortly.

"Okay, good." He coughs again. "Hey, listen, Olivia, me and some guys from track are going to Charlie's tomorrow after school, just to hang out and get some food. Would you... I mean, do you want to come with us?"

I stare at him. Is he *asking me out*? "I..."

The smile on his face falters. "It's no big deal. Either way."

"No, I mean... yes. I would like to come. That would be great. It sounds like... fun. You know."

His brown eyes light up. "Yeah, it's going to be a lot of fun."

"Yeah." My mouth feels almost too dry to speak.

"So... do you want to meet in front of the school at four-thirty? It's after practice, and we need time to, you know, shower and stuff."

I nod. "Okay. I'll be there."

Okay, maybe it isn't an official date. But I really think Liam might like me. I mean, he seemed really happy when I said yes. And he wants to shower beforehand so he smells good. So, these are all a good signs.

Oh my God, I've got a date with Liam. I'm so happy!

Chapter 9

ERIKA

Liam is a brilliant public speaker. He's always been good at getting in front of a crowd and doing his thing. If he were different, he would be perfect for politics. He speaks well, he's good looking, and he's incredibly smart. My son is so many good things.

Before the debate begins, Liam is deep in conversation with a beautiful girl. She seems to also be on the debate team, but she looks like she could be a model. She has blond hair that appears professionally styled. And given how skinny she is, it's amazing how large her breasts are. Do sixteen-year-old girls get implants? I'm horrified by the idea of it.

There's a woman next to me who is fiddling with her cell phone. The gray laced through her hair makes me think she's about my age—probably another parent. "Excuse me," I say.

She looks up and smiles pleasantly. "Yes?"

"Do you know the name of the blond girl on the stage? The one in the yellow blouse."

The woman nods. "That's Olivia Reynolds. She's a really strong debater. But not as good as the boy. Liam."

"Liam is my son," I say, allowing for an instant that touch of pride I often deny myself when I talk about Liam these days.

"Is he?" The woman's eyes light up. "Well, he is absolutely *wonderful*. Very talented. You must be really proud of him. I wish my son could speak half as well."

I smile, trying to enjoy the compliment, but my mind is racing. Olivia Reynolds. That's the girl Liam is interested in. And it's not surprising, because she is absolutely beautiful. Of course Liam would like her.

I've got to fix this.

I excuse myself from this woman who won't stop gushing about my son, and I step out of the auditorium. I just need to make a quick call. I'll be back in time for the debate.

I check the contacts on my phone, searching for the name Frank Marino. My heart is pounding as I click on his name. The phone rings once. Then again.

It's Frank. Leave a message.

Voicemail.

"Frank? It's Erika Cass. I need to talk to you. There's

another... Please call me back. As soon as you can."

Frank is very reliable. He'll call back tonight.

I return to the auditorium where the students are assembled on the stage. Liam is behind the podium. Sometimes I look at him, and I can't get over how that tiny helpless baby grew up into this handsome, intelligent young man. There were times when Liam was an infant when I imagined what he'd be like when he was older.

I was so naïve. I had no idea what was to come.

Liam gives a great performance, as usual. His team wins the debate, as if there was ever any doubt. He is an excellent performer and speaker. When he was in third grade, he had to give a presentation for class, and he insisted on wearing his nicest button-down shirt and pants. He even dug out the black clip-on tie I bought him for a wedding the year before. I thought he was absolutely adorable and took about a hundred photographs. It's almost a decade later, and he still takes public speaking just as seriously.

Liam is also very competitive. I don't know how much he cares about debate per se, but he definitely cares about winning. Whenever he does well in a track meet or a debate, he's in a great mood. But if he doesn't do well, he gets quiet and won't talk much that evening. Fortunately for him, he's very good at winning. And he's very good at getting what he wants.

I won't let him have what he wants this time.

Liam's eyes light up when he sees me walking over to congratulate him. "Did you see, Mom? We won! We get to go to State!"

I grin at him. "You did great."

He loosens his tie, which makes him look older than sixteen. Unlike when he was eight, he knows how to tie his own tie now—no more clip-ons. I watched him practicing it in a mirror a couple of years ago until he could do it perfect. "Thanks."

Before I can say anything else, Mrs. Randall links her arm into mine and pulls me away from my son. Mrs. Randall is a history teacher who is also in charge of the debate team. She taught Liam American history during his freshman year, and was the one who encouraged him to join the debate team. I remember Liam got an A+ in the class, and the comment on his report card was that he was the best student in the class. Hannah has her now for American history, but based on Hannah's recent comment that Mrs. Randall is a "bitch," I have a feeling my daughter won't be getting a similar grade.

"Mrs. Cass!" Mrs. Randall is almost glowing from the win, her gray hair coming loose from her sensible bun. "Liam was great out there, wasn't he?"

I nod, although I'm distracted by the fact that Liam has gone over to talk to Olivia again. "Yes. I know he's been practicing a lot."

"He is so diligent. I wish all my students had that sort of work ethic." She smiles at me. She is solidly in the Liam Cass fan club. "Next stop is Albany! And I bet we'll get to Nationals this year. That will look great on his resume when he applies to college."

Yes, in less than two years, Liam will be going away to college. I can't even think about it. The thought of him being alone and up to his own devices terrifies me.

"That's wonderful," I say.

The smile slips slightly from her lips. "By the way, I hate to bring this up now, but Hannah has missed several of her homework assignments this month."

It's the only thing she could have said to tear my attention away from Liam and Olivia. "She... she did?"

Mrs. Randall nods slowly. "Each missed homework subtracts from her overall grade. And her last test score was..."

"I know." I wince, thinking of the red score on Hannah's history exam that required my signature. Unlike Liam, Hannah has never been a strong student, but high school is proving to be even worse than middle school so far. "I'll talk to her about it and make sure she shows me her homework every night."

"I'm certain she can turn things around." Mrs. Randall looks back over at Liam, then back at me. "I'm sure she has it in her."

I know what she's implying, but Hannah is nothing like Liam. She doesn't look like him and her personality is completely different. Mrs. Randall isn't the first teacher who has been disappointed by the discrepancy.

But not every teacher loves my son. He's gotten so much better at charming adults, but some of them can see right through him. There was one in particular about three years ago. That's a mess I don't want to think about ever again. When I remember what Liam did…

I've got to talk to Frank. Tonight.

Chapter 10

ERIKA

"Mom! Mom, are you listening to me?"

My head snaps up from the dishes in the sink. Hannah is supposed to be unloading the dishwasher while I clean the pots, but instead, she's spent the last several minutes ranting about some girl in her math class named Ashley. I've been so absorbed in the events of today that I guess I tuned her out. I have no idea what Hannah has said in the last several minutes. I close my eyes, hoping I can rewind the ribbon in my brain, but I can't. Whatever Hannah said is gone forever.

"Um," I finally say.

"I knew it!" Hannah looks triumphant. "You weren't listening to me. You *never* listen to me."

"Yes, I do."

"Fine. Then tell me something that's going on with me."

I put down the sauce pan I'm rinsing off. "You're not handing in your American history homework?"

Hannah's cheeks turn pink. "I told you. Those assignments are stupid."

"It doesn't matter. You still have to do them."

"But what's the point? Why do I need to know about some stupid war that happened, like, five-hundred years ago?"

"The revolutionary war happened two-hundred-fifty years ago, Hannah."

"Ugh!" She puts her hands on her hips. She's been doing that when she's upset ever since she was two years old. "What's the difference? It's still a really long time ago."

"It doesn't matter if you think it's stupid or not. It's part of your education. Liam always—"

"Right. Liam. You want me to be just like him. Because he's *so* perfect."

I turn to Hannah, staring at her pale, round face. I'm not entirely sure if she's being sarcastic or not. Most of the worst stuff with Liam happened when he was much younger—I would imagine Hannah is too young to even remember. When we sent him to Dr. Hebert, he was only seven and Hannah was five. I've tried my best to shield her from what goes on, but sometimes I wonder how much she knows.

Does Hannah know anything? *Everything*? What has

Liam told her? Did she mention Olivia in the car to tease Liam or to tip me off?

"After all," Hannah adds, "he's your *favorite*, isn't he?"

My cheeks burn. I hate that it's so obvious how I favor Liam over her. I shouldn't. It's a sign of terrible parenting. I read once that most children long for their parents to be proud of them, so it makes sense that Hannah is struggling in school if she feels like she'll never do as well as her brother.

"Hannah," I say, "you know that's not true. I love both of you equally."

She snorts.

"Look. Why don't we do something together? Just the two of us. I can take you to the mall this weekend and we can get you some new clothes. We haven't had a shopping spree in almost a year. I owe you."

My daughter narrows her eyes at me, but it doesn't take much to win her over. New clothes usually do the job. "Can we go on Saturday?"

"Sure."

"And can we go to Purple Haze after?"

Purple Haze is an ice cream shop that Hannah used to love when she was a little kid. "Of course."

Her lips widen in a smile. "Okay. That sounds good."

Of course, then I start to second-guess myself. I just

discovered Hannah hasn't been handing in her history assignments. Maybe this situation doesn't call for a reward. But now that I've told her we're doing this, I can't very well take it back.

"But," I add, "we'll only go if you hand in all your history homework this week. And I want to *see* it, Hannah."

Hannah looks like she's about to start pouting, but then her shoulders drop. "Okay. Fine."

A small victory.

Before we can make a further dent in the dishes, the front door opens, and the heavy footsteps of my husband and son float into the kitchen. Jason took Liam out for another driving lesson tonight. Apparently, things are going very well—Liam is a natural behind the wheel. No surprises there.

They come to find us in the kitchen, where we've barely made a dent in our chores for the evening. Jason is grinning broadly, and he slings an arm around Liam's shoulders. "What can I say, Erika? Our kid is a great driver. Just like his dad."

I shoot him a look.

"And his mom," Jason quickly adds.

Hannah snorts. "Nice save, Dad."

She has commented on more than one occasion that I've got Jason completely whipped. I don't know if it's true, but he's a good husband. I don't have to nag him to take out the garbage, he always remembers our anniversary, and he changed more than his fair share of diapers when the kids were little.

If there's one thing I would change about him, I'd wish he were a little less laid-back. Especially when it comes to my concerns about Liam. He's always shrugged everything off as "boys will be boys." But I know one of these days it's going to be bad enough that he won't be able to do that anymore.

I look at Liam, and his face has no expression until he notices me watching him. Then he smiles. "I can't wait to get my license," he says.

"And then you can drive me to school in the morning," Hannah pipes up.

"Sure." Liam gives me a pointed look. "If Mom and Dad get me a car."

"We'll see," Jason says. "For now, stick with your mother's Toyota."

I brace myself, waiting for him to add, "We'll probably get you one for your birthday." But he doesn't. Thank God. I think Liam will be a good driver, but something about him having his own car makes me a little uneasy.

"But Liam did do great today." Jason joins me at the dishwasher and starts unloading dishes on his own, even though it's Hannah's job. "He checked his mirrors when he was supposed to. He did the right thing when we got to every stop sign. I wasn't terrified even once."

Liam laughs. "Thanks, Dad."

"You've got to be careful out there," he says. He pulls out a couple of plates from the dishwasher and cocks his head thoughtfully. "Hey. Did you hear about the guy who lost his left arm and leg in a car accident? But he's all right now."

Hannah lets out a groan. Liam and I are silent. "He's all *right* now," Jason says. "Because he has no left arm or leg. Get it?"

"No, I get it," I say.

Jason grins at me. "Well, you're not laughing. So I thought I needed to explain it."

"Nope."

Jason winks. Even before the kids were born, he used to tell his cheesy jokes. But back then, a lot of the jokes involved a saucy double entendre. Now they're straight up dad jokes. But I find it endearing that he persists in making them, even though nobody laughs.

My phone starts ringing from the living room. I use the generic ringtone my iPhone came with, because I can't be bothered to change it. Truth be told, I'm not entirely sure how. My husband is a tech guy and I can't change the ringtone on my phone.

I hurry to the phone and pick it up before it stops ringing. I stare down at the name that pops up on the screen. Frank Marino.

Frank is calling me back.

I quietly slip outside to take the call. And I shut the door behind me.

Chapter 11

ERIKA

"Erika Cass."

Frank's Brooklyn accent rings out on the line. It's so thick that you know he was born and raised there. I found him four years ago—in the Yellow Pages. I searched under private detectives and selected his name randomly. I had no idea what I was doing, and I'm lucky that Frank turned out to be as good as he is.

I don't want to think about what might have happened if not for his help.

"Hi, Frank," I say. "Thanks for calling me back so quickly."

"For you, Erika? Anything. What do you need?"

Frank is a smooth talker. That's what I thought the first and only time I met him in person three years ago, right before the first job I hired him for. He looked just like he sounded—greasy black hair threaded with gray, yellowing teeth from years of smoking, and sharp eyes that didn't miss a thing. The man made me nervous. But he's always done everything I've asked him to. For the right price.

"The girl's name is Olivia Reynolds," I say. "She goes to Liam's school. Same arrangement as last time. Okay?"

Frank is quiet, hopefully scribbling down the information. "Olivia Reynolds. Spelled how it sounds?"

"Yes."

"Got it."

"Same thing as last time. Okay?"

"Okay, you got it." There's shuffling on the other line. "I never seen a woman so eager to cock block her kid. Sometimes I think he's going to be discussing this in therapy someday."

My fingers tighten around the phone until my fingertips tingle. Frank has done this for me many times, and this is the first time he felt the need to comment. "If you don't want to do it, I'll get somebody else."

"No, it's fine."

"Because if you won't do it, tell me now."

"Shit, Erika. Relax. I was just kidding around."

My shoulders relax. "Good."

"One more thing," Frank says. "My prices went up."

"How much?"

He quotes a number nearly twice as much as what I paid last time. My chest tightens. He knows it was an empty threat when I said I would get somebody else. He knows I'm not going to get somebody else. I need him. "Fine."

"It's nice working with you, as always, Erika."

Just do your job, you piece of shit. I grit my teeth, angry I can't say the words that are going through my head. But he's going to do what I need him to do. He's going to help me save my son from himself.

Chapter 12

OLIVIA

Even though it might not be a real date, I could not possibly be more nervous about going to the diner with Liam tonight.

I tried on every item in my closet last night in front of the mirror. Twice. I put on a skirt that was way too short and I would have loved to have Liam see it on me, but it would've looked like I was trying too hard. (Also, I'm not entirely sure my mother would've let me out of the house.) We're just going out for some food after track team practice, after all. In the end, I decide to go with cute casual. I tug on my cutest skinny jeans, paired with a red tank top. And then I spend another hour in front of the mirror, trying to get my hair just right.

Boys are exhausting.

Right now, I'm standing in front of the school in my cute tank top and jeans, hugging my body for warmth. My upper arms are covered in tiny little goosebumps, but my jacket isn't super sexy and I don't want to wear it in front of Liam. I hope he appreciates how much I'm suffering for him.

Madison has decided to wait with me, but I almost wish she didn't. She is not a source of positive energy right now. She's never liked Liam very much, but right now she is downright unsupportive. It seems like she's trying to convince me to blow off Liam before this even gets started.

"And on top of everything else, he's *late*." Madison pulls her phone out of her pocket and shoves it in my face to show me the time. "Is that what you want? A guy who's going to keep you waiting all the time?"

"He told me he might be late." I start jogging in place to keep warm, but then I get freaked out about sweating. "He's at track practice. It's not his fault if he didn't get out on time."

And not to mention Aidan is *always* late. It's almost a guarantee.

Madison sticks out her lower lip in a pout. "I just think he's wrong for you."

"Based on what?"

"Based on…" She glances around to make sure we're the only people standing there. "Look, I didn't want to tell you this, but… you know, Tyler Martinson used to be close friends with Liam."

I cringe at the name Tyler Martinson. He's one of those obnoxious jock guys who plays football with Aidan. Solely because of that, I was spending some time with him at the beginning of the year, and I wasn't all that surprised when he asked me out on a date. But I didn't feel even the slightest bit of attraction to him, so I flat out turned him down. He seemed astonished, like he was doing me a *favor* by asking me out and couldn't believe I said no. His obnoxious response made me even more glad I said no.

"So apparently…" Madison lowers her voice a notch. "Tyler said he had to stop being friends with Liam, because Liam is legit crazy. Like, he would say and do all these crazy things. And Tyler got really freaked out."

I suppress the urge to roll my eyes. "Crazy like what?"

"I don't know exactly," Madison admits. "But apparently, it was some *really* bad stuff. Like, Tyler was actually *afraid* of him. He said Liam is really messed up and any girl who gets involved with him will be sorry."

Now I really do roll my eyes. "Come *on*. You believe that?"

"Yes, I do! Liv, I told you I got a bad vibe about the guy. There's just something about him…"

"Well, I don't see it."

"Then you're blind."

I stare at my best friend and feel a burst of anger in my chest. Why is she doing this to me? She knows how much I like Liam. She's dated two complete jerks and I never said one bad word about either of them. Well, that's about to change right this minute.

"Well," I say, "at least he's better than Aidan."

Madison's mouth falls open. "What are you talking about? What's wrong with Aidan?"

"Are you joking? Aidan is a total asshole. He treats you like crap and he's practically flunking out of school. He bullies underclassmen. And he probably shoots up steroids."

Two little pink spots appear on either one of Madison's cheeks. "He doesn't shoot up steroids."

"Fine. But all the other stuff is true." I look her in the eyes, daring her to contradict me. She doesn't, because I'm totally right. "But *Liam* is the awful one. Because he gives you a bad *vibe*. Oh my God, how *awful*."

The pink spots on Madison's cheeks widen. "Fine. You want to go on a date with a psychopath? Be my guest."

With those words, Madison spins on her heels and stalks off, probably to find Aidan. Her dirty blond ponytail swings aggressively behind her as she walks away. We've had fights before, but this feels like the biggest fight we've ever had. It makes me uneasy.

But I miraculously forget all that when Liam materializes in front of me.

He looks devastatingly handsome in his track team T-shirt, baggy jeans, and a lightweight jacket with his hair slightly damp from the shower. He smiles at me and my heart does a little dance in my chest. So what if Madison and I are fighting? I can't even think about that right now.

"You came," Liam says, as if he's slightly surprised and pleased.

I return his smile. "Of course I came. I said I would."

"Yeah, but..." He ducks his head down. "Anyway, I'm glad you're here."

This guy is *not* crazy. No way. I don't know what Madison was talking about. It's clear Aidan and Tyler are jealous of Liam, because he does so well in school and all the girls think he's cute.

"You look cold," he observes.

I'm not going to lie. I'm pretty freaking cold right now. My teeth are actually chattering a little bit, and my lips feel like they're turning blue. But I don't want to seem like I'm complaining. "Maybe just a little."

And then Liam does something that totally melts me. He takes off his jacket and he holds it out to me. "Here. Take it."

"But then *you'll* be cold."

"Nah. I'm okay. I'm still hot from running."

I've never kissed a boy before, but somehow it seems more significant that a boy has never made a gallant, romantic gesture for me before. I've had a crush on Liam for several months now, but in this moment, I fall head over heels.

I'm totally in love.

Chapter 13

Transcript of Police Interview with Olivia Reynolds:

"Olivia, can you please describe your interactions with Liam Cass?"

"We're on the debate team together. We have been for the last two years."

"Are you friends with him?"

"Yes. I mean, we've been on the team together a while. So we talk a lot. I mean, not just when we're debating."

"Would you describe your relationship with Liam as more than friendship?"

"Um. Well, no. Not exactly, but... look, I feel weird talking about this with, like, the police... it's, like, embarrassing..."

"But you understand why this is important."

"Yes. Of course. I mean, that's why I called you. I thought... maybe if I told you what happened to me, it would help."

"And we appreciate you contacting us."

"Yes…"

"So going back to the original question: did you have any sort of romantic relationship with Liam Cass?"

"Well, no. Not officially. But… I sort of…"

"What?"

"I… I liked him. A *lot*. I thought he was cute. And he's really good at debate, you know?"

"Did he express romantic intentions towards you?"

"Honestly? I mean, sometimes I thought he did. One time he walked me home, but nothing happened. Obviously he liked somebody else better."

"And then what happened?"

"…"

"Olivia, if you could tell us what you told me earlier about what happened next…"

"You mean about that guy?"

"Right. You said that a man approached you on the street."

"Yeah. I was out walking my dog and this old guy—he was, like, maybe fifty—he came up to me and asked me if I was Olivia Reynolds. And it totally freaked me out because, you know, you hear all these stories about some girl going out to walk her dog and she never comes home. And he looked kind of creepy too."

"How did he look creepy?"

"I don't know. He smelled like cigarettes and his teeth

were kind of yellow. Probably because of cigarettes, right? That's why I am not going to smoke ever. Or vape. Vaping is even worse. My health teacher says you can get popcorn lung from vaping, where your lungs look like microwave popcorn."

"Uh, right. So what happened next, Olivia?"

"So I didn't really say anything. I just looked at the guy, but he seemed to know who I was. And then he asked me if I knew Liam, and that was *really* weird."

"What did you say?"

"I said yes."

"And what did he say then?"

"Well, he started telling me all the stuff he knew about me. Like, bad stuff. I mean, not *really* bad. I haven't done anything *that* bad. But, like, he had screenshots of all these text messages on my phone that I wouldn't want my parents or my teachers to see. And some other stuff."

"What sort of stuff?"

"Um, do I have to tell you that?"

"We'd like to have all the information."

"It wasn't illegal. I swear."

"You're not in trouble, Olivia. I promise. Just tell us the truth."

"Okay… well, I was dating this guy last year and I sent him some pictures of myself that I shouldn't have. It was really stupid. And I don't know how that creepy guy ended up getting those photos. God, it's so embarrassing…"

"So what happened next?"

"The guy said if I kept hanging around with Liam, he was going to show everyone."

"So what did you say?"

"What do you think? I mean, I liked Liam, but not enough to get in trouble. So I said I wouldn't hang out with him anymore."

"And did you?"

"Yeah. But honestly, it didn't really matter, because the next day… Well, you know."

"Did you have any thoughts on why that man told you not to hang out with Liam?"

"No. I was just so freaked out about the whole thing. I thought… I don't know. It was the weirdest thing ever, honestly."

"Well, thank you, Olivia. This has been very helpful."

"Detective?"

"Yes?"

"Do you really think Liam did it?"

"I can't share any details of our investigation with you, unfortunately."

"I just want to say… I don't think he did. I've known him for over two years, and he's a really nice guy. I'm not just saying that because he's cute. He's really serious about competing and he's very smart and he just *wouldn't*. I don't think he *could*. I mean, what kind of person does something like that? I just can't imagine it."

"Then why did you contact us?"

"Because... I don't know. I don't think Liam did it. But I guess I'm not absolutely sure. You never know."

Chapter 14

OLIVIA

It's about a mile to the diner, and Liam and I walk together. Well, we're with half the track team and also some of their girlfriends, but Liam and I hang back behind them. His jacket is warm and smells like he does—Dial soap. The sleeves are long enough on me that my fingertips barely poke through.

We talk about math class mostly. Liam says Mr. Gregor smells like old cheese, which is actually pretty accurate. He doesn't seem to like Mr. Gregor much, which surprises me, because a lot of kids act like smartasses in that class, but Liam doesn't. He's really polite to Mr. Gregor—to his face. I get the feeling he's one of Mr. Gregor's favorite students, and not just because he's acing the class.

Liam stands very close to me when we walk. A few times, his hand brushes against my fingertips and I think he's going to try to hold my hand, but he doesn't.

When we get to the diner, there are a lot of kids from our school already there. Even though it's a long walk, Charlie's has the *best* milkshakes. They are so good, I swear. It's like the best ice cream you've ever tasted in shake form. I notice Tyler Martinson is sitting in one of the booths, and I remember what Madison said earlier. That Tyler said Liam is crazy. That Tyler is *afraid* of him.

Could that really be true? Tyler doesn't seem like a guy who would be afraid of anything. And when we walk past him, he and Liam don't make eye contact. He doesn't look at me either, and I wonder if he's still mad at me for not going out with him. I saw him with a different girl a week later though, so it looks like he got over it quick.

We all squeeze into an extra-large booth. There are six of us, and my body is pressed up tightly against Liam. I feel the warmth of his thigh against mine. And I don't mind one bit.

"Are you squished?" He looks at me with concern in his brown eyes. He has such nice eyes. I always was partial to blue eyes, but God, his are nice. And his breath smells like peppermint. I wonder if he swallowed a breath mint before coming. Because I did. I mean, I didn't want to have tuna breath.

"I'm okay," I breathe.

"Good." He grins at me. "Because if I move over one

inch, I'm gonna fall out of the booth."

I return his smile. "Don't fall out."

"I'll try." He flips open the menu. "Do you know what you want to get?"

"Vanilla milkshake," I say without hesitation.

"Hey, that's my favorite too. You stole my idea."

I laugh. "Sorry."

"Do you want to split it?"

Splitting a milkshake with Liam? Yes, please. "Sure."

My doubts about this being a date are starting to fade. He walked me here, we're splitting a milkshake, and I couldn't be closer to him unless I was sitting on his lap. Also, when he orders it for us, he mumbles in my ear, "It's my treat." And even when the other people at the table are talking, he only seems interested in talking to me. His attention is completely focused on me.

Until something happens that spoils everything.

Our booth is fairly close to the bathroom, and when Tyler and his buddies get up to use it, they have to pass by us. Even though Liam and Tyler had studiously avoided looking at each other when he came in, Tyler jostles Liam's shoulder hard as he walks by. It was clearly done intentionally. I know it, and it's obvious that Liam knows it.

When Tyler comes back out of the bathroom, I'm worried he's going to do it again. But instead, as he passes by our table, he stumbles and falls to the ground with a loud thunk. For a moment, everything is quiet as Tyler gets back to his feet.

"You just tripped me, asshole!" Tyler is staring at Liam. There's a scary-looking vein bulging out on his thick football player's neck. "What the hell is wrong with you?"

Liam turns to look at Tyler, blinking his eyes in a picture of mock innocence. "Oh, I'm sorry. That was an accident."

"Like hell it was!"

"You're mistaken, Tyler."

"Say that to my face."

My heart speeds up in my chest. Tyler looks really mad. He's still got that vein in his neck, but now his face is starting to turn bright red. Liam stands up, and I notice that while the two boys are about the same height, Tyler is more broad like the football player he is. Liam has more of a runner's physique. I'm scared that in a fight, Tyler would have the edge.

But Liam doesn't look the slightest bit intimidated. He looks Tyler right in the eyes. "I didn't trip you. You're just clumsy."

Tyler snorts. "What—are you trying to show off in front of your *girl*? Not that you need to do much to impress *her*."

My cheeks burn. The last thing I want is Tyler talking

smack about me in front of Liam. But Tyler's words hit home. What he said seems to upset Liam more than anything so far. "Mind your own business," Liam says in a low voice.

Tyler takes a menacing step towards Liam. Their confrontation has got the whole restaurant watching— everyone is probably hoping there will be a fight. Everybody but me. I just want Tyler to leave us alone. "Does your girlfriend know you're a psychopath?"

Liam rolls his eyes. "Is that all you've got to say?"

"It's true."

"Yeah?" Liam lifts an eyebrow. "Well, if I *am* a psychopath, maybe you should be careful. Because I know pretty much everything there is to know about your family. I know where your mom goes to yoga class. I know your dad parks his car outside the garage at night. And I know what window is your sister's bedroom."

Tyler's eyes widen.

"Also," Liam adds, "you've got a new cat, don't you?"

All the color drains out of Tyler's face. I've never seen anyone look so freaked out. I'm not even sure why. What is Liam talking about? Why is he talking about Tyler's cat? This makes no sense.

But apparently, what Liam said did the trick. Tyler takes a step back, his brow furrowed.

"It wouldn't even be a challenge to kick your ass," he

mutters. He moves past Liam to get back to his seat, but I notice this time he makes an effort to avoid touching him.

Liam drops back into the seat next to mine. There's a satisfied look on his face. A secret smile plays on his lips.

"I think you just scared the shit out of Tyler," I comment.

Liam shrugs. "Yeah, well. He's a jerk."

"Didn't you guys used to be friends?"

"No. Not really."

But that's a lie. Everyone knows that Tyler and Liam used to be tight. Still, he doesn't seem to want to talk about it anymore, and that's fine with me. I didn't come here to talk about Tyler Martinson. I came here to spend time with Liam.

The waitress brings two straws for our milkshake. I wish we only had one straw, so Liam and I could have shared. But two straws is nice too. I try to time it so that I am taking a sip at the same time he is so our faces are inches apart.

"I love the milkshakes here," Liam says.

His leg is pressed against mine and so is his upper arm. If we weren't surrounded by other kids from track team, I wonder if he'd try for a kiss. The thought of it makes my heart nearly beat out of my chest.

But before I can get too excited, my phone starts ringing in my pocket. I recognize the ringtone. It's my mother.

Great.

"Hang on." I reach into my pocket and pull out my phone, which was a present for my birthday last year. But my mom put all these restrictions on it, so I can't play too many games or watch YouTube. Oh, and there's GPS tracking. So that she can know where I am at every single moment of the day. Seriously, why doesn't she just put a microchip in my head? "Hi, Mom."

"Olivia," Mom says. "Are you still at that diner? It's getting late."

Sheesh, she *knows* I'm still at the diner. She's got that GPS thing on my phone.

"It's not that late." I look down at my watch and then out the window. "It's not even dark yet."

"How are you planning to get home?"

"Um." I glance at Liam, who has his eyebrows raised. "I'll just walk."

He'll walk me home. I'm sure of it.

"Walk!" Mom says it like I suggested zip lining home. "Out of the question! I'll drive over and pick you up."

"Mom!" I try not to sound too whiny, but I *really* don't want her to pick me up. Not now. Not when things are going *so* well. "It's still really early. Can't I stay? Please?"

"Don't you have homework to do?"

"I did it at school." (That's a lie. There was no way I could concentrate on my homework when I knew Liam and I were about to have our first almost-date.)

Mom is quiet for a moment, thinking it over. I keep my fingers and my toes crossed that she says I can stay.

"No," she finally says. "I'm going to come get you now. I want you home before it gets dark."

"But Mom—"

"Not negotiable, Olivia."

"Fine," I grumble.

If Liam weren't right next to me, I probably would have fought harder to stay, but I don't want him to hear me fighting with my mother. You know—one of those fights where I explain to her that I am not a baby and she's being absolutely ridiculous. Those can go on for a while, and I've noticed they don't usually end well for me.

I hang up with my mother and shove my phone back in my pocket. "I'm really sorry," I tell him. "My mom is coming to pick me up now."

"*Now*?" His face falls. "You really have to go?"

"She's worried about me walking home alone."

His brows scrunch together. "I would have walked you."

I know he would have. And *his* mother isn't sitting around worrying about him walking me home, then walking home himself. Because his mother isn't crazy like mine.

"I'm sorry," I say.

"It's okay."

And then he reaches under the table with his left hand and finds mine. He gives it a squeeze, and then suddenly *we're holding hands.* Oh my God, we're holding hands! He grins at me, and I grin back. The only thing ruining it a little is that my hand is getting super clammy. I sort of want to pull it away from him and wipe it on my jeans, but I'm not sure how I would explain that one.

"Hey!" One of the other guys on the team is smirking at Liam. "Cass! What are you doing under the table? Hands where we can see them, buddy!"

Liam laughs, but his ears color slightly and he pulls his hand away from mine. My heart sinks in my chest, and at that moment, my mom texts me that she's outside and I better get my butt out there ASAP.

"I gotta go," I say to Liam.

He chews on his lip. "What if I tell her I'll walk you home?"

"She's outside. I really gotta go."

"Okay." He stands up so I can get out of the booth. He rubs at the back of his neck. "I'm glad you came."

I smile up at him. "Me too."

All his friends from track are staring at us. He keeps rubbing at his neck and smiling self-consciously. "Maybe another time then?"

I nod, trying not to let on how disappointed I feel right now. He's not even asking me out for another night. But it's not like we're never going to see each other again. We've got math class together tomorrow. It's my favorite class of the day now, and I don't even like math. "I'll see you tomorrow."

"See you," he says.

I wait one more beat, hoping he'll change his mind and lean in to kiss me, or at least suggest going out again. But he doesn't.

Chapter 15

OLIVIA

I am so mad at my mom.

I was having *such* a great time with Liam. He's, like, the first boy I've ever had a big crush on. And he actually seems to like me back. And she ruined it. For no reason!

"Are you going to give me the silent treatment the whole way home?" Mom asks as she turns onto Maple Street.

I fold my arms across my chest. "You know Liam asked me specifically to come tonight."

"And he'll ask you again."

"What if he doesn't?"

"I'm sure he won't be discouraged that easily."

"You don't know that."

"Give me a little bit of credit, Olivia. Give *him* a little bit of credit."

I let out an angry huff and stare out the window.

Mom knows how much I like Liam. I've been confiding in her about my crush the entire year. Especially since Madison is so anti-Liam, my mother has been my main confidante. She knows how excited I was about tonight.

"I think I saw him through the window," Mom says. She's chosen to ignore me ignoring her. I hate it when she does that, although to be fair, it usually works. "Was he the one wearing the blue T-shirt with the dark hair?"

"Yes," I admit. As much as I want to be angry at my mother, I also sort of want to talk about Liam. I'm very conflicted.

"Oh." She nods. "He's *really* cute. I can see why you like him."

"I know, right?" My palms get all clammy again at the thought of him. "And he's not *just* cute. He is, like, one of the smartest guys in the school. You should have heard him at the debate yesterday, Mom."

"Well, I'm sorry I made you come home, but I'm sure you'll have another opportunity with him."

"He held my hand." I smile at the memory. My whole body gets tingly at the thought of it. "I mean, just for a minute because one of his friends started teasing him. But... it was..."

"You should invite him over to the house."

"You mean while *you're* home?"

"Oh God. Unthinkable."

"Mom…"

Mom winks at me. "What? I'll be cool."

Oh my God, she will definitely *not* be cool. She'll probably drag out old photo albums and show him pictures of potty training.

"You can take him up to your room," she adds. "As long as you keep the door open."

"Do we have to keep it open? It's not like we're going to do anything."

Mom snorts. But I guess maybe she's right. If Liam and I were alone in a room…

God, the thought of it makes me all tingly again. I can't wait to see him again.

Mom pulls up the Honda in front of our house, and by this point, I've mostly forgiven her. Aside from Madison, my mother is my best friend and it's hard to stay angry at her. And she's probably right. I don't think I've blown it with Liam. Aren't you supposed to play hard to get with boys?

So I'm in a pretty good mood when I get out of the car. Until I see who's sitting on the front steps to our house.

Chapter 16

ERIKA

The smell of the meatloaf in the oven fills the kitchen as I chop cucumbers for the salad that will be the green element of our dinner tonight. My mother raised me to always add a green element to dinner. Even though it's a guarantee that Hannah will pick it off her plate with her thumb and forefinger and look at it like it's dog poop. And Liam might also. Actually, it's fifty-fifty that Jason will too.

Still, you have to have a green element.

The front door slams shut, which means Jason is home from work. Right on time. He's removed his shoes by the door—getting him to do that was a victory that was hard won. He wanders into the kitchen, looking pretty dang handsome in his shirt and tie. He offers me a crooked smile. "Smells good."

"Meatloaf."

He joins me at the counter and looks down at the

cucumber I'm chopping. "Funny. It doesn't look like meatloaf."

I roll my eyes and nudge him with my shoulder. "It's in the oven. Five more minutes on the timer."

He walks over to the oven and throws it open to peer at the meatloaf inside. I hate it when he does that because it disrupts the cooking process, but I grudgingly appreciate that he likes my cooking so much that he has to witness it in progress.

"How was traffic?" I ask. I still don't know how he can brave the commute from Manhattan to Long Island during rush hour and keep a smile on his face. Five minutes on the Long Island Expressway and I'm crabby all day.

"Not bad." He sticks his thumb into his tie to loosen it. "Can I help with chopping?"

I snort. Jason is good with computers, but cooking is definitely not his thing. When he's chopping vegetables, he's just as likely to slice off a chunk of his finger—I'd rather not have blood all over my salad. "That's okay."

"What?" He points at the tomato on the counter. "I could chop that up for you."

"Hmm. Could you?"

"Sure. I have great knife skills or whatever." When I give him a look, he grins at me. "Come on. It's just for our dinner. It's not like we're entering the salad in a salad competition."

"How about you set the table?"

"Your wish is my command, m'lady."

I roll my eyes. "Can you yell for Hannah and Liam to come down first?"

"You got it."

Jason pulls his tie the rest of the way off as he wanders over to the staircase to yell for the kids to come down for dinner. Then he obediently comes back to the kitchen to set the table. He's being a five-star husband tonight.

"Did you have a good day at work today?" I say as I start chopping the tomato.

He nods eagerly. "The team is making great progress. Everyone is working really hard, and we're going to have a new product soon. It's exciting."

Jason explained to me some of the software they're building, and I don't entirely understand it. He is definitely some kind of genius. It's a bit intimidating, because I'm definitely not a genius, but after twenty years of marriage, I don't feel insecure about that anymore. At least it means we can afford a nice house and nice cars. And maybe if he gets some time off, we can take a nice vacation as a family.

Hannah wanders into the kitchen in her bare feet just as the timer goes off for the meatloaf. Jason makes a big deal out of how delicious it looks, but Hannah just crinkles her nose. She glares at the gray mound, glistening with tomato sauce and its own juices. "We're not *eating* that, are we?"

"Of course not," Jason says. "That's our new TV. What would you like to watch?"

"Dad," she groans. She narrows her eyes at the dinner I just spent the last hour cooking. "It's just so… meaty. It's like this big hunk of meat."

"Yes, Hannah. That's the definition of a meatloaf."

She sinks into one of the chairs at the kitchen table. "I'd rather have chicken."

"Well, I'd rather be in the Bahamas." Jason shrugs. "We don't always get what we want. Sometimes you have to do horrible things like eat delicious meatloaf."

I smile to myself as I continue chopping the tomato. "Where is Liam? Can somebody tell him to come down?"

Hannah takes out her phone and start thumbing through her text messages. "Liam isn't home."

What? "He isn't?" I try to keep the tremor out of my voice. "Where is he?"

"I don't know. Track practice? What's the big deal? It's not that late."

I glance out the window, where the sun has already dipped in the sky. "The sun is down."

"So?" Hannah keeps her eyes on her phone. "He probably went to eat somewhere with his friends or something. Why are you freaking out?"

"I'm not freaking out."

But she's right. I *am* freaking out. I look over at Jason, who doesn't seem even the slightest bit concerned that Liam is not home. Which makes sense, because our son is sixteen years old and practically driving. He can be responsible for himself. He's not even late yet. He's come home at this time before.

But it's not Liam I'm worried about.

My hands are shaking so badly that I slip with the knife and the blade goes right into my left index finger. Blood immediately pools all over the cutting board.

"Geez, Erika!" Jason winces and goes for the paper towels. He grabs two squares and thrusts them in my direction. "Are you okay? That looks like a bad cut."

I press the paper towels against my finger, and they immediately saturate with crimson. But the cut on my finger is the least of my concerns. Where is Liam? All I can think about is Olivia Reynolds. What if he's with her?

What is he doing to her?

I hope Frank hurries up and does his damn job.

"Erika!" Jason's voice cuts into my thoughts. "That's really bleeding a lot. Maybe we should go to the emergency room…"

"No!" The word comes out too loudly and Jason blinks at me. I clear my throat. "It's fine. Really. I just bleed a lot."

Jason tries to smile, but he looks pale. "And you were

worried about *me* chopping the tomatoes…"

The front door slams, and I let out a breath. Liam is home. Thank God.

My son stomps into the kitchen, still wearing his sneakers that have now tracked dirt all over the carpet and the kitchen floor. I've yelled at him for that many times before, but I'm not going to freak out over it right now. I'm just glad he's home.

"Mom was worried about you," Hannah speaks up before I can pretend the opposite is true.

"You were?" Liam looks surprised. "I just went out to Charlie's with some of my friends from track. You just said to be home by seven. Right?" He looks down at his watch. "I'm not late."

"No, it's fine." I grab another paper towel from the counter to replace the one that's drenched in my blood. "Did you have fun?"

Liam shrugs. "Sure."

The blood seems to have slowed down, which is a good thing. I was beginning to worry I needed stitches. I've never had stitches before, except for during childbirth. "Was it just the guys from track? Or were there girls there?"

I try to say it casually, hoping he might let something slip. But given the way Jason smirks at me, I don't think I was successful.

Liam goes to the cupboard to grab some glasses, which Jason forgot when he was setting the table. Liam has set the table many more times than Jason has. "It was just the guys."

Jason laughs. "He probably wouldn't tell us if it wasn't."

He probably wouldn't. And that's exactly what I'm afraid of.

Chapter 17

OLIVIA

"Tyler." I frown as I say his name. "What are you doing here?"

The last person I expected to see when I got home was Tyler Martinson. He's still got on his football jersey, and he's sitting on the front steps of my house, his elbows on his knees. When he sees me get out of the car, he scrambles back to his feet.

"Olivia," he says. "I've got to talk to you."

"Tyler!" My mother has noticed Tyler sitting there. He knows her because Tyler's mom is this crazy PTA lady. She's always volunteering for this or selling tickets for that. All the other parents are always trying to suck up to her, including my mom. "How are you doing?"

"Good." Tyler shrugs. Liam is always really polite around adults, but Tyler isn't. I'm lucky he doesn't curse my mother out. "Mrs. Mercer, I need to talk to Olivia for a few minutes."

My mother hesitates. Even though she knows his mother, Tyler doesn't look like the kind of guy you want to leave your daughter alone with. He's big, he doesn't look adults in the eye unless he's pissed off, and he resembles the date rapist in some TV movie.

"Just for a few minutes," Mom says. "Then I want you to come inside, Olivia."

I nod, disappointed my mother wouldn't give me an excuse to blow off Tyler. I don't want to talk to him. Not for a few minutes—not for a few seconds. But when my mother goes back into the house, he and I are left alone together for the first time since that day he asked me out and I said no.

The thing is, Tyler isn't bad looking. He's actually pretty good looking. Not as cute as Liam, but who is, right? The reason I didn't want to go out with him had nothing to do with his looks. It had to do with the fact that he's a jerk. And a bully.

For example, when we were freshmen, there was this kid in our class named Greg, who was like the nicest kid *ever*. But he was also really scrawny, wore super thick glasses, and was definitely pretty nerdy. For some reason, Tyler made it his mission to torture Greg. I had gym with the two of them, and Tyler was always trying to find a way to throw the ball directly at Greg as hard as he could.

Which, in Tyler's case, was really hard. I remember one time he threw it at him so hard that his glasses broke and his nose started to bleed.

He also started rumors about him online. I can't remember all the details, but it was pretty bad. I think they also Photoshopped Greg's face on all these embarrassing pictures. Then they sent the pictures to the whole school.

It was stuff like that the entire year. By the time June came along, Greg was so beaten down that he barely spoke anymore to anyone. And then he didn't come back to school in September.

Oh, and last year there was that whole thing with Lily Macintosh. I guess they were going out and he got mad at her, and he sent everyone in the school these photos of her topless that she apparently sent him when they were going out. I felt really bad for Lily, although you have to be really stupid to send naked pictures of yourself to a guy like Tyler Martinson. Anyway, she left school too. Madison told me she tried to kill herself, but I'm not sure if that's true. I overheard Tyler laughing about it in the hallway once.

So yeah. That's Tyler. That's the kind of shit he does.

"What is it, Tyler?" I wrap my arms around my chest, because it's even colder than it was earlier. Tyler is wearing a coat, but there's no chance in hell he would offer it to me the way Liam did. He's too self-absorbed to even notice I'm cold. "What do you want?"

"I need to talk to you about Liam."

I roll my eyes. "Don't bother."

"It's important."

"Liam is a really nice guy." I raise my chin to look Tyler in the eyes. "There's nothing *you* could tell me about him that would change my mind."

"You've got to listen to me, Olivia." Tyler's voice cracks slightly, which surprises me. Is he actually upset? "I'm not joking around. Liam is… he's dangerous."

I snort. "*Liam* is dangerous?"

"I really think…" He frowns at me. "I think if you go out with him, your life could be in danger."

"Oh, come *on*! So you're saying he's a *murderer*?"

"I'm saying… of everyone I know, he's the only one who scares the shit out of me."

"Why?"

Tyler shifts between his thick legs. "It's a long story. You have to trust me."

I just shake my head.

"And anyway," he adds. "Liam has barely any experience with girls. Wouldn't you rather be with someone…" He winks at me. "Someone who knows what they're doing?"

Right. And now he's finally come to the real reason he's here. Because he's pissed off that I went out with Liam after rejecting him.

"I wouldn't, actually," I say.

I start to turn away from Tyler, but before I can, he reaches out and grabs my arm. I try to shake him off, but he holds tight.

"You've got to listen to me, Olivia," he pleads with me. "You're making a huge mistake. I promise you."

Tyler's fingers are the size of sausages. I try again to shake him off again as I feel bruises blossoming on my skin. "Let me go," I say through my teeth.

"You don't understand..."

"Let me go or I'll scream."

That finally gets through to him. He opens his fist and I pull away. My arm still throbs where he was grabbing onto me.

"We'll talk about it more later," he says.

"No," I say. "We won't."

Chapter 18

ERIKA

Jason and I love to binge watch TV series in bed. When we first got a television in our bedroom, it felt decadent. Up until then, we only had the TV in the living room. "What kind of TV addicts are we that we need to have a television in every room?" Jason had said. But we got the television, and it was a flat screen that was just as big as the one in the living room. And we watch it *all the time*. I can't think of a purchase we get more mileage out of than this TV. Even our cars.

Jason has stripped down to an undershirt and boxers, and he puts his arm around me while I snuggle up against him to watch episode five of season two of *BoJack Horseman*. It's this television show about a drug-addicted horse who was on a nineties sitcom. Don't judge.

But it's hard to focus. Frank is supposed to be talking to Olivia tonight. He's supposed to text me when it's done.

So until I get that text, I can't entirely relax. There's a knot in my neck that's throbbing.

"This is the best show on television," Jason says. His eyes are on the screen, and he's completely oblivious to way I keep tapping my fingers against the bed. My nervous habit.

"Even better than *Stranger Things*?"

"Okay. Both good in different ways."

"Hmm."

My phone starts ringing on the table by our bed and I practically jump out of my skin. But it's not Frank—he's supposed to text, not call. I pick it up and see my boss's name on the screen. I look at my watch and see the time is nine-thirty. Still a respectable time to call an employee.

"It's Brian," I say. "Can we pause BoJack?"

"I suppose," Jason grumbles. "But make it quick. This show isn't going to binge watch itself."

I pick up the phone and Brian's nasal voice fills my ear. Brian is my age, but he hates technology and avoids texting or emails if he can help it. He doesn't even have a smart phone yet. He's been running the *Nassau Nutshell* for ten years, and he has a very rigid idea of how things should be done.

"Erika." He has an impatient edge to his voice, which is fairly typical. "Where is my article on the pie contest?"

As part of my incredibly exciting journalism career, I

was assigned to cover a local pie baking contest. It wasn't that bad, honestly, because I got to sample some of the pies. But it's not exactly what I dreamed about when I majored in journalism.

"I thought it wasn't due until tomorrow morning."

"So you were planning to wait until the very last second of your deadline?"

Jason reaches for my belly to tickle me and I swipe him away. "Brian, if you need me to have it by a certain time, why not make *that* the deadline?"

"Erika, just please get me that article."

"I'll have it first thing tomorrow morning."

"Erika…"

"First thing tomorrow morning. I promise."

Brian grumbles, but he has to accept it. There would be some nights when I would get on the computer and bang out the article for him on the spot, but I'm not in the mindset right now. All I can think of is Frank. Part of me was tempted to hide in the bushes outside Olivia's house to see it all go down.

After I hang up the phone, Jason raises his eyebrows at me. "You good to go?"

"Yeah. It's fine."

"You know," he says, "now that the kids are older, you could go look for a better job. One in the city."

I snort. "How am I supposed to do that when I end up

having to drive them to school every other day?"

"Liam will have his license soon. He can drive Hannah." Jason blinks his blue eyes at me. "You should think about it. I know you're not happy at the *Nutshell*."

I take a deep breath. "I'd like to. You know I would. But the kids... They just need me too much right now."

His brow furrows. He doesn't get it. I love my husband—he's been an amazing partner for the last twenty years. But he isn't around as much as I am. He commutes into the city every day and has to travel frequently for work, and that means he misses a lot. When something bad happens, he has to hear it secondhand from me. And he's always certain I'm exaggerating.

He has no clue what our son is capable of.

My phone buzzes on the nightstand. I reach for it, noticing a text message has popped up on the screen. I see Frank's name and the following text:

I spoke to her. It's taken care of.

The tension drains out of my shoulders. Thank God. Disaster has been averted once again, if only temporarily. Olivia Reynolds has been spared, and she doesn't even know it. I shudder to think of what might have happened if I were rushing into the city every day for a job. I might never have found out about this girl.

"I'll think about the job," I lie, as I reach for the remote control.

Chapter 19

OLIVIA

It's an embarrassing fact that my bedroom isn't much different than it was when I was a little kid. I still have posters all over my walls of cute cats and dogs—there's nothing cuter than a kitten sleeping on a puppy. I still need a night light in order to go to sleep. And I still have to arrange all my stuffed animals just so on my bed every night.

Tonight I cuddle with Mr. Penguin as I try to fall asleep. I push my face into his soft black and white fur, squeezing my eyes shut. Sleep, dammit!

No, this is impossible. I can't stop thinking about Liam.

I can't believe I had to leave the diner early. The more I think about it, the more I think Liam would have definitely kissed me. But instead, he didn't even ask to see me again.

The whole thing has left me feeling totally unsatisfied.

Liam is soooo cute. Everything about him makes me all tingly. Every time I close my eyes, I picture him smiling at me. Also, his teeth are nice. For some reason, I'm really into teeth. Perfect, straight teeth are really sexy to me. Is that weird? Maybe. But I just think Liam is really cute.

Liam seemed really disappointed when I had to run out to meet my mother. Maybe he decided I'm not worth the effort. After all, he knows plenty of other girls at school who are prettier than I am. I'm not even the prettiest Olivia he knows.

And the worst part is I can't even talk to Madison about it. Usually, she texts me like a million times during the night, but tonight my phone was oddly silent. It feels like a part of me is missing without Madison.

I'll have to talk to her tomorrow. Try to make this right.

I hear something tapping against my window. I first I think maybe it's rain, but then I realize somebody is throwing pebbles against my window. I put down Mr. Penguin and get up to investigate.

Oh my God.

It's Liam.

He's standing below my window, wearing a light jacket and jeans. His dark hair is tousled by the wind, and he's craning his neck to look up at my window. He waves to me and I open the window enough to stick my head out.

"What are you doing here?" I ask.

He tosses a pebble in the air and catches it. "Target practice."

I stare at him.

"I'm just kidding, Olivia. Could you... Can you come down?"

I glance behind me at the clock on my nightstand. It's a quarter past one. My parents are surely asleep by now, as evidenced by the lack of light coming from underneath my door. They'll never know if I slip out. And anyway, I'll be right downstairs. "Okay, I'll be right down."

I'm wearing only an oversized T-shirt to sleep in, and there's no way I'm going outside in that. Instead, I slip on a pair of jeans and a new tank top. And this time, I grab a light jacket because the temperature has dropped precipitously overnight.

Sure enough, my parents' bedroom door is closed and the light seems to be off inside. I slip past the room, down the stairs, and into the dark kitchen. I unlock the back door and quietly slip outside, making sure not to let the door bang shut.

The light from our back porch casts a shadow on Liam's face. "Hey," he says.

I shiver, despite my jacket. "Hi."

I look at the sky and see the moon is full tonight.

When I was in fifth grade, we learned about all the different kinds of moons. Full moon, crescent moon, new moon. I barely remember it. But I've always loved full moons.

Liam shoves his hands into his pockets and smiles crookedly. "I'm sorry I woke you up."

"You didn't wake me up."

"No?"

"Couldn't sleep."

He nods. "Me either." He rubs at the back of his neck. "I… uh, I couldn't stop thinking about you."

I swallow hard. "You… you couldn't?"

He lifts his eyes, which look even darker than usual right now under the moonlight. "You had to rush out. I'd been… I really wanted to walk you home."

"Oh."

"Look, Olivia, I…" He takes a deep breath. I have no idea what he's going to say, I'm not sure he does either. But then he takes a step forward, ducks his head down, and presses his lips against mine.

Oh. My. God.

It's my first kiss. My first real kiss. And it is *incredible*. Liam is a *really* good kisser. Granted, I don't have any other guys to compare him to, but I don't need to in order to know he's good. I mean, the first time I had ice cream, I knew that was good. And this is indescribable.

When he pulls away, my whole body is shaking. And when he runs a hand through his dark hair, I realize he's shaking too. He gives me a lopsided smile. "I've wanted to do that since the first day of school."

"I'm really glad you did."

"Yeah?" His eyes light up. "Me too."

And then he kisses me again.

Chapter 20

ERIKA

I wake up from a nightmare feeling like I can't breathe.

I don't remember all the details from the nightmare. But I remember being in a deep pit in the ground. And somebody throwing dirt on me, burying me alive. And as they bury me, they laugh. A laugh that echoes throughout the shallow grave.

My heart is still pounding at the thought of it. I have to take deep breaths, trying to calm myself down.

I turn my head to look at Jason, who is sound asleep beside me. He's snoring softly like he always does when he sleeps on his back. His pale eyelashes flutter slightly, but he doesn't stir. Jason has always been a deep sleeper, and he rarely suffers from insomnia. A long time ago, before we had Liam, I could have woken him up to tell him about my nightmare. He wouldn't have been mad. He would have put his arm around me, pulled me close to him, and made me feel like everything was all right again.

But Jason doesn't have the ability to make me feel that way anymore. Nothing can. And he has to wake up early in the morning and commute into the city. I can't wake him up. It wouldn't be fair to him.

It was so simple back when we were young. I met Jason over twenty years ago. I was writing an article on the tech startup company he had helped found that was quickly becoming very successful. His red-tinged brown hair, that our daughter later would inherit, was in need of a haircut and he was also in need of a shave, but he looked adorable. As he explained what the company did, his blue eyes progressively getting wider and more excited, I blurted out, "I have to tell you, I think you're the smartest guy I've ever met."

Jason stopped mid-sentence and blinked at me. "Is that a good thing?"

I didn't hesitate. "Yes."

"Good. Because I think you're the prettiest girl I've ever met."

We were inseparable for a long time after that. We even spent a summer traveling through Europe in style after Jason sold his company for a bundle of money. It was on the Eiffel tower that he got down on one knee and proposed to me. Maybe it was cliché, but it was one of the most romantic things I could imagine.

I love Jason even more than I did that day, but admittedly, the romance isn't what it used to be. I hate that he has to travel so far to get to work every day. And I hate the not infrequent business trips he has to take. And I've hated it even more since an incident that happened two years ago.

Jason told me he had a late dinner meeting at work with an investor. This is something that happens from time to time, and I didn't think much of it. But then when he came home, he was grinning ear to ear and reeking of an unfamiliar perfume. I smelled it the second he kissed me hello. And right after that, he made a beeline for the shower.

He spent the next few weeks being particularly attentive to me. Flowers, expensive dinners out—even some diamond earrings he had caught me admiring on my computer. I couldn't help but think that Jason was filling out every checkbox for signs of a cheating husband.

I considered confronting him about it, but in my heart, I didn't believe my husband was a cheater. I imagined how hurt he would be if I even suggested it. I finally decided I must have imagined the perfume. Or maybe he had dinner with an investor that had particularly strong-smelling perfume and the scent clung to him. It's like when you go out to a bar and come home reeking of smoke, even if you haven't had a cigarette.

And after that night, I never smelled it again. So even if it did happen, it never happened again.

But there's still that worry in the back of my head. Especially now that Jason has gotten "hot." I wish his hours weren't so long. I wish waitresses didn't flirt with him when we go to restaurants, even if he doesn't flirt back. Ultimately, I do trust him though. I don't think he would ever cheat on me—not really.

After all, it's not worrying about my husband that keeps me up at night.

"Jason," I whisper. I don't want to wake him up, but if he happens to be up, then I wouldn't be at fault.

He snores.

Fine. He isn't waking up. And I'm not going to fall asleep again so fast. May as well get up and make myself some tea.

I slide my feet into my slippers and grab my fluffy blue housecoat from the dresser where I throw it every morning. I yawn and pad out into the hallway. I start for the staircase, but something stops me.

The door to Liam's bedroom is ajar.

Liam never leaves the door to his bedroom open at night. Ever. Not even when he was five years old. He always wants the door closed tight. The sight of that door slightly open is as terrifying to me as my nightmare. When it comes to Liam, unexpected is always bad.

I walk over to the bedroom door and push it the rest of the way open. I squint into the darkness of my son's room.

It's empty.

I race down to the living room, my heart pounding. Maybe I'll find Liam on the couch, watching television. Like me, he often has difficulty sleeping. Even though I make him go to bed at ten, I know he's up far later. He told me once that he only needs five hours of sleep.

But Liam isn't in the living room. And he's not in the kitchen. Or either of the bathrooms—downstairs or upstairs. I comb the entire house and even look out on the porch and in the backyard before I race back up the stairs to my bedroom.

"Jason!"

So much for not waking him up. But our son is *missing*. I can't not say anything to him. What am I supposed to do now? Go back to sleep after Liam vanished from his room in the middle of the night?

Jason's eyes crack open. He rubs at them with the back of his fists like he's two years old. "Erika?"

"Liam's gone!" I wring my hands together. "He's not in the house. He went somewhere."

I stare at Jason, waiting for him to get as upset as I am. He rubs his eyes again. Yawns. Honestly, I'm not feeling his fear right now.

"Jason," I try again. "I can't find Liam and it's two in the morning."

"Okay, relax. He's not a baby." He yawns again. "Did you try calling his phone?"

I can't believe that somehow I did not think to do that. I'm amazed by my husband's ability to think rationally in any situation.

I snatch my phone off the nightstand, where it is charging. I select Liam's number from my list of favorites. I press his name, holding my breath, praying he'll pick up.

"Hello?"

I feel a rush of relief at the sound of Liam's voice. Jason mouths: *Told you so.* "Liam! Where are you?"

"Oh." He's quiet for a moment. "I couldn't sleep. So I went out and took a walk."

"At two in the morning? I was worried sick!"

"Dad said I could walk around the block if I couldn't sleep."

I look at Jason accusingly. "Did you tell him he could go outside and walk around the block in the middle of the night?"

Jason taps his chin. "Uh…"

I'll deal with him later. I turn my attention back to the phone. "Liam, I want you to come home right now."

"Now?"

"Yes. *Now.*"

He's quiet again. "Okay. I'll come right home."

We hang up, and now I'm free to yell at my husband. Apparently he has absolutely no common sense. "You told him it was okay to wander the neighborhood in the middle of the night? Seriously?"

Jason sits up straighter in bed. "Okay, look, I know you're mad. But this neighborhood is really safe. It's not like he's a little kid. He's as tall as I am. He's an athlete. He can defend himself."

"Not against a knife. Or a gun."

"You really think somebody is prowling our neighborhood with a knife or a gun?"

"It's just not a good idea."

"Come on, Erika. He's almost an adult. You really think something is going to happen to him?"

No. If I'm being honest with myself, I don't think anything is going to happen to Liam. I don't think he's going to get mugged or attacked. Liam can take care of himself. I'm not at all worried about that.

What I'm worried about is Liam happening to somebody else. Because my first thought when his bedroom was empty was: what does he want to do that he can only do at two in the morning?

What if he's with Olivia Reynolds?

My breaths are coming in quick gasps. I'm hyperventilating. Jason's eyes widen as he realizes what's happening to me. He sprints into the bathroom and I hear him fumbling around the medicine cabinet. When he returns, he's holding a bottle of pills. He fiddles with the childproof cap and finally shakes one out.

"Take it," he says.

I haven't had to swallow one of my Xanax in two months. I had been so proud of myself. But that progress is down the drain. I scoop the pill from his open palm and pop it in my mouth. I swallow it without water. Jason watches me, his brows knitted together. He used to only get a crease there when he was frowning, but now there's a crease there all the time.

"Are you okay?" he asks in a soft voice like I'm some kind of mental patient.

I'm already feeling calmer from the Xanax, even though it's probably a placebo effect. It couldn't work that quickly.

"Listen," Jason says in that same overly calm voice. "Why don't you lie down?"

"Not until Liam is back," I manage.

"What if I go downstairs to wait for Liam? I'll talk to him about not going out in the middle of the night anymore, okay?"

I try to protest, but I feel dizzy and weak. That's what hyperventilating always does to me. And the Xanax probably isn't doing me any favors. "Okay. Thank you."

I lie down in the bed, and even though Jason said he was going downstairs, he lies down next to me and strokes my hair. "You need to relax more, Erika. Everything is fine. The kids are doing fine. You worry much too much."

I wish I lived in Jason's universe. Where the kids are doing fine and my biggest problem is our substantial mortgage. But unfortunately, nothing in my life is that simple.

It's my last thought as I drift off to sleep. I have no idea that my entire world is about to fall apart.

Chapter 21

ERIKA

Liam claims shotgun during the drive to school the next morning. He's in an unusually good mood, in spite of the fact that Jason read him the riot act when he got home, and I repeated the entire performance this morning. But I don't think Jason gave him that hard of a time, and I know I didn't give it my all, considering I was still out of it from lack of sleep mixed with a Xanax hangover.

On top of that, I couldn't get that angry when I knew that Jason had given him permission to leave the house during the night. Really, Jason should've been the object of my wrath. But he had already gone running, showered, and hit the road before I was fully awake. I don't think that was an accident.

Liam has commandeered the radio, and he's got a Maroon 5 song playing. He's humming along, which is very unusual for Liam. Hannah is the one who usually belts out radio lyrics in a painfully off-key voice. In spite of his lack of sleep, Liam is very peppy this morning. I guess he's right— he doesn't need that much sleep. He's still humming when we pull onto the block to get to the front of the high school.

"What's going on at the school?" Hannah pipes up.

It's a very good question. The front of the school is packed with police officers and reporters in equal numbers. It's a bad combination. I try to pull up in front of the school, but a police officer waves me to the side entrance. My stomach sinks. The last thing you want to see around your kids' school is a bunch of cops.

"Is the school even open?" I say. "What's going on?"

Of course, Hannah and Liam immediately whip out their phones to try to figure it out. I pull alongside the side entrance, where there is a teacher manning the door. It seems like they are letting kids inside, although I'm hesitant to let mine out of the car.

"A student disappeared from her bedroom last night!" Hannah exclaims. "Nobody has any idea where she is."

I throw the car into park and look back at Hannah. "Who's the student?"

Not Olivia Reynolds. Not Olivia Reynolds.

"Hang on…" She's still scrolling with her thumb. "It's…" The color drains from her face.

"Hannah?"

Hannah chews on her lip. She glances at Liam, then back down at her phone. "Olivia Mercer."

"Olivia..." I frown at my daughter. "Olivia... Mercer? What year is she?"

She keeps her eyes pinned on the screen of her phone, her hair falling in front of her face. "She's, um, a junior."

I lift my eyes to look at Liam. He is staring at the screen of his own phone, his lips slightly parted. "Liam, do you know this girl?"

"A little," he says. "I've met her. But I don't know her very well."

I narrow my eyes at him. Is he lying? I can't tell anymore. I used to be able to see through him, but he's gotten too good at deceiving me. He sounds like he's telling the truth, at least. Maybe he really is.

So instead, I look back at Hannah, who is an open book. Sure enough, she is looking at the screen of her phone, her brows bunched together, biting her lip hard enough that it's turned white. I get a horrible sinking feeling in my stomach. Oh my God, *did I get the wrong Olivia*? How many Olivias are there in this goddamn school?

"Maybe you two shouldn't go to school today," I say.

Hannah shakes her head. "I've got a math test today. And anyway, why would we stay home? We'll be safe at school."

"If you're sure…"

Hannah manages a smile, but it's strained. "Don't worry so much, Mom."

With those words, she grabs her backpack and gets out of the car. Liam reaches for the bag at his feet and starts to do the same, but I seize his arm. I still remember when his arm was so small and skinny, I could wrap my fingers around it. A lot has changed since then.

"Liam," I say.

He shifts his backpack onto his lap. Hannah has about a million little ornaments hanging off her bag, but Liam has nothing. "I'm going to be late for school."

"Liam." I choke out the next sentence: "Where did you go last night?"

He lifts his dark eyes and looks straight into mine. "I just walked around the block."

"You swear?"

"Mom, stop it. I swear."

When he was younger, Liam had difficulty maintaining eye contact when he was lying—that's how I knew. But his eye contact is strong right now. If he's lying, he's lying right to my face and doing it very well. The truth is, I don't know what to believe. But I keep seeing the way Hannah lost her composure when she read that girl's name off the screen.

"Mom, I've got to go."

"Okay." I release his arm. "Go. But tell Hannah I'll pick you both up at school today."

"I've got track team practice."

"Skip it."

Liam looks like he's going to protest, but he keeps his mouth shut. He puts his hand on the handle of the door, poised to turn it. "Bye, Mom. I love you."

"I love you too."

The hardest thing about Liam is that when he says "I love you," I can't tell whether that's a lie too.

Chapter 22

Transcript from police interview with Eleanor Williams:

"How do you know Liam Cass, Ms. Williams?"

"I was his second grade teacher."

"You were his teacher the entire year?"

"That's right."

"And what did you think of Liam?"

"Well, at the beginning of the year, he was one of my favorite students. Maybe my *favorite*. Second graders… they don't have a great attention span. They get easily distracted or silly and I have to redirect them. But Liam wasn't like that. He was always well behaved, even when the other kids were messing around. And he always finished his assignments first. He understood *everything*. His homework was immaculate. And on top of that, he was very polite. He was also just a really cute kid. Like the kind you'd see in a commercial."

"How did the other children interact with him?"

"For the most part, they all liked him a lot. He was only seven years old, but he was very charming. Almost too charming, if you know what I mean. Like he was putting on an act. That's unusual for a seven-year-old. Usually with kids that age, what you see is what you get."

"So what happened during the year to change your opinion of him?"

"Well, like I said, Liam was an exceptionally well-behaved child. But sometimes he would say the most disturbing things. He had this sweet face, and when he said something like that…"

"Like what?"

"Um, well, it's hard to remember so long ago, but there was one thing he said that stood out to me. And that's why I called you."

"What's that?"

"We were doing a unit about families and marriage and all that. And Liam raised his hand and said that he couldn't wait to get married."

"That doesn't sound so bad."

"He said he couldn't wait to get married, so he could stuff his wife deep in a hole and never let her out."

"…"

"Exactly."

"Did you do anything about all those statements he

was making?"

"I contacted his parents, of course. I didn't take it to the level of the principal, because it didn't seem frequent enough and he wasn't disrupting the class in any way."

"So you spoke to his parents?"

"Just his mother. His father was away on business and couldn't make it for the meeting."

"And what did Mrs. Cass say when you talked to her?"

"She was horrified, of course. I told her I thought Liam would benefit from some sort of psychological therapy, and she agreed. She said she was going to find a child therapist as quickly as she could. But the weird thing was…"

"Yes?"

"She was horrified, but she didn't seem *surprised*. Not really. Not the way you'd think she should've been."

"And why do you think that is?"

"I think she already knew Liam was having these thoughts. I mean, he must have said things to her over the years."

"Do you know if she ever got him into therapy?"

"She told me she did."

"And did his behavior improve?"

"If you're asking if he kept making those disturbing statements, the answer is no. He didn't. He never said anything like that again. But I always got the feeling…"

"What?"

"Well, like I said, Liam was a smart kid. I got the sense that the only reason he stopped saying those things was because he realized he shouldn't say it out loud anymore. I don't think he stopped having those thoughts though. But of course, it's impossible to know."

"Yes, that's true."

"I hope I did the right thing calling you. I wasn't sure if I should, but after I read what happened to that Mercer girl and remembered Liam was in the same grade… well, I just thought I should say something."

"No, it's good you did."

"I really hope you find her."

"We do too."

Chapter 23

ERIKA

I'm jumping to conclusions.

Just because a girl went missing and Liam happened to be out last night, it doesn't mean my son had anything to do with it. Just because her name is Olivia, it doesn't mean she was the girl Liam was interested in. Olivia Reynolds was the girl Liam was talking to in debate team. I confirmed it was her based on her Facebook profile. This is another completely unrelated Olivia.

I'm panicking over nothing. This is going to be okay.

I pull over on a side street shortly after the kids get out of the car and take out my phone. I do a search for "missing high school student" in our town, and the name Olivia and an article instantly pops up. Olivia Mercer, sixteen years old, disappeared from her bedroom during the night. Her mother went to wake her up for school and she wasn't there.

The police are considering the possibility that the girl has run away, but think it's unlikely. All her clothes and luggage seemed to be present, and she also left behind her wallet and her cell phone. On the other hand, there were no signs of struggle or forced entry. Maybe she hadn't run away, but she had left the house on her own accord. With somebody she knew.

There is a color photograph of Olivia Mercer in one of the articles. She's not quite beautiful, but undeniably cute. Round face, lots of freckles, a little dimple on each cheek when she smiles. She looked like a sweet girl. The kind of girl you can't help but like.

I read about ten articles on Olivia Mercer's disappearance, but after the first three, they repeat all the same information. I refresh, hoping to discover a new article about how she was miraculously found.

But no. Olivia Mercer is still missing.

I want to go home and hide under the covers, but we need groceries. Unfortunately, the grocery store near the school will be teeming with parents, wanting nothing more than to gossip about poor Olivia's disappearance. I don't want to talk about it. I don't even want to *think* about it.

There's another grocery store that recently opened up about twenty minutes away. I won't run into any parents there. It's worth burning the extra gas. Maybe driving will clear my head.

I bring up the GPS in the car to lead me to the grocery store. But as I start to type in the name of the store, the GPS brings up a list of recent searches, including one address that is unfamiliar to me. The last search on the list is 41 Green St.

When was I searching for *that* address? Who lives there?

On a whim, I click on it. The British-accented voice of my GPS instructs me to drive straight and then make a right at the next light. I follow the directions, making a right at the light, followed by a left, and another right onto Green Street. I drive down the street, watching the numbers on the right side, which are the odd numbered houses. I'm looking out for number 41.

It's not hard to find. It's the house that has all the police officers and reporters in front. This house is clearly of interest today.

I don't even need to check the mailbox, but I look anyway, just to torture myself. The black letters written on the gray box are like a punch in the gut:

MERCER

I turn the corner and pull over onto an empty street. I sit in my parked car for fifteen minutes, my hands shaking too badly to drive. Liam went out last night. He obviously took my car. And he drove here. To the home of the girl who is now missing. Possibly dead.

I reach into my purse and pull out my phone, but my hands are shaking so much that I nearly drop it. I barely manage to press the button for Jason's phone number. Thank God, he picks up. Jason gets very involved with his work, and we have an agreement that I'll only bother him for level two or worse emergencies. I think this counts.

"Erika?"

"Hey." My voice cracks and I clear my throat. "Jason, we need to talk."

"Jesus, what's wrong? Are you okay?"

"There's a girl from the high school that's missing." I suppress a sob. "She wasn't in her bed this morning when her parents came into the room. And Liam... I think when he went out last night, he took my car and went to see her. Her address is in the car GPS. And now she's missing. She's *gone*, Jason. Vanished!"

"Wait..." Jason is quiet for a moment. "You're saying he took the car out himself—without me?" His voice rises a notch. "That's not okay! He only has a learner's permit."

"*That* is what you're getting out of this? Jason, do you understand what I'm saying?"

"I... I guess not...?"

I take a deep breath. "This girl is missing. Somebody took her, and Liam might be the last person to see her alive."

"So he should call the police and tell them what he

knows so they can find out who did this."

My hands are still shaking, but now it's with anger. How could Jason be this dense? Maybe he's not around much, but he knows the stories about Liam as well as I do. And no, he doesn't believe there's anything wrong with our son. But he has to realize how this looks.

"Wait." Jason's voice breaks into my thoughts. "Are you saying you think Liam has something to do with her disappearance?"

"Yes, that's obviously what I'm saying!"

"Jesus Christ, Erika. Are you serious? You really think Liam would…?"

"You know what I think."

"He wouldn't. This is our kid we're talking about."

"Right."

I hear shuffling on the other line. "Do you want me to come home?"

I let out a sigh. "No. There's nothing for you to do. Not yet, anyway."

"Liam did not do this," Jason says with more conviction than I feel. "She probably just ran away and will turn up in a day or two."

God, I hope he's right. Because the alternative is too horrible to imagine.

Chapter 24

ERIKA

When I get home, there's a white Lincoln Continental in our driveway. I recognize it immediately as my mother's car. She's the last person I feel like talking to right now, but it looks like she's already used her key to get inside and is likely brewing herself a nice hot cup of coffee.

Even though my mother lives all the way in New Jersey, she's currently retired and single, so she doesn't think much of driving out to see us on a whim, without checking if it's okay. Amazingly, Jason doesn't seem bothered by it. His own mother died from breast cancer when he was in college, and his father passed away only a year later from a heart attack. ("He died of a broken heart," Jason told me.) So he likes having the kids' only grandparent around. I like having her here, but I wish she'd call.

Still, I have nowhere else to go. So it looks like I have to deal with whatever she wants.

As soon as I enter the house, I hear her clanging

around in the kitchen. My mother loves the kitchen. She's always buying us some new gadget to use in there. The last thing she got me was an instant pot last month. She spent twenty minutes raving about all the great stuff she could cook with it. Since then, it's been collecting dust in the corner of my kitchen. I know that thing makes great soup, but I don't *like* soup.

"Erika!" Sure enough, my mother is fiddling with our coffee machine. She's the one who bought it for us, along with a year's supply of coffee pods. Her gray hair is gathered into a bun, and she has her tortoiseshell glasses perched on her nose. "I've been waiting for you for half an hour! Is everything okay?"

I don't even know how to begin to answer that question. My mother and I are close—she's the first person I told when Jason popped the question—but I never shared my fears about Liam with her. What can I say? He was her first grandchild—her only grandson. I couldn't bring myself to tell her he was anything less than the perfect little angel she believed him to be. Liam is always oozing with charm around my mother. She can't see through him the way I do.

"Everything is fine," I choke out.

Mom picks up her cup of coffee. She has selected one of the mugs with four-year-old Liam's face on it. He looks so cute in that picture—freckles across his nose and missing one of his front teeth. But all I can think about is how that was the year I first started to realize what he was really like.

"I heard about that girl who disappeared," she says. "How terrifying. I'm surprised you let Hannah out of the house."

I clear my throat. "I'm sure she'll turn up."

"That's the worst thing about having daughters," she says. "You're always worried about stuff like that. With Liam, you don't need to worry."

I think about the map that popped up in my car. The gap of time when he was gone last night. It's got to be a coincidence.

Please, God, let this girl have run away. Or anything that doesn't *involve my son…*

I plop down on the sofa, too upset to attempt to do anything else. My mother joins me with her coffee cup. The sofa shifts as she sits beside me.

"Listen, Erika," she says quietly. "I have to tell you, this isn't a social call. There's something I need to tell you. And… it's… it's not going to be easy."

I sit up straight. What does she want to tell me? Does my mother have cancer? Is that how the rest of this horrible day is going to unfold? I feel like I'm going to throw up. "What's wrong?"

She lowers her eyes. "You're going to hate me."

I look at my mother's face. Even though the wrinkles are new from when I was a child, she still looks the same to me somehow. She's the same brave woman who raised me all by herself after my father was hit by a car and killed. She didn't date all through my childhood, because she said she wanted to focus on me. It's only in the last ten years that she started to have occasional flings and travel. I can't imagine what sort of thing she could possibly say that would make me hate her.

"What's wrong, Mom?"

"I haven't…" She heaves a sigh and looks out the window. "I haven't been entirely honest with you, Erika. There are things you don't know. Things I have to tell you now, before you find out on your own."

She's really beginning to scare me. "Well, what is it?"

"It's… it's about your father."

"My father?" I conjure up the image of a handsome man with dark hair and dark eyes in the one photograph I keep in my bedside drawer. My memories of him are patchy at best. I remember the scratchiness of his face and the smell of cigarette smoke that used to cling to him. He died when I was not quite four years old, so he never lived to see me grow up. He never lived to see the grandson who looks more like him every single day. "What about my father?"

"The truth is…" My mother's hand trembles slightly

on the handle of the coffee mug. She puts it down on the coffee table, ignoring the coaster a mere inches away from where she put the cup. On any other day, this would make me crazy. But today, I couldn't care less. "The truth is that your father isn't... He's actually..."

"What?"

"He's alive."

"*What*?"

Two minutes earlier, I had been thinking there was nothing that could ever make me hate my mother. But now I'm beginning to think maybe there is. My father is *alive*? How could that be? And how could she make me think he was dead for all those years? Daddy was in a car accident. I had accepted her word blindly for over forty years.

"I'm so sorry, honey," she breathes. "I wanted to tell you earlier, but there's no easy way to say something like that."

"How about not lying in the first place?" I grit my teeth. "Why would you tell me he was dead? What happened? Did he run off with another woman?"

I suppose that could make a crazy sort of sense. Maybe my father ran off with some tramp and, in her anger, Mom pretended he was dead instead of a deadbeat. I still don't know if I could forgive her for lying about it for forty years, but maybe I could try.

"No," she says. "He didn't."

I fold my arms across my chest. Am I going to have to pull the story out of her? "Then what happened, exactly? Where has he been for the last forty-two years?"

Mom looks down at her wrinkled hands in her lap. "He's been in prison. For first-degree murder."

Chapter 25

ERIKA

Everything my mother says is another punch in the gut.

My father is alive.

Punch.

My father has been in prison for over forty years.

Punch.

My father is a murderer.

Punch. Punch.

I don't even know what to say. I stare ahead at the wall, my heart jumping around in my chest. This has been the most stressful morning of my entire life. At this point, my day is going to end with me in the hospital with a stroke.

"You can see why I didn't want to tell you," Mom says, her words coming out quickly. "I thought it would be traumatic for you. And if it got out, the other kids might tease you."

"What…?" I start my sentence, but my voice sounds strangled. Ugh, poor choice of words. "What did he do?"

"Well, he killed someone."

"Yes, I gathered that. Who did he kill?" And *why*?

The wrinkles on my mother's face deepen. I can tell she doesn't want to tell the story, but that's too bad. She's kept this secret from me long enough. I deserve to know. "It was a woman," she says. "A woman he was having an affair with."

"Why did he kill her?"

"He claimed it was an accident. He didn't mean to kill her—that's what he said." She shakes her head. "But his story didn't make sense. And obviously, the jury didn't believe it. They thought he planned the whole thing."

Maybe he just wanted to see her suffer. Maybe he just wanted to see her scream.

"Do you think he planned it?" I manage.

Mom is quiet for a moment. "Yes, I believe he did. She was threatening to expose the affair, so he killed her."

"How…" I close my eyes for a moment, imagining my father throwing this mystery woman into a dark hole so she couldn't escape. "How did he do it?"

"He poisoned her."

I feel that tightness in my chest, the same as I did last night when I discovered Liam was gone. I'm on the verge of another panic attack—my second in two days. I take a deep breath, trying to calm myself down.

"Why are you telling me this now?" I say. "After all these years, why tell me now?" And why *today*?

"Because…" She bites down hard on her lower lip. "I just found out. Your father got parole. He's out of prison."

"He's…"

"And I thought he might come looking for you," she says. "So… I wanted you to be prepared for that. If you want to see him. Or not."

"Right."

Today of all days, this is too much for me to take in. My father is alive and he's a murderer. He poisoned a woman. And oh yeah, he's out of jail and might come looking for me.

"I think…" I take a deep breath. "I think I need to be alone right now."

"Of course." My mother's eyebrows knit together. "Do you hate me?"

"No. I don't hate you."

You just have the worst timing in the world.

Mom leans forward and throws her arms around my shoulders. There was a time in my life when a hug from my mother made everything right. But that time has long since passed.

I walk her to the door and stand by the window to make sure she drives away. But even after she's gone, I don't budge from the window. I stare out into my neighborhood, thinking about everything that happened today. A girl has disappeared and it's possible that Liam is somehow responsible. My father is alive and has been in prison for murder.

There's nothing I can do about the former, but there's something I can do about the latter. For all these years, I thought about what it might be like if my father had lived. I thought about the conversations we would have had, him standing proudly at my graduation, shaking his head when he didn't approve of one of my boyfriends, going fishing together out on the lake. And all along, he's been alive— albeit in no position to take me fishing.

And he might look for me.

Of course, I don't have to wait for him to look for me. I could look for him. I bet Frank could track him down in five minutes flat. After all these years, I could lay eyes on my father. The man I believed to be long dead.

Then my eyes settle on my Toyota 4Runner in the driveway. The car Liam took last night out to Olivia Mercer's house. And then lied about it.

My father is going to have to wait. I have much worse problems.

Chapter 26

OLIVIA

I wake up and everything is black.

Where am I? What's going on?

I clutch my face, pushing away a throbbing sensation in my forehead, right between my eyes. How did I get here? The last thing I remember is...

Hop in the car. Just for a few minutes.

No. No, he didn't. He wouldn't.

Oh my God. I think I'm going to be sick.

I retch but my stomach is empty and nothing comes out. I swallow, doubled over on the ground. I blink a few times, trying to adjust to the blackness, hoping the world will jump into some sort of focus, but it doesn't happen.

I can't even see my hand in front of my face. I can't see where I am or one foot in front of me.

Why can't I see?

Oh my God, have I gone blind?

But no. When I look up, there's a tiny slice of light in the distance. There is nothing wrong with my eyes. There is simply no light wherever I am.

My head is swimming, which makes it that much harder to get my bearings. The ground is moist and grainy. Dirt? It's so hard to tell. I sit up and reach out into the distance, feeling for something—anything. My fingers finally touch something solid. It's the same consistency as the ground. Also dirt.

I think I'm in a hole.

Oh God. Oh God. I'm in a hole. I'm in a hole in the ground.

My fingers start to tingle as my panic mounts. I'm not claustrophobic, but it feels like... like I've been buried alive. One minute I was kissing Liam, one of the best moments of my life, and now I wake up here.

Why?

I've got to get out of here. There must be a way out. There's *got* to be.

There is that slice of light above me—a way out. If I could reach it, maybe I could climb out. I get to my feet, but that's when I become aware of another sensation. *Pain.* Agonizing, brutal pain in my left ankle. So severe that I immediately collapse back down into the dirt.

What is *wrong* with me?

I pull up the leg of my jeans to feel my left ankle. It's swollen. *Really* swollen. And warm. And even touching it gently sets off a wave of unbearable pain. My guess is that when I was thrown into this hole, the fall broke my ankle. Or at least, hurt it really badly.

So I can't put weight on my ankle. But I can still try to stand. This time I put my weight against the dirt wall, which collapses slightly under the pressure. It still hurts like hell, but I manage to get to my feet. Or at least, my foot. I stretch out my arm, feeling for something above that I can grab onto.

My fingers fall short.

I can't reach it.

Oh my God, I'm trapped here.

When he put me down here, he knew what he was doing. He knew it would be hard to escape. My only chance is if somebody comes to rescue me.

"Help!" I scream at the top of my lungs. "Help! Help me! I'm trapped!"

Nothing.

I scream until my voice is hoarse and my throat is raw. But I hear nothing. No footsteps. No sound. God knows where I am. Out in the wilderness? Below his soundproof basement?

But it's clear nobody is coming for me anytime soon. Not here.

I collapse against the dirt wall. My throat is parched. I don't remember when I last had anything to drink or eat. A day? If he's planning on trapping me here, will he at least give me something to drink? He will, won't he? Otherwise, I'll die, and I'll be no good to him for whatever he wants.

I hope he brings me food. What will I do if he doesn't?

He hasn't raped me. Even though there's a gap in my memory, somehow I feel certain of this. If he had, I would know it. Right? I'm still a virgin, so I'm sure I'd feel sore if he had done that to me. That's what Madison said, anyway. My jeans are still buttoned and zipped, and nothing is ripped or torn. I'm intact, except for my damn ankle.

God, why didn't I listen to Madison when she warned me about Liam?

Maybe he left me some water. Maybe there's a whole thermos of it somewhere. I need to feel around this space and get my bearings. If there's any chance of trying to escape from here, I've got to figure out what I'm dealing with. After all, women escape from being kidnapped all the time. I've read articles about it. They use their moxie or intelligence or whatever, and they find a way out.

Or else they don't. And years later, their body is discovered half-buried in the woods by some hikers.

Oh my God, I'm going to be sick again.

I double over, retching on the dirt ground. Once again, nothing comes up. I retch hard enough that tears fill my eyes. And then before I know it, the tears are streaming down my cheeks.

I'm trapped here. He trapped me.

I want to go home. I want my mom.

Please…

Chapter 27

ERIKA

Dinner is a very subdued affair.

Jason managed to make it home early tonight, which is something he doesn't get to do very often. Usually when he gets home early, I make a big deal of it and cook something special, but not tonight. Tonight, we're eating Kraft macaroni and cheese. And anybody who says a damn word about it will have their plate yanked away from them and hurled into the garbage.

Not that anyone will care. Both Hannah and Liam have barely eaten anything. Both of them are just pushing the little pieces of macaroni around their plates. Liam has barely said a word since he got home hours ago.

"I'm sorry about dinner," I feel compelled to say.

"What are you talking about?" Jason says. "I love macaroni and cheese. It tastes really Gouda."

Hannah comes alive long enough to groan. She can't

resist complaining about Jason's puns. "It's not *Gouda*, dad. It's that powder stuff that comes out of a package."

"Yes, I realize that, Hannah. Geez, I'm just trying to lighten the mood."

"Well, it's not helping," she says.

Jason gives me a look, then he reaches out and grabs her wrist. "Hey. No phones at the dinner table. You know that."

Wow, Hannah is sneakier than I thought. I didn't even realize she had her phone under the table. She obligingly places it in Jason's outstretched hand. She leans back in her chair, pouting. "I just wanted to see if they found Olivia."

My heart leaps. "Did they?"

Hannah shakes her head. "I don't think so."

I look over at Liam, who is staring down at his dinner plate. I haven't asked him about what I found in the GPS yet. I'm afraid to. Because it's hard to think of any explanation that won't make him look really bad. All I know is that he lied to my face this morning and I couldn't even tell.

"She was in your year, right, Liam?" Jason asks.

"I guess. I didn't really know her."

Then why were you going to her house last night? At two in the morning?

The doorbell rings, which is a relief, because I wasn't

doing much better at eating my macaroni and cheese than the kids were. That relief lasts only until I look through the peephole and see the two uniformed police officers standing at our door.

Oh God. I think I'm going to have another panic attack.

I take two deep breaths before I unlock the door. I plaster a smile on my face that I feel looks very genuine. Maybe Liam is rubbing off on me.

There are two police officers standing in our doorway. One is a man, who is in his late thirties with ruddy cheeks and a gut that's straining against his uniform. The other officer is a thin woman. She looks of Hispanic descent, with sharp black eyes, high cheekbones, and hair pulled back into a severe bun.

"Hello there," the male officer says in a thick Long Island accent. "Does Liam Cass live here?"

Oh no. No no no no…

"Yes…" I manage. "He's my son."

The female officer flashes a smile that doesn't touch her eyes. "My name is Detective Rivera and this is Detective Murphy. We were hoping to ask Liam a few questions. Is he home?"

"Yes?" I say, although I'm not sure why it comes out like a question. I clear my throat. "He's just eating dinner."

"Would you please interrupt him?" Rivera says. The

phony smile has disappeared from her face.

"Um…" I glance in the direction of the dining room. Jason has come out to see what's going on, and his eyes widen at the sight of the police officers. "Does he need a lawyer?"

Maybe I shouldn't have asked that. That sounds super guilty. And we don't know for sure Liam did anything. After all, he's a sixteen-year-old kid.

"No, that shouldn't be necessary," Rivera says. She seems to be the spokesperson. "We just have a few quick questions."

"What's this about?" Jason speaks up, his brow furrowed.

"We're just trying to get some information about the girl who disappeared this morning," Rivera says. "We're speaking with some of her classmates who might be able to help us. We just want to find Olivia."

"Well, Liam says he doesn't know her." Jason folds his arms across his chest. "So I think you might be wasting your time here."

Detective Murphy flashes Jason a disarming smile. "Then this will be real quick. We just want to make sure. A girl's life is at stake, Mr. Cass. We need to do everything we can to find her."

"I'll go get him," I say. I hurry out to the dining room, where Liam and Hannah haven't moved, but Hannah is straining to see what's going on. I put my hand on Liam's shoulder, and he flinches at my touch. "There are a couple of officers out there who want to ask you some questions."

Hannah's eyes widen. "Shouldn't he have a lawyer? Aren't you supposed have a lawyer present if you're being questioned by the police?"

It disturbs me how quickly Hannah—Liam's sole confidante—came to that conclusion. I shake my head. "They say they have a few quick questions. Just tell them the truth, Liam."

"All right." Liam gets to his feet. "I'll talk to them."

Hannah's eyes widen but she doesn't say a word.

When I return to the living room, the two officers are sitting on our loveseat, while Jason is on the couch. He's talking to the officers, but he doesn't look nervous or anything. He doesn't look like he's going to throw up any second, which is the way I feel. He truly believes Liam has nothing to hide.

Liam sits down beside Jason on the couch, sitting up straight as he always does. He doesn't look nervous either. He doesn't fiddle with the hem of his shirt or the hole in his jeans—his hands are completely steady and he flashes the officers a brief, disarming smile. It almost makes me wonder if I'm worried over nothing. If Liam could look that calm around two cops, he must have nothing to hide.

"Liam?" Detective Rivera says.

Liam nods. "Yes."

"Would you mind answering a few questions for us about Olivia Mercer?" she asks.

"I already talked to a police officer at school," he says. "I told him everything I know."

"Yes, but we have a few more questions. Just routine stuff."

"Of course." Liam looks her straight in the eyes. "I'll do anything to help find Olivia. Please go ahead."

Rivera crosses her legs as she leans forward slightly. "Do you know Olivia Mercer?"

"Yes. She goes to my school."

"And are you friendly with her?"

He doesn't hesitate. "She's in my math class. I've spoken to her before."

His answers sound rehearsed. As if he knew what they were going to be asking him and had mentally prepared for it the same way he prepares for his debates. I wonder if they notice.

"Is Olivia your girlfriend?"

"No."

Rivera raises an eyebrow. "No?"

"I don't have a girlfriend."

Rivera lets out a laugh. "A good looking boy like you? That's hard to believe."

"He's only sixteen, Detective," I say.

"When I was sixteen, I had two girlfriends!" Murphy says. His ruddy cheeks grow pinker.

Liam doesn't react to any of this. He flashes a brief smile, but says nothing.

The smile vanishes from Rivera's face again. Her eyes are so sharp, it scares me. I want to tell Liam to be careful, that she isn't going to be taken in by his charm. "So Liam, when was the last time you saw Olivia?"

"Some of the people from track team were hanging out at Charlie's. She was there too."

"Was it a date?"

"No."

"I see." Rivera nods. "And that's the last time you saw Olivia?"

"Yes."

"Do you have any idea at all where she could be right now?"

"No," he says without hesitation. "I'm really sorry. I wish I did." And then, in an incredibly sincere voice, "I'm worried about her. I really hope she's okay."

"We do too," Rivera says.

And then it looks like they're about to get up. And maybe this is over. Maybe they have absolutely nothing on Liam, and he was telling the truth when he said he barely knew Olivia. Maybe they're just going around and questioning everyone in the school. Maybe this is nothing but routine.

But then just as she's about to get up, Rivera sits back down again like she thought of something she had forgotten. "One more thing, Liam," she says.

He raises his eyebrows. "Yes?"

"One of Olivia Mercer's neighbors saw her in her backyard at around two in the morning, talking to a teenage boy."

My stomach sinks. This isn't over after all.

"Do you know who that boy was, Liam?" Rivera asks.

He doesn't answer, but his body stiffens almost imperceptibly.

Rivera smiles grimly. "After some of your friends told us you had brought Olivia to that diner yesterday, we showed the neighbor a few of your school photographs. And guess what? She was able to correctly identify you. She also was able to identify the Toyota that is now out in your driveway."

Liam's eyes widen for an instant, but he quickly regains his composure.

Rivera leans in and looks him straight in the eyes. "Would you like to revise your answer to the question I asked you about when the last time you saw Olivia Mercer was?"

Liam opens his mouth like he's about to answer, but before he does, Jason jumps up from the sofa. "No! No more questions. Not without a lawyer."

"We're just trying to find the whereabouts of a sixteen-year-old girl, Mr. Cass," Rivera says flatly. She looks at Liam. "Liam, if you can tell us where she is—"

"Liam, don't answer them." Jason glares at Rivera, a vein standing out in his neck. "This is a sixteen-year-old boy. He's a great student and a great kid. He did *not* do this."

"With all due respect, Mr. Cass—"

"No, you listen to me." Jason points a finger at them. I'm not sure I've ever seen him this upset. Even during the times I was most freaked out about Liam, he always seemed so calm. If I wasn't so panicked myself, I would think it was a little bit sexy the way he's protecting Liam. "My son has told you everything he knows. If you want to speak to him again, it will be with our attorney present."

Rivera rises from the love seat and Murphy follows. "As you wish, Mr. Cass."

It isn't until the officers are gone that I feel like I can breathe normally again. Of course, this whole thing was a disaster. It is now confirmed. Liam was visiting Olivia Mercer last night. He was probably the last person to see her alive. And he lied about it to the police.

"What the hell, Liam?" Jason snaps at him.

Liam had been maintaining excellent eye contact while the officers were here, but he finally drops his eyes.

The mask of affability he usually wears is gone, and he looks absolutely miserable. I almost feel sorry for him.

"Liam," I say quietly as I sit down beside my son. "Do you know where Olivia is?"

He shakes his head. Lying again. I wish Jason hadn't stopped the officers from questioning him. I wish they had done their police thing and wormed the answer out of him.

"But you were at her house last night...?" Jason prompts him.

Liam's Adam's apple bobs as he swallows. "Yes. I was there. Okay?"

"You took my car?" I ask.

"Yes. I'm sorry."

Jason runs a hand through his graying hair. I think he got ten new gray strands during the last twenty minutes. Of course, if not for my hairdresser, I'd be all gray now, thanks to my son. "What were you doing there?" he asks.

"I just..." Liam squirms on the sofa. "I like her, okay? I wanted to see her. And she came down and... you know..."

Jason frowns at him. "No. I *don't* know."

Liam's ears turn pink. "We made out a little. That's all."

"And then?"

"And then Mom called. So I came home. And that's it."

Jason narrows his eyes at Liam, but I can tell he believes the story. He was genuine in what he told the police officers. He does not believe his teenage son could possibly be responsible for the disappearance of a young girl. He knows Liam is capable of lying, but he doesn't know what else our son is capable of. Only I know the truth.

"Go to your room," Jason says to Liam.

Liam doesn't need to be told twice. He jumps off the sofa and scrambles up the stairs. I wish we could keep questioning him, but it won't make a difference. Whatever else he knows, he's told us all he's going to.

Jason drops his head back against the sofa and lets out a long sigh. "We have to get him a lawyer, Erika. This doesn't look good for him."

"Yes..." I chew on my lip. "It's kind of a big coincidence though, don't you think?"

"What do you mean?"

"I mean, he just *happened* to be around this girl's house on the night she disappeared? Do you really believe that?"

He frowns. "What are you saying?"

"You know what I'm saying."

He raises his eyebrows. "What? You're saying you think our son murdered this girl? Really, Erika?"

"Maybe not murdered..."

I wish I had a wife, so I could keep her deep in a hole. I can still hear Miss Williams's words in my ear. Liam said a lot of disturbing things, but that one was way up there. That was one of the ones I won't forget. Or his answer when I asked about him about it later that night:

I'd just like to see what would happen to her, Mommy. If I put her in a hole and didn't feed her, what would happen? And if she were my wife, I could do what I wanted and no one would even look for her.

That was the day I made our first appointment with Dr. Hebert.

"You know the kind of comments Liam has made in the past," I remind Jason.

He shakes his head. "You've always made too much of that. He's precocious. It's just words."

"It's not *just* words."

Jason blinks at me. "I can't... I can't have this conversation with you, Erika. This is our *child* we're talking about. He didn't do it. And I'm not going to let them pin it on him."

"Fine," I say. "Get him a lawyer."

Jason spends the rest of the night looking up criminal attorneys. He's convinced that a good lawyer can make this problem go away. But I know he's wrong. The only one who can make this go away is Liam.

Chapter 28

OLIVIA

I don't know how long I stay crouched in a little ball on the ground, sobbing my eyes out.

When I'm done, my eyes are raw and my face feels puffy. There's dried snot on my cheeks and hands. But that's the least of my problems.

I can't sit here feeling sorry for myself. If I don't want to die here, I've got to do something. I've got to figure out a way to escape. Or at least, figure out a way to survive until I'm rescued.

I've got to be smart. It's the only way.

I feel along the ground, hoping to locate something that might give me a clue as to where I am or how to get free. I have to crawl, because my ankle hurts far too much to put any weight on it. It's definitely got to be broken. Even when I'm not putting weight on it, it's throbbing like crazy.

I discover another wall across from me. I would guess this hole is about four feet by four feet. Maybe six or seven feet deep. Not very big. I wonder if he dug it himself. It would've taken him a long time if he did. I remember reading that book *Holes* when I was in ninth grade. It was about some kid who had to dig holes as part of a punishment. It was pretty good, as I remember. I think they made it into a movie.

In the third corner I check, my heart leaps when my fingers close around a tiny thermos. I pick it up, and it makes a noise when I shake it. There's liquid inside! I fumble with the cover, desperately trying to open it, even though I can't see a thing. If I spill this thermos, I'm toast. It's not much water, but I want it more than anything I've ever wanted in my life. Even more than I wanted Liam to kiss me when we were at the diner.

I hear a pop, and my fingers make contact with a straw sticking out of the container. I put my lips on the straw and take a sip. Oh my God, it's heavenly. Even though it has a slight metallic aftertaste, it's the best thing I've ever tasted. The water is cold in my mouth and my parched throat and my empty stomach. I want to guzzle the whole thing, but at the same time, I'm not sure when I'll get more. I should save it. Ration it. That's what a survivor would do.

I reluctantly close the top and gingerly put it back in

the corner, now half empty. I'm not going to drink more until I feel really desperate. I need to know what the situation is. Will he come back? Will he give me more water? Food?

With the water tucked away, I explore the final corner of the hole. This corner isn't empty either. I feel something there, something long and smooth. My fingers close around it. I squint as hard as I can, desperate to see something. Anything. But it's too dark.

I keep feeling around, and I realize there are more objects in this corner. They have a similar feel and consistency. Sharp or round edges. Mostly long and thin.

Then I come across something that feels a little different. It's round, roughly the size of a melon. But it's not a sphere. As my fingers round the curve, I feel two large holes. My chest tightens as I realize what I'm touching.

It's a skull.

I can't stop screaming, even though nobody can hear me.

Chapter 29

Transcript of police interview with Dr. Alice Hebert:

"Thank you so much for speaking with us today, Dr. Hebert."

"I thought it was my obligation to do so."

"Can you state for the record your profession?"

"I am a child psychologist. I've been in private practice for the past twenty-three years."

"So I guess you've seen it all then?"

"Just about, yes."

"And what made you come forward?"

"When I found out a young girl's life was in danger, I felt it was my moral obligation to say something. To save her life. Even if it meant breaking patient confidentiality."

"That's the reason we were so eager to speak with you today. We don't know how much time Olivia has left. We're desperate to find her."

"I understand. I'll do what I can."

"Based on the fact that you're willing to speak with us

about confidential issues, I assume you believe Liam Cass is responsible...?"

"Obviously, I can't say for sure. It's been many years since I treated Liam. But... yes, I believe he's capable of this."

"When did you start treating Liam?"

"When he was seven years old. His mother brought him to me because of several disturbing statements he made in class and at home."

"What kind of statements?"

"More than once, he mentioned the idea of wanting to trap a girl and watch her starve to death. He actually did play this out once when he was in kindergarten. He duct-taped a girl in a closet.

"I spoke to the principal at the school, and she told me about that incident in the closet."

"It was very disturbing, obviously, and his mother was quite upset over everything."

"What about the father?"

"I only met him once. He had a very busy job in the city, and he seemed to think we were making a big deal out of nothing. He didn't get it. But the mother was almost hysterical. We had a session without Liam, and she ran down a list of things he had done that had scared her."

"Such as?"

"Liam was, in many ways, mature for his age. He was

very responsible. For that reason, Mrs. Cass was persuaded by him to purchase a pet hamster. Unfortunately, the first hamster allegedly escaped and she had to buy him another. Liam told her the second hamster escaped as well, but then she caught him burying it in the backyard."

"Was the hamster dead?"

"Yes, but Liam finally admitted that he was the one who killed the hamster. He let it slowly starve to death."

"Jesus."

"Yes. It was quite upsetting. After a few months, it was very clear Liam was suffering from antisocial personality disorder. Do you know what a sociopath is, Detective?"

"That's the personality disorder when you don't feel emotions. Weren't Jeffrey Dahmer and Ted Bundy sociopaths?"

"Most likely. As early as the 1800s, doctors who worked with mental health patients noticed some patients demonstrated outwardly normal behavior, but they had no sense of ethics or empathy. These patients weere called 'psychopaths,' but then it was later changed to 'sociopaths' because of the effect these people had on society. Now both terms are used but 'sociopath' generally refers to a milder form of the disorder. Psychopaths are much rarer."

"So what does that all mean?"

"Well, for starters, sociopaths don't have normal

human emotions like empathy. They have no concern for the feelings of others. They also have a very high threshold for disgust, which has been measured by lack of reaction in these patients to photos of mutilated faces. But sociopaths don't care about faking emotions. Psychopaths, on the other hand, are excellent actors. They're intelligent, charming, and fantastic at manipulating emotions. They can make you believe they care, when in fact, they feel nothing."

"So they're good liars."

"They are pathological liars. They can tell the most outlandish stories without blinking an eye. And the other salient characteristic of sociopaths is a weak conscience. They feel very little guilt or shame or remorse. Psychopaths, on the other hand, have *no* conscience. Can you imagine what that's like? To feel no remorse whatsoever for your terrible actions?"

"…"

"On top of that, sociopaths have a very low tolerance for frustration or for discharge of aggression."

"Meaning…?"

"It takes very little for them to become violent."

"I see."

"And they're fearless. When a normal person is put in a situation where they anticipate a painful stimulus, such as an electric shock, their sweat glands will increase in activity. But in psychopathic subjects, no skin conductance responses were emitted. They don't feel fear the way we do."

"Right."

"So if you put it together, Detective, you've got an individual who feels no empathy, no remorse, no fear, and is prone to violence. It's not surprising so many serial killers are diagnosed as psychopaths."

"So are you saying Liam Cass is a psychopath?"

"It's hard to say. He was only nine years old the last time I saw him, and most of these personality disorders technically can't be diagnosed until eighteen. But…"

"Yes…?"

"He was definitely a sociopath, but my gut feeling was that he was also a psychopath. Even at such a young age, he was an amazing liar and manipulator. But at the same time, when I first met him, my instinct was to like him. It took several sessions before I could see through him. And I am a professional."

"So he's a serial killer?"

"Be careful making that jump. Nearly all serial killers are likely psychopaths, but not all psychopaths become killers."

"But you believe Liam is capable of murder?"

"Well, psychopaths are capable of murder. So if Liam is a psychopath, then yes, he is capable of murder."

"How long did you work with Liam?"

"Two years."

"That doesn't seem very long, everything considered."

"Liam didn't want to be helped. He had no interest in changing for the better. When I tried to talk with him he simply lied to me about what he was feeling. If there's one thing my sessions with him did was to make him realize what he should and shouldn't say out loud. And the truth is…"

"Yes?"

"I was scared of him."

"Scared?"

"Detective, I used to keep a photo on my desk of my daughter, who was about Liam's age. During one session, he kept staring at the photo and smiling in this very disturbing way. Then he started asking questions about her."

"What sort of questions?"

"Innocent questions. Like what foods did she like and what were her hobbies. It wasn't anything terrible, but the way he asked was very upsetting to me. And I think he meant for me to feel uncomfortable. I put the photo away after that."

"Did he cause her any harm?"

"No. But soon after that, I told Mrs. Cass that I didn't think I was helping her son, and we terminated our sessions. I didn't want to work with him anymore."

"Because you were scared."

"Yes."

"Of a nine-year-old boy."

"If you knew what was going on inside that kid's head, you would be scared too."

Chapter 30

ERIKA

Right after Jason and I finish loading the dishwasher, an alarm goes off on my iPhone. I pull it out of my pocket and look at the alert:

PTA meeting at 7:30. Traffic is light. You should arrive in ten minutes.

Damn. That stupid PTA meeting is tonight. And I told Jessica I would go because I'm the one in charge of movie night, the most important event of the year.

"What's wrong?" Jason asks me.

"I was supposed to go to this PTA meeting tonight."

"The PTA?" He frowns. "Is this really a good time to get more involved in the PTA?"

"Jason..."

"Can't you skip it? Didn't you say you hate those things?"

"Yes, I did say that. And I *do*. But Jessica is counting on me to do movie night. And I feel like... maybe I shouldn't be antagonizing anyone now..."

Jason gives me a look. "You really think you need to worry about what Jessica Martinson thinks of you?"

No. I shouldn't. But I still do. I've always longed for that woman's approval. "I won't stay for long. Okay?"

He shrugs. "Whatever you want, Erika. I'm going to go look up lawyers for Liam while you're organizing movie night or whatever it is you feel is more important than our son…"

He's right. I shouldn't be organizing movie nights right now. If I'm in a position where I'm looking up attorneys for my sixteen-year-old son, my life is too complicated to be doing movie night. Maybe I'll talk to Jessica when I get there. I'll explain to her that I can't do movie night and I'm sorry.

But then again, I don't want her to think I'm backing out because Liam is guilty of something.

I drive over to the school, and sure enough, traffic is light and it takes only ten minutes. I see the cars of all the other moms parked outside the school. Jessica's minivan is right by the entrance in the primo parking spot that she always seems to nab.

PTA meetings are held in the library on the second floor. I charge up the stairs, glancing down at my watch to find that I am now five minutes late somehow. Stupid iPhone didn't alert me soon enough. Oh well. I'll slip in the back and it won't be a big deal. Jessica usually spends the first twenty minutes going over minutes from last meeting anyway. These things are torture.

The door to the library creaks loudly when I push it open. I'm clearly the only latecomer, and everyone is already gathered around the conference table set up in the center of the room. Jessica is standing at the front, wearing a blue and white dress that looks fantastic on her. She always looks fantastic. Under any circumstance, I might feel a twinge of jealousy, but that's the last thing I'm feeling right now.

I remember the first time I saw Jessica Martinson, back when the boys were in first grade. We had just moved to the town and were starting over after that awful incident in kindergarten. Jason thought I was being silly when I said we should move, but too many people knew what had happened. I could feel them whispering about me when I went to the supermarket. We had become pariahs there and needed a fresh start.

I showed up at a quarter to three that day to pick Liam up from first grade. Jessica was waiting as well and looked hopelessly glamorous, even in her T-shirt and yoga pants. She was surrounded by a group of women who were hanging on her every word. She loves being the center of attention—that hasn't changed. I watched them laughing at a joke Jessica had made, but I was too intimidated to try to approach them. I was never one of the popular kids back when I was in school, and I didn't expect that would change in adulthood.

It wasn't until Tyler and Liam came out of the school together that Jessica took a sudden interest in me. She walked over to me purposefully, a charming smile on her red lips. She was looking at me, but her eyes were on my son. "You must be Liam's mother. I'm Jessica—Tyler's mom."

"Erika," I said.

"Tyler talks about Liam nonstop," Jessica said, as if she was impressed.

"That's wonderful," I said, although in the back of my mind I was thinking that I hoped Liam didn't end up duct-taping him in a closet.

"Seems like the boys have gotten to be good friends." She looked down at Liam, who was standing patiently beside me with his SpongeBob SquarePants backpack on his shoulders while the other boys were running around like crazy. "Hi there, Liam. I'm Tyler's mother."

Liam held out his right hand, which Jessica accepted. "It's very nice to meet you," he recited.

Jessica laughed, utterly charmed by my son. "What fantastic manners. You trained him well, Erika!"

Amazingly, I hadn't trained him at all. Liam learned all on his own what to say to adults to make them love him.

After that day, Jessica was my best friend. Liam and Tyler had play dates once or twice a week, and we learned to count on each other if we had an emergency where we needed someone to pick up one of our sons from school. It wasn't until the end of grade school when that abruptly changed. The boys barely spoke to each other anymore. Jessica and I were still friendly, but no longer friends. I never quite understood why.

And I have a feeling things are just going to get worse.

I try to slip into the library quietly, but as the door swings shut behind me, Jessica abruptly stops speaking. Everyone in the room turns to look at me.

"Oh, um, hi," I stammer.

"Erika!" she exclaims in a flat voice. "I didn't expect to see *you* here."

"Yes, I… I'm sorry I'm late…"

Jessica's ice blue eyes remain on my face. "No worries…"

I slip around a few of the other mothers (and one lone dad) to get to the only empty seat. Everyone in the room is staring at me. I thought nobody would be aware of Liam's connection to Olivia, but it's painfully obvious that's not the case. *Everybody* knows. Maybe they don't know the police were at our house tonight. Maybe they don't know Liam was at Olivia's house at two in the morning. But they know *something.*

Jessica clears her throat. "All right. Let's go back to reviewing the minutes."

I've always found PTA meetings to be a form of torture. Even though I love my kids, I just can't bear going through the planning of events for them for the entire year. I'm fine with planning one event, like movie night, although I'd rather just be a minion handing out movie tickets or pizza on the night in question. But Jessica and I go way back. If she needs my help, I have no choice but to offer it.

"We still need more volunteers for the book fair," Regina Knowles complains. "Nobody wants to do cleanup. And that's when we need the most help."

Yes, the eternal problem. Everybody wants to help out at the events, but nobody wants to be on the cleanup crew.

"I'm sure we can find somebody to help with cleanup," Jessica says. Her eyes scan the room, as several women try to look in other directions. "Rachel? Maria? Will you help out?"

Rachel Richter and Maria Sheldon look absolutely unenthused at the idea of cleaning up after the book fair. I've done it before, and it's an exhausting job to pack up all those books. We all know it. But Jessica stares them down, and they both nod an affirmative.

"Wonderful." Jessica claps her hands together. "Now that we have book fair settled, let's talk about movie night."

Finally. She looks over at Alicia Levine. "Alicia, I want to thank you so much for stepping up as chair of movie night."

What?

"Happy to help, Jess," Alicia says.

Is she joking with me? What's going on here?

I clear my throat and say as delicately as possible, "I'm sorry, Jessica, but didn't you ask me if I could be in charge of movie night?"

Jessica tucks an errant strand of blond hair behind her ear. "Yes, but I *know* how busy you are, Erika. And Alicia was *so* nice to step up. So... I'm letting you off the hook."

The room has gone silent again as everyone stares at me and Jessica. What she said was a bald-faced lie. She asked *me* to be in charge of movie night. And she changed her mind about it when she found out about Olivia.

She could have at least given me the courtesy of telling me in advance, so I didn't waste my time driving out here when my son needs me at home.

And now the silence is broken by the sound of people whispering. I don't know what the hell they're saying, but I can only imagine. I want to yell at them that if they've got something to say about my kid, they can say it to my face. But I don't actually want that. I just want to go home.

I rise unsteadily to my feet. "I think maybe I'll just take off then."

"Feel free," Jessica says. "I *do* appreciate you offering to pitch in though, Erika. Honestly."

There have been times during my friendship with Jessica that I have wanted to slap her, but never so much as at this moment. But I'm capable of controlling my impulses. So I grab my purse and run out of the room before these women can see me cry.

Chapter 31

Transcript of police interview with Madison Hartman:

"How long have you been friends with Olivia Mercer?"

"Practically my whole life. We became friends the first day of kindergarten. We were wearing the same dress and we bonded over it."

"So you're very close with her?"

"Uh, yeah! We're best friends."

"Did Olivia ever give you any indication she might run away?"

"No. Never. Olivia would never run away. She wouldn't do that to her parents."

"Did she do drugs or alcohol?"

"Are you kidding me? Olivia was a good girl. One time, me and Aidan—that's my boyfriend—offered her a drink of some beer Aidan swiped from his dad's stash, and she wouldn't touch it."

"If she were planning to run away, would she tell anyone about it?"

"Yes! She would tell me… But she didn't run away. I'm telling you. There's no way… It was Liam. That bastard, Liam Cass."

"You think Liam is the one responsible for her disappearance?"

"I don't think he is. I *know* he is."

"Why do you say that?"

"Um, because Liam is a crazy person?"

"Why do you think he's crazy?"

"Okay, well, I wasn't totally sure before. I mean, there were rumors about him. Like, I went to a different middle school than he did, but people sometimes talked about that English teacher and what they thought he did to him. Some kids believe he did it, although I honestly didn't believe it until now. Do you guys know about that?"

"Yes. We know."

"I mean, mostly it was just a vibe I got from him. Obviously, he's pretty cute, but he just seemed so phony. Like, a lot of girls thought he was really charming, but I just thought he was a fake."

"How so?"

"So here's an example. One day, I saw him messing around with some of his friends before first period, and then he was late for class. I had first period with him, and the teacher asked him why he was late. He told her his mom was driving him and she had a flat tire and that's why he was late."

"A lot of kids tell lies."

"Yeah, I know. I mean, I lie to teachers or my parents all the time. But they always seem like they sort of know that I'm lying. It's hard to tell a really good lie to an adult in a believable way. But Liam was so good at it. He looked right into the teacher's eyes and said it with a straight face, and the teacher didn't even suspect for a second. I would have believed it too if I didn't see him outside messing around. You know? And there was other stuff too."

"Like what?"

"Like I was at the athletic field after school because I was waiting for Aidan to finish football practice, and the track team guys had a meet. Liam was racing and he lost, and I could tell he was really pissed off about losing. He walked right up to this fence and kicked it so hard, it broke. I was kind of shocked at how angry he seemed."

"Did you tell that to Olivia?"

"No…"

"Why not?"

"Well, because last year Aidan punched a wall and broke his hand, so I thought if I told her that story, she'd bring up the story about Aidan and act like it was no big deal. Or tell me I should break up with Aidan."

"Olivia told you to break up with Aidan?"

"Yes… I mean, not in a serious way. But she didn't like him."

"Why not?"

"I don't know. She thought he was a football player thug, but… what does this have to do with Liam?"

"Has Aidan ever been violent towards you?"

"No! Never! Aidan isn't perfect, but he's a good guy. Not like Liam."

"Was Liam ever violent toward Olivia?"

"No. He could be really nice when he wanted to be. That's what I'm saying—he was such a fake. And she was totally taken in by it. She was so into him… and she's not even like that. She doesn't get that into boys. He totally did a number on her."

"Do you think he had any reason to hurt her?"

"No. I mean, she already wanted to go out with him, and I bet she would've done just about anything for him."

"So why are you so certain Liam is responsible for her disappearance?"

"Because he's crazy! Crazy people don't need a reason to do something crazy, right?"

Chapter 32

ERIKA

When I get back home, Jason says Liam hasn't come out of his room since the cops left, so I decide I should go check on him. It's a relief when I knock on the door and he tells me to come in.

Strangely enough, I find him at his desk, hunched over one of his textbooks. He's reading and outlining the book, as if this was any other day. As if the police hadn't been here, only hours earlier, essentially accusing him of murder.

"Liam?"

He doesn't look up from his textbook. "Yes?"

"What are you doing?"

"Studying. I have a history test tomorrow."

"Could you stop for a few minutes? I'd like to speak with you."

If it were Hannah, she would have moaned about how

I shouldn't interrupt her when she's trying to study, even though she gets distracted every five minutes by her phone when she's studying anyway. But Liam obediently turns away from his history book and looks up at me, blinking his brown eyes innocently.

"What is it, Mom?"

I take a deep breath. My hands are shaking, and I feel like I'm about to burst into tears. I remember back when Liam was younger and he used to see that psychotherapist. She used a term that I had contemplated but was afraid to ever say out loud:

Sociopath.

He doesn't feel empathy like you do. He doesn't feel love. He's just faking it.

As a mother, it was one of the worst things anybody has ever said to me. *Your son doesn't love you. He's not capable of it.* At the time, I refused to believe it. But as the years passed, I realized how true everything Dr. Hebert told me was.

"Where is she, Liam?" I say. "Where is Olivia?"

He looks me straight in the eyes, the same way he did to the officers as he lied to their faces. "I don't know."

"Liam…" A tear escapes from my right eye and I wipe it away before he can see it. Being vulnerable in front of a person who has no empathy is always a mistake. "The police know what they're doing. Whatever you've done…

They're going to find out. If you tell me where she is, I can help you. I'll let her go. I can pretend I just stumbled onto her…" I take a shaky breath. "But if you kill her…"

"Mom." He scrunches up his eyebrows, which makes him look younger. "I swear to you. I didn't do anything to Olivia."

"I don't believe you, Liam."

His eyes darken. There are moments when I feel frightened of my son. Such as when I found him with that hamster when he was only six. He let it starve to death right in front of his eyes. The poor hamster was so withered, you could see all of its little bones sticking out. You could tell it had suffered. And Liam didn't care. No, worse—he enjoyed it.

"I didn't do it, Mom." His voice is firm, almost angry. "I don't know where she is. Now can I go back to studying?"

I nod wordlessly, and Liam swivels on his chair to turn back to his history book. He starts outlining again, like his mother wasn't just in the room, accusing him of kidnapping and murder. That's how Liam is. He doesn't let anything bother him.

After Dr. Hebert came up with a diagnosis, I asked her how this could have happened. Liam grew up in an upper middle class, happy household. We provided firm, but very fair discipline. He had a wonderful childhood.

How could he turn out this way?

"There's often a genetic component," she had said.

But that didn't explain it any better. Jason and I were about as boring and normal as you could get. It didn't make any sense. How could a nice, normal couple like us produce a child like Liam? I never got it.

Not until this morning. When I found out my father had been in jail for murder for over forty years.

Chapter 33

OLIVIA

I have no idea how long I've been down here.

I finally stopped screaming. It went on for a long time. And even after I stopped, I was still shaking. I sat down in the corner of the hole, across from the skeleton, and just hugged myself. For hours, maybe. I don't know who this skeleton belongs to, but I can't kid myself it's a good sign that it's here. Somebody else was down in this hole. And that person died here.

Or more likely, was murdered.

The memories of how I got down here start to return more vividly. The handkerchief shoved in my face that smelled funny. Not being able to breathe. And then… nothing.

He's going to kill me. That's why I'm here. And I can only imagine the reason he put me here instead of killing me outright is that he has other plans for me before he kills me.

But everyone has got to be looking for me. My mom… I want her so badly, it hurts. I can't imagine how scared she must have been when she came into my bedroom and found me missing. She would have called the police immediately. She'll never stop looking for me. She'll have every policeman in the whole state out searching.

And then when the police find me, they'll throw his ass in jail. And I'll get to go home to my warm, comfortable bed. And Mom will make me chocolate chip pancakes. And I'm not leaving my bed for a week. Well, maybe I'll go to the doctor to have them take a look at my ankle, which is still throbbing.

I'm going to get out of here. I know it. My parents will find me.

My stomach lets out a low growl. I'm starving. And thirsty. *So* thirsty. I finished the water an hour ago. I knew I should ration it more, but I couldn't help myself. I picked up the thermos and emptied it down my throat without a second thought. And now it's gone.

I wonder how long it takes for a person to die from dehydration.

Maybe that's how Phoebe died. That's what I have named the person who the bones in the corner belong to. Mom and I used to watch the TV show *Friends* in reruns, and Phoebe was my favorite character. So that's what I have called her. Phoebe. She deserves a name. I wonder if her parents are still looking for her. When I get out of here I'll tell people she's down here. Maybe her parents can have some closure.

I'm going to get out of here. I will.

I'm going to find a way. I won't give up.

I hear a noise coming from above. Is that footsteps? Is it the police? I start to scream, but my throat is so parched, I have one false start before anything comes out.

"Help! Help me, please!"

It's footsteps. Definitely footsteps. There is a sound of metal just above my head, and then creaking of hinges. Finally, a bright flash of light fills my vision.

After sitting in the dark for so long, the light is agonizing. I clasp my hands over my eyes to shut it out. It's a flashlight. Someone is shining a flashlight on me.

"Olivia?"

It's *him*. It's not the police. He's come back.

"Help!" I shriek, hoping a neighbor or passerby might hear. "Somebody! Help me! Let me out!"

He cocks his head to the side. "I'm afraid you're wasting your breath, Olivia. We're in a cabin in the middle of nowhere. Nobody's going to hear if you scream."

I stop screaming and stare up at him as I catch my breath. I'm not entirely sure I believe him, but he doesn't seem at all concerned that I'm yelling. So it's probably true.

"I'm sorry it took me so long to get back to you," he says. Although he doesn't sound sorry. Actually, there's no expression at all in his voice, like he's a robot. He sounds so different than usual. It's freaky. "The police are everywhere. I had to wait until night."

"Please let me out," I croak.

I peek through my fingers, up at his face, squinting through the bright light. I can't believe I ever thought he was handsome. I must have been out of my mind.

"I'm afraid I can't do that," he says.

Tears spring to my eyes, but I try to keep them from falling. I have a feeling me crying won't make him feel any sympathy. "Why not? I won't tell anyone. I *swear*. I'll just say that I ran away. I promise."

"Yes. I'm sure."

"I swear!"

He smiles in a way that makes my skin crawl. "I'm sorry, Olivia. I can't let you out."

I take a deep breath. "Please… if you let me out, I'll… I'll do anything you want. *Anything*."

He lets out a laugh, loud enough that I know he must be telling the truth about us being the only people out here. "You'll do whatever I want anyway. It's not like you have a choice."

That's probably true. He's not a big guy, but he's much bigger than me. He could overpower me easily, even if I wasn't weak from lack of food and water with an injured ankle.

"What do you want then?" I ask in a tiny voice.

He doesn't answer me.

I glare up at his face. "You better let me out right now. If you don't, when the police find me here, I'll tell them everything."

He flashes that smile again. "Oh, will you?"

"You bet I will!" A muscle twitches in my jaw as I shout up at him. "I'll tell them what you did! You'll go to jail for the rest of your life!"

I watch his expression, waiting for him to react. But his face doesn't show even a flicker of fear.

"Are you threatening me, Olivia?" he says. "I really hope you're not threatening me."

There's something in his eyes that's even more terrifying than the rotted corpse in the corner of the hole. My mouth is so dry, I'm not sure I can even manage a response. But I clear my throat. "I'm not threatening you. I'm just telling you what's going to happen."

"Well," he says, "I better make sure they never find you then."

I clutch my knees, my heart pounding in my chest. He means it. He's never going to let me out of here. Ever.

Oh God…

He lifts a large brown paper shopping bag into the air

and drops it into the hole. It falls beside me, making a loud enough impact that I flinch and let out a yelp.

"That's food and drink," he says. "I don't know when I'll be able to get back here, so you better make it last."

And then the light goes out.

"Wait!" I cry. "Wait!"

His voice again, cutting through the blackness: "What?"

I swallow, hoping I can appeal to his sympathy one last time because threats obviously don't do the trick. "Can you leave me the flashlight? Please?"

He's quiet for a moment, as if considering it. Dare I hope he might say yes? I would give anything for that flashlight.

"It's so dark down here," I say softly, "and it's so hard to tell what everything is. It's driving me crazy. If you could leave me the flashlight—"

"No," he says.

And then the trap door above my head creaks shut. And I hear the sound of the lock being turned, trapping me down here once again. I bury my face in my knees and let out a sob.

I don't want to die down here. There's got to be a way out.

Chapter 34

ERIKA

I considered keeping the kids home from school, but both of them wanted to go, and Jason said we should try to keep things as normal as we could. But Jason did stay home from work. He locked himself in the spare bedroom to work from home, even though I know he's in the middle of an important project and has a ton of meetings. He's trying to do all his meetings on the phone.

"You can go to work," I tried to tell him. "Liam will be okay."

"I think it's better I stay home," he insisted.

I didn't want to admit how grateful I was that he stayed. Nothing else happened after the police stopped by last night, but the whole night I kept jerking awake after having nightmares. I couldn't remember any of them when I woke up in the morning, but my body was covered in sweat.

I try to get my own work done, but it's difficult. I'm supposed to be writing an article about the best local playgrounds, but my head isn't in the game. Besides, Hannah and Liam have been too old to go to playground for years. I'd like to be nostalgic about the simpler times, but I can't. Ever since Liam was four years old, he was a ticking time bomb.

I hope they find Olivia. That's all I can think about. I hope she ran away. I hope they find her in some motel, tearful and wanting to come home.

What little concentration I have is broken by the doorbell ringing. When I see Jason coming down the stairs, I realize that the doorbell has been ringing for several minutes. I don't know what's wrong with me if I don't notice a doorbell ringing ten feet away from me.

Jason reaches the door before me. He squints through the peephole, and his face turns pale. "Shit. It's the police."

Jason squares his shoulders and cracks opens the door. It's Rivera and Murphy again. But there are more people behind them. This doesn't seem like a good sign. When the police come with a squad of people behind them, you know you're in trouble.

"Hello, Mr. Cass." Rivera doesn't bother smiling this time. "We have a warrant to search your home and your wife's Toyota."

I step forward. "Liam is at school."

"We don't need Liam right now," she says. "But we do have a warrant for his phone."

God only knows what's on his phone. I don't want to think about it. "Can you come by later for the phone?"

Jason is busy inspecting the warrant, but I'm not sure why he's bothering. These are police officers. If they need to inspect our house, we're not going to stop them. I only hope Liam was smart enough not to leave something behind.

My own phone starts ringing within my pocket. I pull it out and see the name of the high school. My stomach sinks. "Detective, can I take this call? It's the school."

She nods curtly and I swipe to answer. "Hello?"

"Mrs. Cass? It's Principal McMillan. I'm afraid we have a situation."

She has a situation? She should see what's going on in my house. "What's wrong?"

"I need you to come here as soon as possible. Liam and another student were involved in a fistfight in the hallway. They're both in my office."

Oh God.

"Is Liam okay?" I say.

"He's fine." Her voice softens slightly. "But we don't tolerate fighting on school property. I'm going to need you to come here right away."

I don't know how I'm going to manage that, but I can't say no to Mrs. McMillan. "I'll be right there."

Jason has lowered the search warrant and is staring at

me. So are the two detectives. I wish I didn't have to have this conversation in front of the detectives. The timing couldn't be worse.

"Liam got into a fight at school," I say, trying to ignore the way Rivera is looking at me. "I need to go there to pick him up."

"Jesus." Jason frowns. "Okay. I... I'll stay here and you go get Liam."

I look behind the detectives at the team of people who are going to rip apart my home. I wish I could stay. I can't deal with Liam fighting at school on top of everything. I've gotten a lot of calls about Liam over the years, but nothing like this. He's never done anything to get his hands dirty before.

I grab my purse, but Detective Rivera stops me. "You can't take the Toyota. We need to search it."

"But I'll just... I'll be right back..."

"Take my Prius, Erika." Jason grabs his keys off the hook on the wall where he keeps them and tosses them to me. "Send me a text after you talk to the principal, okay?"

I nod. It's probably better anyway. I have a feeling this is not a conversation that will be quick.

Chapter 35

ERIKA

When I get inside the school, my daughter is waiting for me by the entrance. I'm sure she's supposed to be in class, so I assume she's skipping. But that's the least of my problems right now. Hannah has red-rimmed eyes and her auburn hair is in disarray—even more than usual. She looks like somebody just died.

"Mom!" she cries. And she throws her arms around me, which is something she hasn't done in public in a very long time. Although to be fair, I don't think there's anyone else in the hallway. "I saw the whole thing. It wasn't Liam's fault."

I pull away from her. It's hard for me to believe that anything that's happening right now isn't Liam's fault. "Are you sure?"

"Yes!" She swipes at her eyes with the back of her hand. "Tyler jumped him out of nowhere. What was Liam supposed to do? Just stand there while Tyler beat him up?"

"Why did Tyler do it?"

"Isn't it obvious?" Hannah blinks at me. "Everyone thinks Liam is responsible for what happened to Olivia. But he *isn't*. I *know* it."

I'm not sure how Hannah knows it. I sure don't.

"Tyler is telling *everyone* that Liam is some kind of psychopath," Hannah says. "*Tyler* should be suspended. It wasn't Liam's fault."

I have a bad feeling Mrs. McMillan won't see it that way. And either way, Liam can't go to school right now. That's very obvious. Not until this whole thing blows over.

"I'll see what I can do, Hannah," I promise her. I don't tell her about the police officers at our house, who are currently searching through her brother's belongings. And my car. There's no point in making her even more upset. "I'm going to go talk to the principal now. But you need to go back to class."

But Hannah clearly has no intention of going back to her class. She follows me to the principal's office and I don't stop her. This is hard on her too.

When I get into the administration office, Jessica Martinson is already there. The last thing I want right now is to have a conversation with Jessica, but the principal's door is shut, so I have no choice but to sit down next to her to wait. I still feel the burn of how she shunned me at the PTA meeting. After all those years, how could she do that to me?

"Hi, Erika," Jessica says in an unreadable tone. "Quite a scuffle our boys had, didn't they?"

"Yes," I say vaguely. I don't mention the fact that my daughter told me that her football player thug of a son jumped my kid. Somehow I suspect Liam will get the blame for all of this. "Boys fight, I guess."

Jessica smiles tightly. "Yes. I'm sure they're making too much of this. Hopefully, they'll just get a warning and that will be the end of it."

That's impossible. They were fighting in school. There's no way they won't be punished severely. But I appreciate Jessica's optimism.

The door to the principal's office cracks open and Mrs. Kristen McMillan stands at the entrance. She's around my age, but much taller with a strong jaw and her hair styled into an immobile shoulder-length helmet. The last time she and I spoke was during parent teacher night, when she ran into me in the hallway and told me how brilliant Liam was at his last debate, and how he's on his way to becoming valedictorian. She's not smiling this time as she waves us both into her office.

The two boys are sitting in chairs in front of her desk. Tyler is slumped down, holding an ice pack to his face, but Liam is sitting up straight, staring at the wall. He doesn't look great though. Tyler got in a good punch to his cheek bone, which is dark red, on its way to black and blue. His shirt is ripped and his usually neat dark hair is in disarray. He looks like a kid who just got beat up. In spite of everything, I wanted to throw my arms around him.

He's my son, after all. No matter what.

"They had to be pulled apart by two teachers," Mrs. McMillan says. "It's one of the worst fights I've seen during my time as principal."

"It was his fault." Tyler pulls the ice pack away from his face, revealing a split lip. "He started it."

"No, I didn't," Liam says calmly. "I didn't do anything."

"The hell you didn't!"

"Boys, calm down!" Mrs. McMillan snaps at them.

But Tyler isn't about to be subdued. "You started it when you murdered Olivia Mercer, you psychopath. Everyone knows you did it!"

Liam doesn't respond to that. He just stares straight ahead.

"That's enough," Mrs. McMillan says sharply. "Tyler, I don't care who started it. Both of you were involved in this fight."

"He deserved it." Tyler nearly spits the words. "That and more."

Mrs. McMillan looks between the two boys, her eyes narrowing. "Tyler, Liam, I'd like both of you to step outside while I speak with your mothers."

Liam immediately obeys, while Tyler tries to protest. But Mrs. McMillan has her secretary escort them outside and apparently babysit them while she talks to the two of us. Once the door closes, her lips form a straight line and she peers at us over the edge of her spectacles.

"Obviously, there's no excuse for this behavior," Mrs. McMillan says. "Fighting is not tolerated. We can't have a repeat performance of this."

"Of course not," Jessica says. "I'm so sorry about Tyler's behavior. He just got… emotional."

I keep my mouth shut, just as my son did.

"Tyler will be suspended for a week," Mrs. McMillan says. She looks at me and hesitates. "Liam will receive one day's suspension."

A week ago, I would've been worried about how this would affect Liam's college admissions. Now I couldn't care less. She may as well have suspended him for a week. I can't send him back to school after this.

But Jessica is absolutely furious. A pink spot forms on either of her cheeks. "A *week*? How come Tyler gets a week and Liam only gets one day?"

"For one thing," Mrs. McMillan says, "this is Tyler's second offense. I told you after he was in that fight last year that it couldn't happen again. Also, there were several witnesses who confirmed that your son initiated the fight. Liam has an impeccable record. He's a straight-A student—"

"But he's crazy!" Jessica bursts out. She glances at me, then quickly looks away. "I'm sorry, but that's the elephant in the room. Liam is *crazy*. He kidnapped that girl, and he's probably going to kill her. Tyler was just upset about it."

I stare at my former friend, shocked she would say such a thing. Even when Tyler and Liam stopped being friends, she never said a negative word about Liam.

"I'm sorry, Erika," she says. "But you know it's true. Liam has serious mental health issues. The reason he and Tyler stopped being friends was because Tyler was afraid to have him in the house. *I* was afraid to have him in the house." She shakes her head. "He needs to be in therapy. Or better yet, locked up."

"Mrs. Martinson!" Mrs. McMillan exclaims. "I know you're upset, but please. This is uncalled for."

I stare down at my hands. I don't know what to say. I want to defend my son, but the truth is, I agree with her. But before she can say another word, we hear shouting outside the office. Mrs. McMillan rises to her feet and we follow her. What is it *now*?

Liam and Tyler are still sitting right outside the office, but another girl has joined them. She has dirty blond hair that's loose around her chubby face, and she has tears streaming down her cheeks. She's pointing at them, her hand trembling.

"Where is she, you asshole?" she shouts at Liam. "Tell me what you did with Olivia!"

"Madison!" Mrs. McMillan snaps. "Please settle down right this instant!"

The girl's hands curl into fists and I'm scared she's going to come at Liam. But instead, she stomps her foot against the ground. "He did this! The bastard did something to my best friend. And look at him! He doesn't even *care*!"

I look at Liam, who is watching Madison's temper tantrum without any expression on his face. He hasn't said a word in protest. He just stares at her like she's an insect crawling on the wall. Like he really doesn't care.

They end up having to call the school security guard to take Madison away, because she won't stop shouting at Liam. Mrs. McMillan takes me aside, a concerned look in her eyes. "It may be best for Liam to stay home until this blows over."

"Yes," I murmur. "I was thinking the same thing."

She frowns. "Liam is a good boy. It's terrible that he got caught up in this tragedy."

As it turns out, Mrs. McMillan has been successfully charmed by my son. During his two years and change in high school, he has been very well behaved. There have been no incidents during this time. The last incident he had, in fact, was involving that English teacher in eighth grade. I don't like to think about that. But Mrs. McMillan clearly doesn't know about Mr. Young. She only sees what Liam allows her to see.

"Good luck," she tells me.

Chapter 36

Transcript of police interview with Tyler Martinson:

"Tyler, how long have you known Liam Cass?"

"Forever. Like, first grade."

"And you used to be friends?"

"Best friends, actually. I was always going to his house, or he'd go my house. We used to be really tight."

"And what was your opinion of him at that time?"

"Well, he was my best friend. So obviously, I liked him. He was cool. But he had a dark side, if you know what I mean."

"What do you mean?"

"Like, he was really good at manipulating people to get what he wanted. Especially teachers. He could blow off his homework and he would never get in trouble. I couldn't get away with *anything*."

"And what did the other students think of him?"

"They liked him too. Especially the girls. They were all, like, in *love* with him. It was really annoying. But Liam just thought it was funny."

"Were you jealous of him?"

"Me? No. I mean, I wasn't interested in girls back then. Now it's more annoying. They all still love him. He's like Ted Bundy. Wasn't he that serial killer women liked so much?"

"You mentioned he would manipulate other people. How did he do that?"

"So here's an example. In fourth grade, we had this roly-poly farm in our classroom. Liam got this idea to dump the farm on the floor and smash all the worms. That was his idea of fun stuff to do. And I went along with it because... I don't know. I thought it was fun too, I guess. Anyway, there was this other kid in the class named Michael. Nobody liked Michael because he was gross and fat and picked his nose. But Liam invited him to come with us, and Michael was so happy. But it was all a trick, you know? Because the only reason Liam wanted him to come was so Michael would get blamed for what we did. And it worked. Liam told the teacher Michael did it alone, and she believed him. And Michael didn't even rat us out, probably because he was hoping we'd still be friends with him after. But we weren't."

"Did you feel bad about it?"

"No. I mean, not at the time. But looking back, yeah, it was a shitty thing to do to Michael. But it was Liam's idea."

"At what point did you stop being friends with Liam?"

"Um, that would probably be sixth grade."

"Was there a particular reason?"

"Hell yeah. So Liam came to my house, and he had this little chipmunk trapped in a piece of Tupperware. He poked a couple of holes in it so the animal could breathe. And he told me he wanted to cut off the air and watch the chipmunk through the glass as it suffocated."

"..."

"Yeah, exactly. I was freaked out, and I told him I didn't want to do it. He tried to convince me, but I refused and told him he was a weirdo. Finally, he got angry and left."

"Did you tell anyone about it?"

"I told my mom because I wanted to make sure he didn't come over again."

"What did she say?"

"She didn't look that surprised. She just told me to stay away from him."

"You mentioned before you had another interaction with Liam that was very unsettling for you."

"Yeah. That was last year."

"What happened?"

"Okay, so Liam's sister—you know, Hannah—she's a

huge pain in the ass. She got all pissed off at me for some reason, and I guess she told him about it. So he felt like he had to avenge her or something. Even though I didn't even do anything wrong."

"What did he do?"

"So there was this stray cat that used to hang out by our house. My sister used to feed him, so he kept coming back. I didn't really care either way. I never fed the cat—I mean, that's not my responsibility, to feed a damn stray cat. And sometimes he'd be right in front of the door, so I had to kick him out of the way. Anyway. I got home from school one day and the stupid cat is in my bed. Can you imagine? I thought Emma let him inside. But then when I tried to shoo him away, he didn't move. So then I tried to pick him up to move him and…"

"Yes?"

"His insides fell out."

"…"

"Shit, I feel sick thinking about it. Somebody sliced him through the belly, and then when I picked him up… BAM, cat guts all over my bed!"

"That must have been very upsetting."

"Damn right. Oh, sorry. Am I allowed to say that?"

"Say what?"

"Damn. Because it's, like, a curse word."

"It's okay. So what did you do next?"

"I told my parents obviously. And I told them I thought Liam did it. But they asked if I had any proof, and I didn't. So we didn't do anything. My mom just kept saying to stay away from him and his family."

"And that was your last serious interaction with Liam?"

"Yeah. Well, if you don't count me kicking his ass the other day."

"Tyler, how do you know Olivia Mercer?"

"Oh, just from around. She was in my year. And she was friends with Madison Connor, who's dating my buddy Aidan."

"Are you friendly with her?"

"I don't know. A little."

"Did you ever ask her out on a date?"

"No…"

"Some of your friends from the football team said that you did ask her out. And she told you no."

"That's not… That's not what happened at all. Some of us were going out for burgers and I just invited her along. No big deal. And she was busy."

"Did it bother you when you saw her out with Liam?"

"Hell no. She's not even that hot. She could go out with whoever the hell she wants. Liam… half the football team, for all I care."

"So you weren't jealous?"

"What the… I thought we were talking about *Liam*. Liam is the crazy one."

"Tyler, how many times have you been suspended for fighting?"

"Jesus Christ, just twice. Is that a lot?"

"It's more than any of your peers."

"Yeah, but… The first time wasn't my fault. The guy stole my girlfriend. You don't do that to someone."

"But you threw the first punch."

"Yeah. I did. But—"

"And you were the one who punched Liam in the hallway first. Weren't you?"

"Fine. Yes. Look, I was mad at Liam because I thought he killed Olivia. That's the reason… I'm not crazy like he is. Yeah, we used to be friends. But after I realized what he was like, we stopped being friends. I'm not like him. And I sure as hell didn't do anything to Olivia."

Chapter 37

ERIKA

Jason texts me that the police are still searching the house, so I take the kids to McDonald's for lunch. I want to warn Liam about what's happening, but I'm not quite sure how to tell him.

Hannah agonizes over the menu at McDonald's, complaining about how it's going to ruin her diet. Then she goes ahead and orders a bacon double cheeseburger with large French fries. Liam says he's not hungry, but he reluctantly orders a Big Mac and Coke. I don't have much appetite either, but I pick something randomly from the menu. We've got to eat.

Hannah is the only one who manages to eat anything. She stuffs French fries into her mouth absently, almost automatically. Liam stares at his burger. His right cheek looks worse than it did in Mrs. McMillan's office. I can only imagine how bad it will look by tomorrow.

"Do you want me to get you some ice for your cheek?" I ask him.

"No."

"It's going to get more bruised if you don't ice it."

"I don't care." He regards his burger with a look of disgust. "Mom, I'm not hungry. Can I go sit in the car?"

Somehow I get the feeling I shouldn't let Liam out of my sight right now. "No. We're all going to stay right here."

"But, Mom—"

"You don't have to eat, but you have to stay here."

"Fine." Liam slumps down in his seat and pouts. Wow, the kid's acting like a real teenager now. Hannah has always been the expert at moping when we tell her what to do, but Liam always accepted everything without argument.

"Also," I add, "there's something you should know."

Liam lifts his eyes.

"The police are at our house right now. They're searching the house and my car."

Hannah puts down her burger, eyes flashing. "*What*? Don't they need a warrant or something to do that?"

I nod. "They do. And they came with one." I look at Liam again. "They also want your phone. And just so you know, they'll be able to read anything you've deleted."

He's quiet for a moment, playing with the wrapper on

his sandwich. "Fine."

"How bad is that, Liam?"

Before Liam can say a word, Hannah speaks up, "Liam didn't do anything. So they're not going to find anything incriminating."

I'm not so sure about that. But Liam doesn't give anything away with his expression. I get the feeling that my kids have been discussing this together. Sometimes I wonder what sorts of things Liam says to Hannah. Clearly, he trusts her in a way that he doesn't trust me or Jason. If only I could be a fly on the wall.

"We'll go see the attorney Dad hired this afternoon," I say. "He'll tell us what's likely to happen next."

I force myself to chomp down my salad. I don't have any appetite, but I need to eat if I'm going to get through what's going to happen next.

Chapter 38

OLIVIA

I have catalogued the inventory of the bag.

He has left me two plastic water bottles, four slices of bread, two apples, and a granola bar. If he's coming back within a day, I'll be fine. But he made a comment about how he wasn't sure when he could get back here. So how long is this food going to have to last me? Two days? Three? *A week?*

He could have brought me more food. He did this purposely. Maybe to make sure I was weak enough that I won't be able to fight him off or escape. As if being plunged into darkness twenty-four hours a day isn't bad enough.

I have divided the corners of my small space into their various purposes. One corner is for Phoebe. You can bet I'm not touching *her*. A second corner is for me to do my business. I was able to hold off for several hours, but you can't stop bodily functions. Of course, it's not making this dank hole smell any better. A third corner is for the food. And the fourth corner is for me to sit or sleep. I amazingly managed to sleep last night, although it was broken up and interspersed with nightmares.

I woke up sobbing. All I can think about is my home. How much I want to be back there. How much I want my mom.

I've got to find a way out of here.

In the meantime, I have divided the food into rations. I'm allowing myself one slice of bread total per day, half an apple, and half a bottle of water. I've already eaten the granola bar—I couldn't help myself. But the rest needs to last me for several days. It's not going to be nearly enough, but it will be enough to live on. Until I can get out of here

I've been devising a plan.

If he dug this hole, he did it when the soil was warmer and more pliable. And presumably, he had a shovel. But I can make a dent in the soil with my fingers. If I scrape at it hard enough, it comes free. My plan is to dig out enough to form a mound for me to stand on to reach the trap door above me. And once I can reach that, maybe I could find a way to break the lock.

He's never going to let me go. I saw the look in his eyes yesterday night. He's *crazy*. He wants to keep me here, for whatever reason. So that means if I'm going to get out,

I'm going to have to do it on my own. I can't count on the police to save me.

I'm getting out of here. If it's the last thing I do.

Chapter 39

ERIKA

Jason texts me that the police are almost done, but they still need Liam's phone, so I herd the kids back into the car and head home. The kids both look startled by the number of police cars around our house. I can't even imagine what the neighbors are thinking. But if they've been reading the local papers, they could probably take an educated guess.

Detective Rivera is talking to Jason when I unlock the door. She looks at Liam's bruised face and her eyes widen. "What happened?"

"Just a little scuffle at school," I say. I hate that she has to see him like this. Liam has never been in a fistfight before in his life. He's not a violent kid. At least, not in the way that Tyler is.

"Liam," Rivera says, "I'm going to need your phone."

Liam reaches into his pocket and hands it over to her without argument.

"It goes without saying," Rivera says, "you don't leave town without letting us know. We'll be in touch about anything we find."

With those words, she takes off, leaving my family alone again. I survey the living room, which doesn't look like much has been disturbed. I wonder what they've been doing here all this time.

"They were mostly in Liam's room," Jason says, as it reading my thoughts. "And the car. They spent forever going through your car."

"Are we going to see the lawyer?" I ask.

He nods. "Yeah, he fit us in for an hour from now." He looks Liam up and down, at his ripped shirt and bruised face. "You better change clothes."

Liam nods and goes upstairs. Hannah goes up to her room too, leaving Jason and me alone in the living room. Jason glances at the stairs and lowers his voice. "The attorney has a connection in the police department," he murmurs. "He said they're close to an arrest. They're hoping to find something here today that will make it a slam dunk."

I push away a sick feeling in my stomach. I can't believe this is happening. I can't believe there's a good possibility Liam is about to get arrested.

"But they won't," he says.

I wish I believed in Liam's innocence the way Jason

does.

———

Our attorney is named John Landon. He looks tall and capable, with a full head of gray hair, and a suit that looks very expensive. I didn't even ask Jason what this guy is going to be costing us. I don't want to know. But I know what attorneys charge, and if this guy is any good, he's probably charging us a fortune.

Liam sits down between us in front of Landon's mahogany desk. Not surprisingly, his cheekbone looks even worse than it did earlier in the day. He's going to have one hell of a shiner. It will be his first. He's never even needed stitches or had a broken bone before.

"What happened to your eye?" Landon asks him.

"I ran into this kid's fist," Liam says.

Jason rolls his eyes. "Some of the kids are giving him a hard time at school. They think he's guilty."

"Who does?" Landon asks.

Liam drops his eyes. "Everyone."

Landon nods, unsurprised. "I'm afraid it's going to get worse before it gets better. I just spoke to my contact at the police department, and it sounds like they found something during their search."

All the hairs on my arms stand at attention. "What did they find?"

Landon spreads his arms apart. "I don't know yet. But it's something big, apparently. They said to expect an arrest in the next twenty-four hours."

Liam's face pales. "You mean they're going to take me to *jail*?"

I always thought of Liam as a kid who could deal with anything. For the most part, everything seems to always roll off his back. Even when he got expelled from kindergarten all those years ago, he didn't seem all that bothered by it. But at this moment, he looks absolutely terrified. I don't blame him. I would be terrified too in his shoes. I'm terrified *for* him.

"I'm afraid so," Landon says. "But I'm hoping based on your age and lack of priors, you'll be able to make bail. They're hoping to make a big deal out of some complaint from a guy named Richard Young—a teacher Liam had."

Liam looks like he's going to be sick. Of course, we all remember Richard Young. That was the first time the police ever showed up at our door, and I thought there was a reasonable chance Liam could end up in jail. But nothing ever came of it. What Young had claimed Liam did was horrible beyond words, but the man had no proof.

As for me, I was never sure.

"Do you know what Mr. Young accused him of doing?" Jason says.

"Yes. I do."

"So you recognize that was completely blown out of proportion." Jason folds his arms across his chest. "That guy was really paranoid. I mean, Liam was only thirteen at the time. Can you imagine? There's no way he could have…"

Landon looks at Liam for several seconds. We made him put on a dress shirt and nice pants prior to this visit, and aside from the bruise on his face, he looks like his usual handsome, clean-cut self. "No, I agree. It seems unlikely."

I let out a breath.

Landon folds his hands in front of him and focuses his gaze on my son. "Liam, I'm only going to ask you this one time. Do you know what happened to Olivia Mercer?"

Liam glances at me and then at Jason. "No," he says.

Landon lifts an eyebrow. "You should know that anything you tell me stays in this room. Knowing the whole truth will help me to defend you. I don't like surprises."

"I don't know what happened to her," he insists.

I watch my son proclaim his innocence. As the words leave his mouth, I get this strong sensation that he's lying. But then again, he's always lying. Nothing he says anymore has any basis in reality. It makes me want to grab his shoulders and shake him.

Landon considers his words. I wonder if he's thinking

the same thing I am. "Mr. and Mrs. Cass, may I speak with Liam alone?"

Jason found. "Why?"

"Because *Liam* is my client. The two of you are not. And the attorney client privilege doesn't apply to you. If he gets charged, they'll almost certainly try him as an adult. So I think we should treat him as an adult."

"Is that all right with you, Liam?" I ask him gently.

I place my hand on his shoulder, even though I know he doesn't like being touched. Not that he ever complains about it when I'm affectionate, but he never came to me for hugs the way Hannah used to. He just didn't care. He never needed physical affection like other children.

"It's all right," Liam says.

Even though it almost kills me, we leave Liam in the room with Landon. Jason is just as unhappy about it as I am. As we sit in the waiting room, he keeps sneaking looks back at the closed office door. "What do you think they're talking about in there?"

"I don't know."

I glance around Landon's small waiting room—at his attractive, blond receptionist and the few people occupying seats across from us. Landon is a criminal attorney, so presumably everyone here has been accused of committing some sort of crime. The woman across from me is about my age, with schoolmarm glasses and hair gathered into a bun. I watch her flick through a copy of *Good Housekeeping* magazine.

What crime could this woman possibly have committed? She looks like someone I'd run into during a PTA event.

Then again, if there's one thing I've learned in the last sixteen years, it's that looks can be deceiving.

Jason bounces his right foot against the carpeting, casting a look back at the closed door to Landon's office. "I can't believe they're bringing up that garbage with the English teacher," he mutters. "If that's all they've got, they're grasping at straws."

"That was really bad, Jason. Liam is really lucky he didn't get charged."

"Charged? He didn't do anything!"

I don't know what to say. I should probably agree, but I can't bring myself to say the words.

"If he really did that…" He furrows his brow. "Erika, our kid isn't a monster."

I can see in my husband's eyes that he means it. I wonder what it is they found in our house that's so significant and if it will be enough to change Jason's mind.

Chapter 40

Transcript of police interview with Richard Young:

"You say you were Liam Cass's English teacher?"

"That's right."

"And when was that?"

"It was about three years ago. He was in eighth grade."

"And what was your opinion of him?"

"Honestly?"

"Of course."

"I hated him. I feel terrible saying that because what kind of teacher hates one of his students? But there was something about Liam that I instantly disliked. And I have to say, I was alone in my opinion. Universally, all the teachers adored him. Middle school kids aren't easy, but Liam seemed like a good kid—the kind teachers hope for in our classes. He was obviously very bright, well-behaved in class, and always handed in assignments on time."

"But you didn't like him?"

"He just rubbed me the wrong way—I can't even say why. There was something very fake about him. And also…"

"Yes?"

"I have a daughter. She's Liam's age, and she had some classes with him. And a few times, I saw them talking in the hallway and it drove me crazy. My wife told me I was overreacting, but given current circumstances, it sounds like I was reacting very appropriately."

"So did you do anything?"

"…"

"Mr. Young?"

"I'm not proud of this…"

"It's important to be honest right now. A girl's life could be at stake."

"Fine. I took Liam aside after class one day and told him to stay the hell away from my daughter."

"Did he?"

"No. He did not. In fact, he started showing more interest in her after I said that to him. Right when he knew I was paying attention. Like he was taunting me."

"Well, that's not an unusual response of a teenage boy to authority."

"I'm also not proud to say that I took my frustration out on his grades. English is very subjective, and I started grading his essays very harshly. He went from an A to a C."

"Did he do anything about it?"

"He complained. But I refused to change his grades. I also told Lily, my daughter, that I would ground her if she spoke with him again."

"And how did that go?"

"Initially, I thought it was successful. Lily stopped talking to Liam, and he just ate the bad grades. I thought it was over and done with."

"But it wasn't?"

"Obviously, I can't prove Liam did anything to me."

"What do you *believe* he did?"

"It was a Saturday night around two in the morning. My wife and I were fast asleep until our dog came into our bed. She vomited all over the bed and woke us up. But once I was awake, I found it very hard to think straight, and my wife and I both noticed we had splitting headaches. I called 911 and went to Lily's room to check on her. I couldn't wake her up at all. And then I passed out in her room."

"What happened?"

"Carbon monoxide poisoning."

"But you recovered?"

"Yes. Thank God for my dog. We spent several days in the hospital, but we were okay. But if Daisy hadn't woken us up, we would've been dead by the morning. All three of us."

"Did they find out how it happened?"

"There was a crack in our radiator. Supposedly, this sort of thing can happen, but we have a relatively new house. It was suspicious, to say the least."

"Didn't you have a carbon monoxide detector?"

"Yes. That's the other thing. Our detector was disconnected."

"That's a little suspicious."

"Exactly."

"Did you suspect Liam Cass?"

"No. Not at first. I mean, I didn't like the kid, but he was only thirteen years old. I didn't even think he knew what carbon monoxide was."

"So what made you suspect him?"

"One of my neighbors told me and the police they saw a kid skulking around my house shortly before it happened. I found a photo of Liam from his school records, and they confirmed it was him."

"Did the police investigate further?"

"They questioned Liam, but apparently he had a friend living in my neighborhood, so that was his excuse for being there. There was no other evidence he did anything. If he was ever inside my house, he left no trace."

"But you believe it was him?"

"I absolutely do."

"So he got away with it?"

"He sure did."

"Did you do anything further?"

"I'll tell you, Detective, there is one thing I did."

"What's that?"

"I gave the kid an A in English. Some things are not worth dying over."

Chapter 41

ERIKA

Liam barely said a word during the drive home. I made a few attempts to get him to talk, but he only answered in monosyllables. I wanted to know what Landon said to him when they were alone. Or more importantly, what he said to Landon. Did he tell the attorney the truth?

It's a relief to find Hannah is in her bedroom where we left her when we get home. After the way Olivia Mercer disappeared, I was almost scared Hannah might be gone too. Of course, why would she be? The monster was in our car.

As soon as I get into the bedroom, I dig around in the medicine cabinet for my Xanax. If there was ever a time I've needed it, it's right now. This is too much for me to deal with. My son getting arrested? You don't see that in many parenting books.

Damn it, where's my Xanax?

It's not in the medicine cabinet. I fumble through bottles of Tylenol, Motrin, Benadryl, triple antibiotic cream, antifungal cream, face lotion, hand lotion, expired antibiotics—God, why do we have so much crap in the medicine cabinet? But no Xanax.

Then it hits me. I shoved the bottle back in the drawer of my nightstand last time I took them. I wanted them next to my bed for easy access the next time I woke up in a cold sweat.

I make a beeline for the nightstand and open the drawer. The pill bottle rolls to the front, and I feel a jab of relief. I grab the bottle, wrench it open, and pop one in my mouth. I swallow it dry.

There's something else that catches my eye from within the drawer in my nightstand. At first, I think it's a photo of Liam. But then I realize it's the photo of my father. The one I always keep in my nightstand, so I don't ever forget him.

Of course, I put it there before I realized who he really was. What he did.

I pulled out the photograph to get a better look at it. My father looks like he's in his late twenties, about ten years older than Liam, but God, they look so much alike. The photograph is like looking into a time machine showing my son in the future. Same hair, same eyes, same crooked smile, same build. It's uncanny.

I can only imagine what else Liam inherited from this man.

I don't remember much about my father. I have a vague memory of holding his large hand as he walked down the street with me. I also remember when there was a mouse in our home and my father put out a trap to catch it. He showed me the trap, the mouse's tail captured by the metal bar, as the tiny animal squealed in distress. He laughed when I cowered behind my mother's legs. It's one of my first memories.

I always looked at that memory as an example of my father taking care of our family by getting rid of our rodent problem. But now I wonder if there was more to it than that. Did he enjoy torturing that little mouse the same way Liam enjoyed starving those hamsters to death?

In the past, when I've looked at this photograph, I experienced a rush of affection for this man who never got to see his daughter grow up. But right now, I feel something very different. Jason and I tried to do everything right as parents, but we couldn't change our son. There was something innately wrong with him. Something in his genes.

Liam is, after all, the grandson of a murderer.

I pick up my phone and punch in my mother's number. She answers after the second ring. "Oh, Erika, thank God. I was scared you were never going to speak to me again."

She has no clue what we've been through with Liam in the last twenty-four hours. Any resentment I might have felt for her keeping a secret from me takes a backseat to everything else. "You did what you felt was right. I can't be angry at you for that."

"I only did it to protect you. Because I love you."

She was protecting me because she loves me. The same way I want to protect Liam, even if he doesn't deserve it. Even if he doesn't love me. Even if he can't. "Mom, can I ask you a question?"

"Of course, darling. What is it?"

"What was my father like?"

"What... what do you mean?"

"His personality. What was he like?"

"Oh." She hesitates. "Well, he was... very charming. As you can imagine. All the women loved him. Liam, I think, takes after him in looks. Don't you think?"

I think he takes after him in more than looks. That's what I'm afraid of, anyway.

"Would you say he was... manipulative?"

My mother's laugh sounds hollow. "He manipulated me into marrying him, that's for sure. It was... well, I don't want to say it was mistake because I got you. But he wasn't a good husband, even before."

"Why not?"

"He was just very self-absorbed. He wasn't really ready to settle down. He wasn't the sort of man who wanted to stay in on a Saturday night and watch television. He always wanted to be out doing something. And when we had a child, that only made it worse."

I take a breath. "Was he cruel to you?"

She's quiet for a moment. "Yes, he certainly could be. Very cruel." She sighs. "He just wasn't a good person, Erika. Probably the best thing that ever happened was him exiting our lives. He wouldn't have been a good father."

I look down at the photograph in my hand. My mother has answered some of my questions, but I have more. I have a feeling that the only way I can possibly understand my son is to understand my father.

And there's only one way to do that.

"Thanks, Mom," I say. "I better go now."

"Are you okay, Erika? You sound funny."

"I'm fine."

"Have they found that girl yet who went missing? Such a tragedy."

"I've got to go, Mom," I choke out.

I hang up the phone before my mother can ask again if I'm okay. I'm not okay. I don't know if things will ever be okay again.

I stare at my phone for a moment. I feel slightly calmer. It must be the Xanax.

I looked back at my list of calls from the last several days. I select Frank Marino's number from the list before I can chicken out. I've got a new job for Frank.

After five rings, when I'm about to give up, Frank picks up the phone. "Erika! What's going on? Your little town is all over the news."

"Yeah." I swallow hard. Frank hasn't mentioned Liam, which means his name isn't in the news. Of course, since he's underage, the media can't mention him by name. But I have a feeling if he gets arrested, it will all come out somehow. The media can't mention Liam's name, but it can trend on Twitter or be shared on Facebook. Or whatever it is people do on Instagram. "Frank, I need you to find somebody for me."

"Find somebody?"

"Yes, like where he lives. An address." I take a deep breath. "His name is Marvin Holick."

"Okay…"

"Just so you know," I say, "he's my father."

Chapter 42

OLIVIA

I don't think he's coming back tonight.

Part of me is scared maybe he'll never come back. Not that I want to see him—the thought of seeing him again makes me physically ill—but I've only got left three slices of bread, one apple, and one bottle of water. I'm doing my best to hold off on eating or drinking, but my throat is painfully parched. All I want is to guzzle the entire bottle, but I know that would be stupid.

What if he doesn't come back for two or three more days? Then what?

If he doesn't come back soon, I'll die.

I can't let that happen.

I'm making some progress with the mound I'm building. It's hard to tell how big I need to make it, because I can't actually see where the trap door is aside from that tiny dim slice of light that disappears entirely at night. It's very hard to tell how high up it is. Also, I am essentially doing this blind. The hole is pitch black—it makes no difference if my eyes are open or closed.

And I'm so weak. All I want to do is lie on the ground and sleep. It would be easy to do. To let starvation and dehydration take me.

Every time that happens, I think about my parents. My friends. My bedroom.

But I can't think about it too hard, or else I'll start crying.

I've been doing all the digging with my fingers, and now they've become painful and raw. I can't see what they look like, because I have no light, but I imagine they're very red. I imagine pinpoints of blood.

I pat the mound with my palms. It's not big enough— I can tell that much. It needs to be at least a few inches higher. I scrape at the ground with my fingers and wince. God, my fingers hurt. I don't know what's worse—my fingers or my ankle.

If only I had a tool to help me dig.

I've got the empty water bottle. That's better than nothing, but it's hard to grip. And other than that, the only thing down here even resembling a tool is...

Oh no, I'm not going to do *that*.

Yes, one of those bones lying in the corner would be ideal for digging. Not as good as a shovel, but much better than a water bottle and light years better than my poor fingers. But I can't do that.

Can I?

I reach into Phoebe's corner until my fingers touch the smooth surface of one of her bones. A shudder runs through me. I lean forward a little more until my fingers close around the bone.

It would be so perfect.

But I can't. It's bad enough I'm stuck down here. It's bad enough I'm starving to death. But I won't do *that*.

Of course, it might be the only way I'll ever get out of here. The only way I'll ever see my family again.

I pick up the bone, feeling the weight in my hand.

I have no choice.

I'm going to get out of here for both of us, Phoebe.

I'm going to let your family know you're down here. Give them closure. Give you a real burial.

And I'm going to make sure that asshole goes to prison for the rest of his life.

Chapter 43

ERIKA

It's at five o'clock in the afternoon the next day that I hear a crash coming from the kitchen.

I was in the living room, trying desperately to focus on getting an article written for the next edition of the *Nassau Nutshell* when the sound of broken glass stole what little was left of my concentration. I slid my laptop off my legs and got up to investigate.

There's a rock lying on the floor, in the center of our kitchen. The window above the sink is shattered, and there's glass everywhere. I take a step and feel a sliver slice into my foot. I wince at the pain and crouch down to pick up the rock. There's a piece of paper taped to it with a word scribbled in red magic marker:

MURDERER

It's starting.

"What was that, Erika?" Jason is standing at the

entrance to the kitchen, still in his boxers and a T-shirt. He insisted on staying home again today, and I am intensely grateful. If Liam gets arrested today, I don't want to be alone here. Of course, if the police show up, I feel like maybe Jason doesn't want to be in his underwear. But I don't want to give him a hard time. Jason's underwear is the least of my problems.

I hold up the rock. "Somebody had a message for us."

"Shit," he breathes. "Should we call the police?"

"What's the point?" I say. The truth is, Liam probably deserves it. And the last thing I want is to invite the police into our home. "Just be careful where you step until I can clean up. There's glass everywhere."

Jason glances down at his watch. "It's getting late. No police yet. Maybe they're not going to arrest him after all."

I snort. "You're joking."

"Look, I know they think he did it. I'm not an idiot. But they have to have evidence to arrest him. They can't do it on a gut feeling."

I close my eyes. I wonder where Olivia Mercer is right now. I hope to God she's okay.

The doorbell rings, and my eyes fly open. Every time I hear that ring, I feel like I'm going to have a heart attack. Jason and I exchange looks.

"Maybe it's the person who threw the rock, coming to apologize?" he suggests.

I don't dignify that with a response.

I reach the door first. I peer through the peephole and see Detective Rivera's face. Oh no.

My hands are shaking too badly to open the door. Jason has to work the lock for me. When he gets it open, I immediately see the handcuffs in Rivera's hands. I think I'm going to faint.

"Is Liam home, Mrs. Cass?" she asks me.

"You're arresting him," I say numbly.

She nods slowly. "I'm sorry."

Jason looks down at the handcuffs, his face growing pale, but he doesn't protest this time. He walks to the foot of the stairs and calls out, "Liam? Get dressed right now and come down here."

I watch as my son emerges from his bedroom, wearing a plain T-shirt and a pair of clean blue jeans. In spite of the bruise on his cheekbone, he looks so young and handsome now. When he catches sight of the detectives at the door, he stops walking. I watch as he takes a deep breath, then forces himself to move forward.

I get seized by the desperate urge to throw my arms around him and tell him it's all going to be okay. But it would be a lie.

When Liam gets to the bottom of the stairs, Rivera steps forward. She holds out the handcuffs, and Liam's eyes widen as he takes a step back.

"Liam Cass, you are under arrest for the kidnapping and murder of Olivia Mercer."

She reads him his rights as he listens silently with a dazed expression on his face that likely mirrors my own. I can't believe this is happening. My legs are jello—they feel like they're going to collapse under me.

I wonder what they found in their search. It must be something really big.

When Rivera finishes reading his rights, she holds out the handcuffs. Now Liam looks really panicked. He looks like he's about to burst into tears, but he's holding it back. I haven't seen Liam cry since he was three years old. He very rarely cried as a baby. He was such a good baby. I remember thinking to myself that it was unfair any woman should be so lucky.

"Do you have to put those on me?" he asks, unable to hide the note of desperation in his voice.

"I'm afraid so," she says, without any sympathy in her voice.

At least she cuffs him in front rather than behind his back. I flinch as the cuffs snap into place. This is it. They're really arresting him. They're really taking him away to jail. My baby. In *jail*. How could this be happening?

"Liam, please just tell them where she is!" I blurt out.

For a moment, everyone goes silent.

Jason stares at me, open-mouthed. "Erika…"

The officers are staring at me too. Liam's face is bright pink. "Mom," he says, "I didn't—"

But before he can finish saying whatever it was he was going to say, Rivera puts an arm on his back and leads him out the front door. The sun is still up, and it's obvious several of our neighbors are watching him get led to the police car in handcuffs. Everyone knows what's going on. I expect more rocks through our window tonight.

And then they drive away. I follow them outside and watch the police car until it becomes a speck of dust in the distance. Jason comes out to join me. I expect him to yell at me for my little outburst in the house, but he doesn't say a word.

When we get back in the house, Hannah is standing in the middle of the living room. Her eyes are bloodshot, and she looks like she hasn't showered today. I'm fairly sure those are the jeans and shirt she was wearing yesterday. "Did they take him? They arrested him?"

Jason sighs heavily. "Yes."

A tear escapes from her left eye. "Dad! How could you let them?"

He frowns. "I didn't have much of a choice. They had a warrant for his arrest."

She stomps her foot on the ground. "This is bullshit! He didn't do it. You know he didn't!"

"Hannah…" I say.

"Don't even, Mom!" she snaps at me. "I know what *you* think of him. I see the way you look at him. At least Dad thinks he's innocent."

They both look at me, waiting for a response. I don't know what to say. Hannah is absolutely right.

"Even if he's guilty, I still love him," I finally say.

And that is the truth. Hannah and Jason might think Liam is innocent, but they're wrong. I'm the only one who can see through him. All I can hope for now is that Olivia Mercer is still alive. Maybe if he tells them where she is, they'll go easy on him.

"You have no idea, Mom," Hannah says. "Liam would never have done this. He really liked Olivia."

I wish I had a wife, so I could put her deep in a hole.

Unfortunately, Hannah is the one who has no idea what she's talking about. I know my son. And I know this won't end well.

——

When I first saw those two blue lines on the pregnancy test seventeen years ago, I never would have believed the baby growing inside me would end up behind bars.

Everything about Liam's early life was easy, starting with my pregnancy. I got knocked up on our first try—and in contrast to my pregnancy with Hannah, where I was sick for the entire time, I felt great when I was carrying

Liam. People used to tell me I was glowing. And the labor was similarly easy. Five good pushes and he was out. Screaming and pink and perfect.

Liam was a really mild-mannered baby. He rarely fussed or cried. He ate whenever I offered him my breast, and he slept nearly through the night as soon as we brought him home. He was a beautiful baby too. He looked like one of the children in the magazines with his chubby cheeks and sweet smile. Other women were always stopping me in the street to admire him.

And Liam was fantastic at playing the part. When people would ask him how old he was, he would hold up one finger and cry, "One!" He loved to perform. Sometimes I would look down in his crib at night at his sleeping face and wonder how I got so lucky.

It was when he was barely four years old that I first noticed something different about him.

We were at the park. I had Hannah in her carriage and she was sobbing as usual. I was lucky that Liam could be trusted to play independently, because Hannah required all my attention. So I didn't notice what he was doing until I found him crouched in the corner of the park. I pushed Hannah's carriage over to see what was going on.

Liam was playing with a large carpenter ant. He had built some sort of enclosure, and he would allow the ant to leave, then trap it again. I watched him do this for a minute, trying to figure out the rules of his game. Finally, I said, "What are you doing, Liam?"

He lifted his big brown eyes and smiled at me—that smile that made all the women fall in love with him. "The ants thinks he's gonna get away, but he can't! He doesn't know I'm gonna smoosh him."

Those words said in Liam's four-year-old baby voice made me feel really uneasy. "Liam," I said in a choked voice. "You're being mean to the ant."

He scrunched up his little face. "But it's just an ant, Mommy. Who cares?"

"It's a living creature, Liam."

But he just looked at me blankly until I told him to go play at the monkey bars again. He obligingly went back to the jungle gym, but I couldn't get the incident out of my head. That night, I told Jason about what he said, but Jason wasn't at all concerned. "Boys like to play with bugs," he said.

But he wasn't playing with the bug. He was *torturing* it.

It only got worse after that. More disturbing statements that got harder and harder to shrug off. And then that girl found duct-taped in the closet when he was in kindergarten. He got kicked out of school for that one. I told him he could never do anything like that ever again, and technically, he didn't. I finally took him to that child psychologist, Dr. Hebert, but I don't believe she did anything to help him. He just got smarter about keeping his mouth shut.

And not knowing what he was thinking was the hardest part of all.

After the police take Liam away, Jason immediately calls Richard Landon. We sit on the sofa and he puts our lawyer on speaker phone, so we can both listen in. We have to order Hannah to go upstairs, because she shouldn't be listening to this, and also, she's almost hysterical.

"John," Jason said. "They just took him. The police. They cuffed him and put him in the car. They're taking him to jail."

"Yes." Landon's voice jumps out of Jason's phone. "I had a feeling that was going to happen today."

"What are they going to do now?" I ask.

"They're going to bring him to the police station and book him," Landon says. "They'll photograph him and fingerprint him, and then put him in one of their holding cells."

My son behind bars. Tears spring to my eyes. I can't bear it.

"We'll get him a bail hearing tomorrow morning," Landon says. "Hopefully they'll set bail and he can go home until the arraignment."

Jason looks up at me, his brow furrowed. "You think

they won't set bail?"

"It's possible. They're charging him with murder."

"But they don't even know if Olivia Mercer is dead!" Jason says.

"Right. They have to prove that a crime was actually even committed, so that's in his favor." Landon pauses. "Also, he's only sixteen. I'll argue all that at the bail hearing."

"So there's a chance they might not even be able to charge him?" I ask hopefully.

Landon is silent for several seconds. "I'm not going to lie to you, Erika. They may not have a body, but they've got a strong case against him."

My stomach drops. "What have they got?"

"Well, for starters, it was known that they were at least dating, if not boyfriend and girlfriend. We have the neighbor who is testifying not only that Olivia and Liam were together that night, but that she got into his car." He clears his throat. "But it was what they found in your car that was the nail in the coffin. They found traces of blood that matched Olivia's blood type and three of her hairs. In your *trunk*."

"In my trunk?" I say numbly.

"Yes," Landon says. "If they were just in the seat, we could argue she was in the car, but the trunk is a bit more damning."

"But it's a hatchback," Jason points out. "If she was in the backseat, her hair could've gotten into the trunk. It's not like the trunk is an enclosed space."

"I can argue that. But it doesn't explain the blood, does it?"

Jason leans back against the sofa, shaking his head. I think he has just checked out of this conversation.

"Are you still there?" Landon asks.

"I'm here," I say.

"I'm going to go over to see Liam now. He's probably very scared so I'll tell him what's going to happen next. Also…"

"What?" I say.

Landon sighs. "I'm going to try to convince him to tell me where Olivia Mercer is. Whether or not she's alive. We can use that as a bargaining chip."

I swallow a lump in my throat. This is the last thing I wanted to hear. "Did Liam tell you he did it?"

"You know I can't tell you that, Erika. Confidentiality."

"Please, John! He's only sixteen year old and he's in jail and—"

I'm sobbing now into the phone. I'm two seconds away from completely losing it, if I haven't already. I don't know how this could be happening. I was so careful. How did I get the wrong Olivia?

"Erika, Erika…" Landon's voice cuts through my sobs. "Look, calm down. He… he didn't tell me anything. Okay?"

I gulp, trying to catch my breath. "But you think he did it."

It's not a question.

Our attorney is silent for a moment. "Yes, I do. Come on, Erika. He obviously did it. The evidence is overwhelming." He gives me a second to absorb this. "But look, even if she's dead and he buried her, he can offer to lead the police to her body in exchange for leniency. A life sentence as opposed to the death penalty."

"Do you think she's dead?" I ask in a voice that is barely a whisper.

Landon is silent for what seems like an eternity. "Honestly? Yes. I think she's already dead. If she wasn't at first, he probably realized he had to get rid of her to destroy the evidence."

"God," I whisper. I wipe my eyes with the back of my fingers.

"But I'll do my best for him," Landon says. "Whatever he did, I'll fight for him. That's my job."

Why? That's the question I want to ask. Because if Liam really killed that girl, he *should* be locked away in prison. He should be in a place where he can't hurt anyone ever again.

I spent his entire childhood trying to protect him from himself. I have failed.

Chapter 44

ERIKA

When I come downstairs later in the evening to force myself to eat some dinner, I find Hannah sitting on the sofa in the living room, slouched down as she watches television. I get close enough that I can see what's on the screen. It's *The Princess Bride*.

The Princess Bride used to be my favorite movie when I was a kid. When Hannah was four years old, I showed it to her and Liam for the first time. Liam didn't think much of it, but Hannah loved it. It became her favorite movie, and I think it still is. It's a comfort movie. It's her bowl of chicken soup.

I stand there for a moment, watching Hannah watch the movie. Her eyes are pinned on the screen, and she mouths the words along with the characters. She could probably recite every line in this movie from memory. Actually, so could I.

"Can I join you?" I ask.

Hannah looks up at me with her blue eyes rimmed with red. The last time I saw her, she was screaming at me. But now she lifts one shoulder. "As you wish."

It's a line from the movie. An olive branch?

I sit down on the sofa next to Hannah, but leaving a respectable distance between us. If I sit too close, she'll complain I'm stifling her. But sitting too far away will make her unhappy too. I can't figure out how to make Hannah happy—I never could. Even when she was an infant, she would howl her lungs out while I would beg her to tell me what was wrong. Even two-year-old Liam commented once, "My baby sister is always sad."

Fourteen years later, nothing has changed.

"I'm sorry you had to see that happen earlier," I say to Hannah.

She doesn't take her eyes off the screen. "It wasn't your fault."

"I know, but…"

She turns to look at me. "You really think he did it, don't you?"

I clear my throat. "Well, I don't know for sure. I mean—"

"That's why you hired that guy to scare off all the girls Liam likes."

My mouth falls open. Hannah knew about that? It

hadn't even occurred to me she might know. I thought that was my deep dark secret.

"One of them told me." Her eyes flick back at the television screen. "I assumed you were behind it. Considering you were the one who sent him to the shrink."

"You know about that?"

"Liam told me."

I suck in a breath. "I'm really sorry, Hannah. I'm sorry you got caught up in all of this. I promise I'll do my best to keep you out of it from now on."

Hannah picks up the remote control and shuts off the television. She faces me now, her eyes filling with tears. "I don't *want* to be kept out of it. I just want my brother back home."

Hannah's loyalty to Liam is understandable. Whatever else anyone can say about Liam, he's a good big brother. People warned me when I got pregnant that bringing a newborn home when you've already got a two-year-old is a recipe for jealousy. One of my girlfriends told me she constantly had to protect her infant from her toddler.

But it was never like that with Liam and Hannah. The first time I brought Hannah home, he couldn't stop staring at her. When we finally let him hold her under careful supervision, he was so gentle. He kept stroking her little face with open-mouthed awe.

When she was about four months old, we took her to the park and a big dog rushed to the stroller, barking loudly enough to make Hannah burst into tears. Liam jumped in front of the dog, bravely holding up his hand. "Doggy, no!" he cried. "No hurt my sister! *No!*"

I don't know what Liam did or didn't do to Olivia, but he has always protected his sister.

"It's going to be okay," I tell Hannah. "We're going to get him home."

Hannah wipes her eyes with the back of her hand. "Do you really believe that, Mom?"

I wish I could say I did. I wish I could tell my daughter that the truth will come out and Liam will go free. But the real truth is, whether or not the truth comes out, I believe Liam will spend the rest of his life in prison.

Chapter 45

ERIKA

Jason and I get ready for bed in absolute silence.

The only thing we could possibly talk about at this point is the fact that our son is in jail, and it's all we've spoken about for the last several days. It's the last thing I want to talk about now. I know Jason is still peeved at me for what I said when the police showed up to arrest Liam. But it's not like I meant to make my son seem guilty. If I could take it back, I would.

I join my husband in the bathroom while he's brushing his teeth. He's got the electric toothbrush whirring in his mouth. Five years ago, Jason had a root canal, and after swearing he would never go through something like that again, he purchased an electric toothbrush and about a crate full of dental floss. He's used them both religiously, and he's had such good dental visits since then, I switched over to the electric toothbrush last year. I do feel like it gets my teeth cleaner, but the annoying part is that we can't both brush at once anymore. I have to wait for him to be done, then swap out the toothbrush heads.

As I wait, I rinse off my face, although there's not much to rinse since I didn't bother with makeup this morning. I let the hot water wash over my skin, trying not to think about what's going to happen tomorrow. Liam's bail hearing. Every time I imagine it, I get a sick sensation in the pit of my stomach.

What if he doesn't make bail? I can't conceive of not getting to take him home tomorrow. But Landon says I have to accept the possibility that Liam might be in jail for the duration.

Liam in jail. My little boy in jail. Surrounded by murderers and thieves.

"Done," Jason says, as he hands me the handle of the electric toothbrush.

"Thanks," I say.

We are so polite.

My hands are shaking as I try to get electric toothbrush head in place. Jason watches me for a moment until he takes it for me and secures the brush.

"It's going to be okay," he says. He furrows his brow. "It's just a misunderstanding. In a week, this will all have blown over."

I snort. "Do you genuinely believe that?"

He stares at me, a sad look in his blue eyes. "Erika, do you genuinely believe our son killed that girl?"

The bathroom feels stiflingly small. I've got to get out of here. I put down the toothbrush, even though I haven't brushed yet, and scurry back into our bedroom. Jason follows me, apparently still waiting for an answer to his question. I wish I had his faith in Liam. But I know things he doesn't know. As much as he wants and needs to hear it, I can't tell him I believe Liam is innocent.

"I know it doesn't look great for him." His tone is almost pleading. "But Liam wouldn't do this. He's a good kid. He comes from a good family."

Arguably, Jason and I are good parents—both of us are so normal, we're boring. But Jason doesn't know my history. He doesn't know the secret about me that I only recently found out myself. And maybe I owe it to him to tell him the truth. Maybe that's the only way to make him understand. Even if it makes him look at me differently.

"Jason," I say. "There's something I need to tell you."

His eyes widen and he takes a step back. After the number of revelations he's had to deal with in the last few days, I feel bad dropping this one on him. But I owe it to him to be honest.

"You're scaring me, Erika," he says. "Should I… should I be sitting down?"

I reach out and take his hand, which is unsurprisingly clammy. I lead him over to the bed, and we sit side by side. Jason is staring at me intently, his brows knitted together.

"I recently found out something... kind of surprising."

He shakes his head. "More surprising than the police arresting our kid?"

I take a deep breath. "It's about my father. He's... he's alive."

His mouth falls open. His face looks about how mine probably did when my mother dropped the bombshell on me. "Are you serious? How?"

It's harder than I thought to tell him the truth. Because I know what it means. I have always believed that while Liam had his issues, it wasn't my fault. But now I know the truth. Liam is the grandson of a murderer. This is in his genes. And it doesn't help matters that he looks exactly like my father. The spitting image.

I explain it to Jason as best I can, considering all I know is from my mother. He listens, his face growing paler by the second. When I finish telling him everything, he mutters, "Jesus."

"I know."

"How could your mother have kept this from you?"

"I guess she thought it was easier to think he was dead. That knowing he was in jail might traumatize me."

He frowns. "Are you going to go see him?

"Do you think I should?"

"It's your decision, Erika."

"Yes, but what do you think?"

He hesitates for only a second. "If I were you, I wouldn't."

"But he's my father…"

"So what? The man is a murderer. Do you really want to have anything to do with him after that?"

The conviction in his voice unsettles me. After all, there might be a time in the near future when we have to visit our own son in jail. If it comes out that Liam really did kill Olivia, will Jason disown him?

The truth is, I know deep down, whether Liam did it or not, I'm going to support him. I'll visit him every week in jail if it comes down to it. I hope it's not true, and I pray to God that Olivia is okay, but no matter what, Liam is my son. No matter what he does, that isn't going to change.

I'm not sure Jason feels the same way.

"I haven't decided yet." I chew on my lip. "Obviously, this isn't the best timing. But… I'm curious. What if Liam is the way he is because…?"

Jason cocks his head to the side. "Because of what?"

"Because of me. Because he's inherited it from me?"

He blinks a few times. "You're not a murderer, Erika."

"But my father is."

My husband stares down at his hands for a moment. My stomach fills with butterflies as I try to figure out what he's thinking. When I can't stand it another second, he looks back up at me. "Liam didn't kill that girl."

"But what if he did?"

"No." He squares his shoulders. "I'm sorry, Erika. But just because your father was a crazy murderer, it doesn't mean Liam is too."

But I can see in his eyes the shred of uncertainty. For the first time, he doesn't look so sure that our son is innocent. He had no idea when he married me that I was the daughter of a convicted murderer. A *psychopath*. Now that he knows what's running through my blood and what I might have passed down, he's finally starting to believe that our son isn't the perfect child he thought him to be.

And it's all my fault.

Chapter 46

OLIVIA

It's night now. I know that because the slice of light has vanished, plunging me back into the worst kind of pitch blackness.

I have almost no food or drink left. One slice of bread. Some part of the last bottle of water. I'm so thirsty, I could drink my own pee. I never understood how people did that during those survival stories. But I totally get it now. I'm dizzy with hunger and thirst.

With the remaining strength I have left, I've been working on building up the mound using Phoebe's bone. My little tower is about a foot high based on feel. Possibly high enough to reach the trap door.

I've got to give it a try. Before he comes back.

I step up on the mound with my right foot. I try to lift myself to the top, leaning against the side of the hole, but I accidentally put weight on my left ankle.

Oh my *God*.

I howl and double over in pain. My left ankle feels worse every day. It's definitely broken. It's very swollen and warm, and I'm having trouble wiggling my toes. But then again, it's just pain. People get shot and keep moving. I have to get past it. That's my only chance of survival.

Think of happy things, Olivia.

My parents. My mom.

My room.

Madison.

I can only imagine what Madison must be thinking right now. She warned me. She warned me and I didn't listen.

I've got to get out of here. I've got to see my family again.

I take a deep breath and get back up on the mound. My left ankle touches the ground and it's agony, but I don't allow myself to collapse again. I stand up straight, lifting a long bone in my hand over my head. It scrapes against the roof of my enclosure.

I did it! I can reach the top!

I bang on it with the bone, and I hear metal. The trap door is locked.

Of course.

I shouldn't be surprised, because I heard the lock turning the last time he came, but my whole body sags with disappointment. I thought I was going to get out of here. I thought this was it. I'd escape and be home within the hour.

This is just a setback. Don't give up.

I take a deep breath, pushing away a wave of dizziness. This isn't hopeless. After all, it's just wood above me. If I can break through the wood, I can get out of here. I've got all the time in the world to pound against the wood until it breaks.

Here goes nothing…

Chapter 47

By the morning, the papers are all reporting an arrest has been made in the disappearance of Olivia Mercer. It's not just local news, but the national papers have picked up the story as well. They can't print Liam's name, because he's only sixteen, but it doesn't matter. They can't keep people from saying his name in the online comments.

I sit in bed, reluctant to get up and face the world, reading through the comments until I can't bear it anymore. Overwhelmingly, the general public thinks Liam is guilty.

I don't care if this kid is sixteen. He deserves the electric chair. Some people are too sick to live.

I heard he has a long history of mental problems. Parents deserve to go to jail too for not making sure he

got the help he deserves.

Lock this kid up and throw away the key!

Tragic and horrible! This is what lethal injections are for!

But the worst are the comments from people who obviously know Liam in real life. It looks like the majority of the town has decided he's guilty. Or at least, the ones who are posting online.

I've known Liam Cass since grade school. He's nuts! I could totally see him murdering someone. He's definitely guilty!

Liam used to play with my son, but I told him Liam wasn't welcome anymore. I knew that kid was trouble.

Olivia was a beautiful girl. She was stupid to go out with Liam Cass, just because she thought he was good-looking. Now she's paying the price.

The family has been hiding Liam's mental problems for years. He's a psychopath but they'll do anything to

protect him!

The kid was kicked out of kindergarten for raping a girl. That says it all!

Great. Now the Internet has convicted him of rape when he was five years old. It's hard to read all these comments, but somehow I can't look away. There are a few positive ones at least, intermingled with the awful ones.

OMG, Liam is in my Spanish class and he is sooooo nice. He would never do this! I don't believe it's true!

Liam is one of the best students I've ever had in all my years as a teacher. I may not know all the evidence, but it's hard to imagine such a fine young man could be capable of this.

Liam is a great teammate and great guy! This is bullshit! Someone must be framing him!

I finally put down my phone and stop reading when Jason appears at the doorway to the bedroom. We haven't spoken since our conversation last night, and I wonder if he's still angry with me. He doesn't look angry though. He looks pale. "I don't want you to freak out, Erika…"

"Then don't start a sentence with those words." I sit up straight in bed, clutching the covers in my fingers. "What's going on? What happened?"

"Somebody spray-painted something on our front door."

I can only imagine what somebody's written on our house. Right in front of our all our neighbors, who I'm sure saw nothing. I have been doing my best to keep the tears back, but now they threaten to spill over.

"Erika…" He sits down next to me at the edge of the bed. "It's okay. Don't cry. I'm taking care of it. Just stay inside the house."

But this is about a hell of a lot more than some words spray painted on our door. That can be painted over. The bigger problem isn't as easily fixed. I wipe my eyes, trying to get control of my tears but I can't.

Jason's eyes soften. He puts his arms around me while I sob for our son. It's hard to stop. I just keep thinking of my little baby. The tiny, helpless bundle I brought home from the hospital sixteen years ago. In jail. He must be terrified. I'm his mother and I'm supposed to be there to look out for him, and I failed.

"It's all my fault," I murmur into Jason's damp shirt.

His warm hand strokes the back of my head. "No, it's not. Stop saying that. You're a great mother. It's not your fault."

How could he say that though? Especially now that he knows about my father?

He squeezes me tighter. "Liam's going to be fine. This is all a mistake. He'll be home before you know it." He kisses me on the top of my head. "Look, why don't you take a shower so we'll be ready for the hearing? I'll take care of the graffiti."

Right—Liam's bail hearing is at eleven. I've got to get out of bed and shower before that happens. I don't know if I can muster up the energy though. I just keep thinking about Liam spending the night in jail. Or worse, spending the next thirty years' worth of nights in jail.

"Okay," I mumble.

Jason pulls away from me. When I look up at him, his brow is furrowed. "Are you going to be okay?"

I nod wordlessly.

"You sure?"

I swallow a lump in my throat. "Go do what you need to do."

Jason almost looks like he's going to insist on staying, but then my phone rings on my nightstand, so he takes the opportunity to go downstairs. I look over at the screen and see my boss's name flashing.

Oh God—I've got an article due today. It's been the last thing on my mind lately, but Brian is going to go nuts that I don't have it ready. I don't want to lose my job on top of everything. Especially since it's clear Liam's legal bills will be substantial.

"Hi, Brian," I say. I try not to sound as terrible as I feel. If Liam can be charming when he doesn't mean it, so can I. "I'm so sorry about the article being late. If you could just give me until tomorrow…"

Brian is silent for a moment before he says anything. "That's the thing, Erika. I need to talk to you about your article."

"I could probably have it by tonight if you really need it… Things have just been really crazy here."

"Yeah," he breathes. "I heard."

Oh no.

"Oh. I didn't realize you knew."

"I'm a reporter, Erika. It's all over the news."

"Not his name," I squeak. As if it matters.

"I think…" Brian's voice lowers a notch. "I think would be for the best if you took a hiatus from the paper. Until this blows over. You need to be there for your family right now."

"It's okay. I can still do my job."

"This isn't optional."

Oh, I get it. Nobody wants to read parenting tips from the mother of a murder. I guess that makes sense. "For how long?"

"Let's play it by ear."

So... forever. Basically, I'm fired. There's probably some law against this, but I don't have the energy to fight this battle. I'm sure Brian knows it. "Fine."

"I'll be in touch," he promises.

No, he won't.

I put down the phone. I hadn't imagined it was possible, but I feel even worse now than I did five minutes ago. On top of everything, I've lost my job. At least Jason can't get fired, since he's his own boss. It's a small comfort.

I finally drag myself out of bed and into the shower. I let the hot water wash over me, not wanting to ever get out again. I want to live in the shower. What would Jason say if I refused to get out of the shower? But no. I have to be there for my family. It would be selfish to have a mental breakdown right now.

As I'm toweling myself dry, my cell phone starts ringing in the bedroom. I run out of the bathroom, dripping wet, and reach for my phone just before it goes to voicemail.

A voice hisses at me from the other line: "It would be a shame if somebody murdered your pretty little daughter like your son murdered that girl."

My heart nearly stopped in my chest. I stare at the phone. "Who is this?"

Not surprisingly, they hang up.

I close my eyes, wishing I could go to sleep and this would all be a horrible dream. But no. I've got to get dressed and go to this hearing. I've got to be there for Liam, no matter what horrible thing he's done.

Chapter 48

ERIKA

There are reporters outside the courthouse, so we follow Landon's instructions and go around to the back. Thank God they can't use Liam's name, but I'm not sure where the restrictions end. Certainly if the entire Internet knows who he is, the reporters do too. They're not by our house, but maybe soon they will be. And if Liam gets tried as an adult, which Landon says is a strong possibility, I'm worried all of those protections will vanish.

The last time I was in a courtroom was when I served on a jury nearly a decade ago. There are rows of benches in the back for people to sit. A wooden table for the defense and one for the prosecution, and then a bench at the front where the judge presides. As Jason, Hannah, and I slide into the bench in the back, I'm reminded vaguely of going to church. It's been longer since I've been in a church than a courthouse.

Maybe we should have been more religious. Maybe that would have saved Liam.

The judge is already seated in the front of the room. The Honorable George Maycomb. He's old—old enough to be my father, with a full head of white hair and a neatly trimmed beard to match. Landon said that Judge Maycomb tends to be lenient, although when it comes to the murder of a young girl, all bets are off.

After about ten minutes, a bailiff leads Liam into the courtroom, and I get my first look at my son since the police took him away. He's wearing a wrinkled orange jumpsuit that's a size too big on him, and he looks *awful*. His cheekbone is still purple from where Tyler hit him, and there are dark circles under his eyes. He looks like he didn't sleep at all last night. He looks so bad, Hannah lets out a gasp when she sees him.

For a moment, he doesn't look like a sixteen-year-old, on the verge of adulthood—he looks like a scared little boy. *My* little boy. The same boy who sported a gap-toothed grin for a whole year and would hold up fingers to tell his age. I want more than anything to run up to him and throw my arms around him. I want to protect him from this.

But I can't. I did my best, and I failed.

We don't even get a chance to talk to him. Liam is led straight to his seat, but he sees us. He doesn't wave, but he nods his head—I suppose an enthusiastic hello would be unbecoming coming from an accused murderer. I cringe as I recall that the last thing I said to him was to beg him to tell us where Olivia is. How could I have said that in front of the police? Yes, I meant it, but it was the wrong thing to say. I wonder if he hates me.

Landon explained to us what would happen today. There will be no jury, but the charges will be listed, Liam will enter his not guilty plea, then Judge Maycomb will set bail. *If* there's bail. Given he's accused of murder, there's no guarantee.

The prosecutor is a woman named Cynthia Feinstein, who is around forty, with black eyes and an angry frown permanently etched on her lips. She looks like she wants to strap my son into the electric chair personally. When she stands up to speak, her voice is deep for a woman—intimidating.

"Your honor." She addresses the judge, her black eyes darkening further. "There is ample evidence that Liam Cass is responsible for Olivia Mercer's disappearance. He was confirmed by multiple other students to be dating her. He was seen at her house at two in the morning, and she was witnessed entering his vehicle. Her hair and her blood were both found in the trunk of the vehicle when it was searched later. There are no other suspects in the case or persons of interest. Olivia Mercer has been missing for three days now, and given the blood in his vehicle, there is compelling reason to believe that he has killed her and hidden the body." Feinstein pauses. "Given the seriousness of these charges and the overwhelming evidence, the defendant has ample reason to leave town to avoid conviction."

When the prosecutor says it like that, it sounds very convincing. If I were the judge, I wouldn't give Liam bail. I look at my son, who is sitting quietly at the defense table, his shoulders rigid, staring straight ahead.

I wish I knew what he was thinking.

Landon gets to his feet. "Your Honor, every piece of evidence that the prosecution has is circumstantial. We don't even know at this point if Olivia has run away. Yes, they were together that night and there was evidence she was in his car. But is that so surprising if she was his girlfriend? Moreover, the defendant is a sixteen-year-old *child*. He's just a boy."

At Landon's words, every eye in the courtroom goes to Liam. I'm glad he's in the rumpled jail jumpsuit and not in a suit. In a suit, he would have looked older. But now, he barely looks sixteen. He looks like a scared little boy.

"He has never been away from his parents for more than one night," Landon continues in a gentler voice. "Not even for a school trip. His mother works from home and she can be with him at all times. We'd be happy to hand over his passport or whatever else you need. But this is a bail hearing to determine flight risk, and I think it's clear my client is in no risk of elopement."

Judge Maycomb strokes his white beard. He looks Liam over and sets the bail at $200,000.

This is cause for celebration—the judge could have easily denied bail entirely and Liam would be locked up again until the trial. Instead, after we put down ten percent of the $200,000 to the bail bond company, we can have Liam home by this afternoon. It also means that Maycomb doesn't think much of the prosecutor's evidence against Liam.

But none of us are in a celebratory mood during the drive home. The car is so silent, it feels like we're coming home from a funeral. Jason drives and I sit shotgun, staring out the window. Hannah and Liam sit in the back, so quiet that I could forget they're there.

"How was last night?" Jason asks Liam, in a pathetic attempt to break the silence.

Liam tugs at his collar as he squirms in his seat. He's back in the same T-shirt and jeans he'd been wearing when he got arrested. "Fine."

"Were you able to sleep at all?"

"A little."

"Did they feed you?"

"Yeah. It was fine."

"What was the dinner?"

"I don't know. I don't remember."

I nudge Jason to try to get him to stop. Obviously, Liam doesn't want to talk about his night in jail. I can only imagine it must've been horrible for him. But isn't it what he deserves?

When we get to our front door, I sense something just as Jason is turning the lock. I don't know what it is exactly, but I have a feeling like we shouldn't go inside. It's like a hand against my chest, pushing me backwards. Instinctively, I step in front of Liam. Even after everything that's happened, my instinct is to put my own life in front of his.

Especially when we step inside and see the glint of a knife.

Chapter 49

ERIKA

She appears out of the shadows, her hair wild, her face streaked with tears. She's holding a carving knife—one of ours. I recognize the handle. It's a knife that somebody gave us as a housewarming present when Jason and I first moved in here. Jason carves the turkey with that same knife every Thanksgiving. I've used it enough times to know the blade has dulled over the years, but it's far from harmless.

She rushes at us with the knife. I take a step back, my arms outstretched to protect Liam and Hannah. Although I have a feeling Liam is the real target here. She goes right up to him, not caring that I am between them, and shakes the knife in his face.

"Where is she?" the woman shrieks at him. "Where is my daughter?"

Liam's eyes widen. His mouth falls open and he

manages to say, "I... I don't know."

"You're a liar!" The woman, apparently Olivia's mother, Mrs. Mercer, shakes the knife at him. "I know all about you, *Liam Cass*. My daughter used to talk about you all the time. But Madison told me what you're really like."

There's only one of her and four of us, but she's the one who has the knife. On the other hand, her right hand is shaking like a leaf. I don't think she could stab him if she tried. But I'd rather she didn't try.

"Mrs. Mercer," Jason says with his best attempt at a smile. "Please put down the knife and we'll talk."

She doesn't make any attempt to lower the knife. "I'll put down the knife when *he* tells me where she is."

Jason pulled his phone out of his pocket. "If you don't put down the knife, I'm calling the police right now."

Fresh tears sprout in Mrs. Mercer's eyes. "Call them. I don't care. He's already taken the only thing that's important to me in the whole world."

I look at Liam's face. His brows are knitted together. As much as I don't want this woman threatening my son with a knife, there's part of me that's hoping this might work.

Tell us where she is, Liam! Please!

But he doesn't say a word, and Mrs. Mercer collapses into tears. She drops the knife on the ground and buries her face in her hands, sobbing. "I wish she never met you. I wish…"

I don't know what else to do, so I try to put my hand on Mrs. Mercer shoulder, but she shakes me off roughly. She lifts her tear-streaked face and looks at Liam one more time. "Please tell me where she is. If you have any ounce of humanity left inside you, please…"

Liam's eyes meet mine. And he just shakes his head.

Jason is the one who gently leads Mrs. Mercer out of our house. He calls a taxi for her and gets her safely inside. She seems to have calmed down, but she's still crying.

Liam watches the whole thing, his face devoid of any emotion. And when the taxi pulls away, he goes upstairs to his room and shuts the door behind him without another word.

Chapter 50

Transcript of police interview with Hannah Cass:

"How close are you with your brother, Hannah?"

"I'd say we're very close. He's my best friend."

"Your best friend?"

"Well, yeah. He's my big brother. He looks out for me."

"You understand the charges against him."

"Yes, I understand. But you guys are totally wrong. Liam didn't do anything."

"You're aware of his history of antisocial behavior?"

"You mean that hamster he killed? Yeah, I know about that. Mom makes such a big deal out of it. Out of everything. She's such a drama queen."

"There were other incidents."

"Nothing big."

"Did he talk to you about his former English teacher, Mr. Young?"

"I heard about it. But that was ridiculous. Liam didn't

do that. He was thirteen! How would he possibly know how to give someone carbon monoxide poisoning? I barely even know what that is."

"But you knew he disliked that teacher?"

"Yeah, but… Listen, Liam didn't do this to Olivia. He didn't kidnap her and didn't kill her. He *liked* her. He was so excited she agreed to go out with him."

"Why was he excited?"

"Um, because he's sixteen and a girl he liked agreed to go out with him? Is that a serious question?"

"Several of his classmates warned Olivia to stay away from him."

"Like who? Tyler Martinson? He is, like, the worst person alive."

"Why do you say that?"

"Because he is? He liked Olivia first, and he was mad that she wanted to go out with Liam and not him. Because Liam is handsome and charming, and Tyler is butt ugly and a jerk."

"It sounds like you don't like Tyler very much."

"Let me tell you something about Tyler. One of my friends went out with him one time, and he was a jerk and she wouldn't go out with him again. But he kept bugging her, so I told him to stay away. And then he started giving *me* a hard time."

"What did he do?"

"Mostly stupid stuff. Yelling obscenities at me… Like I care. But one time when I was coming out of school, he grabbed me and wouldn't let me go. That one kind of scared me, because he's a big guy. A football player, you know? He could have… Well, I don't want to think about it."

"So what happened?"

"Liam found out about it and he was really mad. I mean, *really* mad. He told me he was going to make sure Tyler never bothered me again."

"What did he do?

"I don't know. But after he said that, Tyler left me alone. So."

"You never asked him what he did?"

"I'm sure it was less than what Tyler deserved. Honestly, I bet Tyler is the one who killed Olivia. I wouldn't be at all surprised. Liam was there, but Tyler was the one with the motive. He would have killed someone just to get Liam in trouble. I swear to God."

"Olivia was in your brother's car. There was a witness."

"Right. Exactly. Liam goes on a date with Olivia, then he shows up at her house at night and isn't at all subtle about it. After doing all that, don't you think he'd realize if she disappeared, he'd be the first one blamed?"

"Sixteen-year-old boys are stupid."

"My brother isn't stupid. Whatever else you can say about him, he's really smart. If you really believe that stupid story about Mr. Young, he got away without a trace. Do you really think he would do something like that when it was so obvious he'd get caught?"

"Maybe Olivia wouldn't do what he wanted her to do when he came to see her."

"No way. Olivia was *totally* infatuated with him. She would have done anything for him. He didn't *need* to kidnap her. I'm telling you, Liam didn't do this. You'll see. The truth will come out."

Chapter 51

ERIKA

My phone hasn't stopped ringing all day. I wish I could turn it off entirely, but I'm too scared of missing an important call. That said, I don't answer any numbers I don't recognize. At least eighty percent of the phone calls are threatening. People likely in my own town—my neighbors—telling me my son should be locked up, that my family should be murdered.

Even the nicer calls leave me with a bad taste in my mouth. A mother I used to be friendly with, Nancy Jeffers, called me an hour ago. She told me she didn't think Liam was guilty and that I had her "full support," but I imagined after the call, she went back to her friends to report how tired and stressed out I sounded. *Erika sounds like she's falling apart. I wouldn't want to be in her shoes.*

As I'm settling into bed for the night, my phone rings again. I pick it up and see Jessica Martinson's name on the screen.

I shouldn't answer. Nothing good can come of this call.

Then again, if anyone knows the gossip, it's Jessica.

Before I can stop myself, I press the green button to take the call. "Hello?"

"Erika!" Jessica's voice is syrupy sweet. "It's Jessica. Jessica Martinson."

As if I might not know who she was. As I haven't had her number programmed into my phone for the last decade.

"Hi." I swallow hard. "What is it, Jessica?"

"I just wanted to see how you're doing."

"Fine." I'm not even remotely fine, but she's the last person I want to unburden myself to. "Thank you for asking."

"Of course."

I wait for her to say some pleasantry and end the call. *If you need anything, let me know.* But she doesn't say it. She just waits on the other line, as if she's got something to say but isn't sure how to say it.

"Is there anything I can help you with, Jessica?" I finally say.

She's quiet for a moment. "I wasn't going to say anything, but I feel like I need to. Erika, I think you did the wrong thing by bailing Liam out of jail."

I suck in a breath, my head spinning. "Jessica…"

"I know you're going to say it's none of my business," she says, "but we used to be friends and I need to say my piece. We all know Liam did this. He deserves to be in jail."

"We don't know that…"

"Come on!" she bursts out. "Don't insult my intelligence. I know Liam very well. He murdered a cat in my home, Erika. I know you took him to see that psychologist. Clearly, it didn't work."

My throat feels so dry, when I open my mouth, nothing comes out.

"Erika, you need to let the police lock him away, and then you should *walk away*. If you support that monster, then you—"

I press the red button to end the phone call. I can't listen to another word of this. Especially because I know she's right. My son is a monster, but how can I walk away?

I sink down on the bed and bury my face in my hands. I don't know what to do anymore. My instinct is to protect Liam, but I'm not sure if it's the right thing to do. I don't know what's right anymore.

The phone rings again, and I want to throw it across the room. I crack my eyes open to look at the screen. Frank Marino. He's calling me back. This is a call I need to take. But my hands are shaking so much, I have trouble hitting the green button.

"Hello? Frank?"

He chuckles darkly. "Having yourself an interesting day, aren't you, Erika?"

He knows. Of course he knows. He's a detective. "Yes. I have."

"Well, I finally understand why you were trying to scare off all those girls."

My jaw twitches. This is not a time for jokes. "Did you get that address for me on Marvin Holick?"

"Yeah. I got it. Nice guy." There's an edge of sarcasm in his voice. "Like grandfather, like grandson."

I want to slam the phone down and never call Frank Marino ever again. But more than that, I want to find my father. He could be the answer to everything. "What's the address?"

He recites it for me and I scribble it down on a piece of paper on my nightstand. He lives in Queens, probably less than an hour drive from here. Really, right around the corner. I could pop over to see him tonight, if I wanted.

Maybe I should.

I wonder what Marvin Holick will say when I show up at his door.

Chapter 52

OLIVIA

I am absolutely *exhausted*. I have spent the better part of the day hammering away at the trap door. My arms are aching, and I'm not even sure I've made any progress. At one point, I was sure the wood was splintering, but then when I felt it with my fingers, it was intact. Of course, it's hard to know for sure because I can't see a damn thing.

I also finished the last of my food and drink today. I was trying to hold out, but I was so desperately hungry and thirsty after all the work I did. Before I knew it, everything was gone.

I have no food. No drink. Nothing.

The worst part is I have devoured every morsel there is to eat, but my stomach still feels completely empty. There's a dull ache in the center of my chest. I feel like I don't have the energy to move, much less go back to hammering at the trap door.

But it's my only hope.

Well, that's not true. The police might find me. As I lie in one corner of my cell, trying to ignore the ache of emptiness in my belly, I imagine what it will be like when the police storm in here. They'll find me and bring me back to my family. And best of all, they'll punish *him*. My parents will never give up on me. They'll keep looking until they find me. I *know* it.

I don't know what time it is when I hear the footsteps. I've lost all track of time, but that slice of light is gone, which means it must be dark out. I know in my heart that it's probably him, but just in case it's not, I scream out, "*Help! Help me please! I'm down here!*"

It happens just the way it did last time. I hear the locks turning and the flashlight blinding me. It occurs to me that if I had spent my time building the mound higher instead of pounding on the lock, I might have been able to be ready to jump at him when he opened the trap door.

Damn. It's too late now.

"Olivia," he says. "How are you doing?"

"Awful," I spit at him. "I'm starving. I need food. And water."

"Yes," he says patiently. "People need water to live. Did you know that a person can survive only three to five days without water? Without water, your organs will eventually start to fail and your brain will swell up. But people can survive longer without food. Weeks. Your body will break down excess fat, and when that's gone, it will break down muscle. Your body will effectively consume itself."

I blink up at him, trying to ignore the shooting headache that resulted from the flashlight in my eyes. There's a look of fascination on his face as he recites these facts. Like I'm some sort of rat in a science experiment.

"How does it feel, Olivia?"

My hunger and thirst evolve into anger. I am not a science experiment. I am a human being. And I'm not going to play his perverted game. "Fuck you."

My anger only seems to amuse him though, just as my threats did. "Just tell me. How does it feel to be starving to death?"

"Go to hell."

He reaches into a paper bag next to him. I hear crackling of paper, and then his hand emerges from the bag. At first I think he's going to point a gun at me. But it's not a gun. It's a piece of bread.

He grins at me. "Tell me how you feel and I'll give you this bread."

I want that bread so badly. Like it's a decadent piece of chocolate cake. I stare at it, wanting to tell him to go to hell again, but wanting that bread even more. After all, the bread means survival. If I die, nobody can tell the police what he's done.

"I feel like something is clawing away at my insides," I say. "And I feel dizzy. A little nauseous."

Is that enough? Is that enough for you, you bastard?

I suppose it is, because he tosses the bread into the hole. I make a halfhearted attempt to catch it, but it falls past my fingers into the dirt. I don't care. I'm close to literally eating dirt. He also tosses in another plastic water bottle, but this one is only half of the size of the others. And there's only one.

"If you cooperate, you'll live longer," he says. He nods at the bones in the corner. Under the light of his flashlight, I can see them clearly for the first time. The outline of ribs and a pelvis. What used to be arms and legs. "*She* didn't cooperate."

I wonder what's happening on the outside. I've been gone for days—people must be starting to assume I'm dead. How long will he let me live down here? It feels like eternity, but I know it can't go on forever. If he keeps feeding me so little, I'll die in a month or two. But I have a feeling he won't drag it out that long. As he said, people can only survive three to five days without water.

And if he does somehow get arrested, but he doesn't tell the police where I am, that will be it. I'll die of dehydration in days.

"I'll try to come back in a few days," he says.

"A few days?" My panic escalates at the realization that all I have is one piece of bread and barely a pint of water. "But…"

"And don't waste your energy trying to escape," he says. "The wood is sturdy and so is the lock. You won't get out of here."

With those words, he shuts the trap door again, plunging me back into blackness. I wrap my arms around my knees and let out a sob, but the tears don't come. I'm too dehydrated to even cry.

He's killing me.

Chapter 53

ERIKA

After everything that happened yesterday, I couldn't summon up the energy to go visit my father. I spent half the night tossing and turning, but then around two in the morning when I kicked him awake, Jason sleepily suggested I take another Xanax. I have rules about how much I can take in one day, and I'm over my limit, but I didn't want to spend the entire night awake. So I took one, and it did the trick.

I don't even attempt to make breakfast for the family. When I get into the kitchen, Liam is sitting at the kitchen table with a bowl of cereal. But he's not eating. He's just sifting it around with a spoon.

"Do you want frozen waffles?" I ask him.

"No."

"You've hardly eaten anything in the last few days."

"I'm not hungry."

"You've got to eat. You'll be sick if you don't."

Liam lifts his brown eyes with those long eyelashes that make his sister jealous. "What do you care? You think I'm a murderer."

I open my mouth, but nothing comes out. What am I supposed to say to that? He's right. Ever since I found Olivia's address in our car GPS, there hasn't been one moment when I didn't think Liam was guilty.

"I still love you," is all I can say.

Liam snorts. "Why?"

"Because you're my son."

He just shakes his head. But I don't expect him to understand. That was one thing Dr. Hebert told me repeatedly. *Liam is not capable of love.* He tells me he loves me, but he's only saying it because he knows it's expected of him. And he knows it makes me happy. And it's in his best interest to make me happy.

I wonder if my father ever loved me.

I've got to see him. Somehow I feel like reconnecting with him will be the answer to everything.

I leave Liam in the kitchen, and I head upstairs to shower. Jason is coming out of the bathroom, his hair damp from the shower, a towel wrapped around his waist. After all the running he's done, he looks so fit. Still very sexy, maybe even more than he was when he was younger. Under different circumstances, I might have been tempted to initiate some morning fun. But under these circumstances, it seems inconceivable.

"Hey," I say.

He rubs his eyes. He looks tired, and I feel bad for having kept him awake half the night with my restless sleep. "Hey."

"I was wondering if you could stick around the house with Liam. I… I need to go out."

"Where?"

"I need to take care of some things at the newspaper." The lie rolls off my tongue easily. I never told Jason that Brian fired me. "It shouldn't take too long."

"Okay." Jason slips a shirt over his head. "Take your time. I'll take care of things here."

He accepts my lie so easily, I feel guilty. Jason is so trusting. He believes me, and he believes Liam. Why am I the cynical one?

I go past him into the bathroom to use the shower. Before I jump in, I stare at myself in the mirror. A week ago, I would have said that I had aged gracefully, but now I look ten years older than my age. These have been the worst few days of my life. When Liam got kicked out of kindergarten, it felt like the worst tragedy ever. What I wouldn't give to go back to that time.

I squint in the mirror at my brown eyes, which now have purple circles underneath. They are the same brown eyes that Liam has. I say that Liam looks like my father, but really, he looks like me. *I* look like my father.

Sometimes I wonder what else the three of us have in common.

What am I capable of?

Chapter 54

ERIKA

I get in my car by nine in the morning, and I'm on my way to pay a visit to Marvin Holick. Given I haven't called him, I recognize there's a reasonable chance he might not be home. But I go anyway. I need some time alone, and the drive will clear my head.

You think I'm a murderer.

I can't stop picturing Liam's face as he said those words. He looked hurt. I always believed nothing ever got to my son but maybe I'm wrong. But I have this feeling that his hurt expression is yet another act. After all, Hannah and Jason believe he is innocent, and I'm the only one who can still see through him. He needs to win me over.

While I'm driving, my phone rings. I see my mother's voice pop up on the screen and I almost let it go to voicemail. But at the last moment, I send the call to the car speakers.

"Hi, Mom," I say.

"Erika!" Mom is talking much too loud, which is what she usually does on the phone. She doesn't seem capable of controlling the volume of her voice when she's on a cell phone. "Why didn't you call me? I just found out from Jeanne during our bridge game that my grandson was arrested!"

"It's okay. He's home now."

"Okay? You know what they're saying he did, right?"

"Nope. I have no idea what crime my son has been charged with."

"Erika…"

"We're dealing with it, Mom. He's got a good lawyer."

"But… God, they're saying that he…"

"It will be okay," I say with confidence that I don't feel. But at least I can keep my mother from worrying. "It's all blown out of proportion. Our lawyer says it will be fine."

"He does?"

"Yes." If by fine, I mean the lawyer thinks he's guilty and should show the police where the body is. But I already lied to my husband today. Might as well lie to my mother too. "Anyway, I've got to go."

"Will you call me if anything else happens?"

"Yes."

Wow, another lie. I'm on a roll.

The address Frank gave me is an apartment building. It looks more like a tenement, with graffiti scribbled all over the brick walls, and a small awning covered in holes. Just looking at it makes me want to clutch my purse tighter to my chest. Then again, it's understandable my father couldn't afford a nicer place to live coming right out of jail. It's unfair to judge him. At least, not for where he lives.

According to the scribble on the paper lying on the seat next to me, my father lives on the second floor. I pull into a parking spot right in front of the building, and sit there, trying to work up the courage to go see him.

I have to do this. I have to do this today.

I take a deep breath and get out of the car. I walked unsteadily to the building, glad I wore my ballet flats for the trip, because I'd probably face-plant in heels. There's an intercom at the entrance, but I happen to arrive just as a man is leaving, and he holds the door for me to go inside. And just like that, I'm in.

I walk up the two flights to get to the second floor. When I emerge into the hallway, there's an odor of urine, the paint on the walls is peeling, and the light above is flickering. My father's apartment is 203. I walk down the hallway until I reach the doorway. The numbers 203 are etched into the paint. Before I can lose my nerve, I reach out and ring the doorbell.

Then I wait.

I wait a minute. Two minutes. By the third minute, the butterflies in my stomach are settling down. Obviously, Marvin Holick is not here right now. I'll return to meet my father another day.

But then the door is yanked open.

Chapter 55

ERIKA

"Whatever you're selling, I'm not interested."

An old man glares at me from behind a chain. I can barely see him, but I can make out his eyes. My eyes. Liam's eyes. This is him. My father.

"I'm not selling anything," I say.

He narrows his eyes at me. "Then what do you want?"

"I…" I clear my throat. "Could I come in and explain?"

"No. You tell me what you want and then I'll decide if you can come in."

This isn't how I wanted to have this conversation—through a door chain. But he's not leaving me much choice. "I… I'm your daughter. I'm Erika."

The suspicion in his eyes deepens for a moment, but then something changes. He shuts the door and I hear him fumbling with chains. When he opens the door again, the chain is gone.

He just looks like an old man now. The dark hair that was thick in the photo from my drawer is now almost gone, and what's left is white and wispy. His teeth are yellow and he has big jowls. He's wearing a checkered shirt and suspenders. He's a shadow of the handsome man he used to be.

"Erika." His voice quakes. "I can't believe you're here. Come in."

I step into his tiny apartment, which is sparsely furnished with an old ratty couch that looks like it came from the curb, an unfurnished bookcase, and a coffee table with one short leg. Also, the living room is beyond messy. There is laundry strewn all about the room and food cartons all over the coffee table. I suppress the urge to tidy it all up myself. He probably hasn't lived here long enough to be a hoarder, but he's moving in that direction.

"Sit down!" he says anxiously, gesturing at his ratty sofa that looks like it's crawling with worms or bedbugs. "Can I get you something to drink?"

"No." I'd be terrified to drink out of one of the glasses in this place. "Thank you."

My father, Marvin Holick, sits down beside me on the couch. He has a nervous smile on his lips that makes him look younger—he looks a little bit like Liam when he smiles like that. He's not what I expected at all. I was expecting a Sean Connery type who would be smoking a cigarette and explaining casually in a possibly Scottish accent about the murder he committed. But this man is far from Sean Connery. He's more like Mr. Magoo.

He blinks his watery eyes at me. "I'm so glad you're here, Erika."

I smile tightly.

"I wanted so badly to contact you after I got out of prison," he goes on. "But I knew what your mother told you about me. And I thought… well, I thought you'd be better off without me in your life. But I'm really glad you're here."

I nod.

"I want to hear everything about your life." He starts to reach for my hand, but I pull away before he can make contact. "Are you married? Do you have children?"

"I'm married," I say stiffly, "and I have two teenage children."

"I have grandchildren?" His face lights up. "Do you have photographs?"

I study his wrinkled face. Is this all an act just to get on my good side? Is he actually excited to see photos of my children? Because the truth is, Marvin Holick does not seem like a sociopath. At *all*. But he committed a murder. And the description my mother gave of him sounded just like Liam.

I slowly pull out my phone from my purse and bring up some recent photos of the children. My father gets out a pair of glasses and looks at the photos for far too long for it to be an act. When he gets to the one of Liam right after his debate, he lets out a gasp.

"My God!" he says. "The boy looks just like me!"

"Yes," I say vaguely.

That's not all he got from you.

"What's he doing there?" my father asks. "He's all dressed up."

"He's on the debate team."

"Debate team!" His face lights up. "What a smart kid. Wow. Your husband must be smart. He sure don't get that from me."

"Mom is pretty smart."

The smile fades from his lips. "You're right. She is." He hands me back my phone, a troubled expression on his face. "I'm so sorry, Erika. About… well, about everything. I really screwed up."

"Yeah," I mumble.

He lowers his eyes. "You probably want to know what happened."

I don't want to know. But I *have to* know. I need to know what made him kill a woman. And what I can do to keep his grandson from suffering the same fate as him—if it isn't too late. "Yes," is all I say.

He nods and sighs, sinking deeper into his ratty sofa. He runs a hand through what's left of his hair. It's hard to imagine it was ever as dark and thick as Liam's.

"I was young and stupid," he finally says. "It's a really bad combination. I met this girl. Nancy. Christ, I wish I could take it all back. I loved your mother, but… I was too young and too good looking for my own good. And then the girl told me she was knocked up—she threatened to go to tell your mother. I thought your mother would leave me, and I'd lose the both of you."

"So you killed her."

"No!" His watery brown eyes fly open. Those eyes used to be the same color as Liam's but now they've lost their vividness, like a shirt that's been washed too many times. "I didn't want to kill Nancy. I swear. I just… this buddy of mine gave me some pills I could slip her that would make her lose the baby. And after that, I was going to end it with her and be faithful to your mother. I never wanted to kill her. I *swear* it."

I stare at him.

"You don't believe me." He shakes his head. "I don't blame you. The police didn't believe it either. Maybe they would have if she'd really been pregnant, but she lied about that. There was never any baby." He takes a shaky breath. "And then I lost you both anyway."

I look away, unable to meet his eyes. Do I believe

him?

"It was a terrible mistake," he says. "I wish I could take it back. I would have faced up to the music—whatever it took. But Christ, I paid for it. I missed your whole life. I missed out on having a grandson who looks just like me. I missed holding my grandkids when they were babies. And Angela… She never came to visit me. She wanted to forget I existed. Raise you herself."

"She did a good job."

"Yes. She sure did." He pulls off his glasses and rubs his eyes. "I don't deserve it, Erika, but I was hoping maybe I could meet your family sometime. Do you think there's a chance of that? Someday?"

"Maybe." I know it would make him the happiest man in the world to tell him yes, but I can't do that right now. He obviously has no idea about the mess Liam is in. I can't forge a relationship with my father with that going on. And I still don't know how to feel about his confession. "I'll be in touch."

"Okay." He gives me a nervous smile. "You don't by any chance have a photograph of you and the kids that I could… have?"

I have wallet-sized versions of Hannah and Liam's school photos. I slip my father copies of both of them. He spends an extra few seconds looking at Liam's, his lips parted. He really did miss out. He would've loved being a grandfather to those kids.

And what would my life have been like if he had been in it? If he hadn't done such a stupid thing and gotten himself locked away? Everything could've been different.

I glance at my watch and realize I've been here for an hour. I've got to get back home before Jason starts wondering where I really am. The last thing I need is for him to talk to Brian. So I tell my father goodbye and hurry back to my car. He insists on walking me downstairs, and he waves at me until I drive away.

I don't know what I expected when I went to visit my father. I wasn't expecting a lonely old man, that's for sure. I have no idea if Marvin Holick really wanted to kill that woman or if he was telling the truth and it was all just a horrible accident. I want to believe he isn't a murderer. I want to believe that more than anything.

But I know one thing: if he is a sociopath, he's the best actor in the history of the world.

Chapter 56

ERIKA

I've stopped answering my phone entirely. I don't know where people got my number, but I've been getting death threats all day. They keep getting worse and worse. People are calling me up, telling me that they're going to kill me, my daughter, and especially my son. If I don't answer, they leave messages. It's awful.

To some extent though, I know how they feel. They blame me for what Liam did. I blame myself. It feels like there's something I could've done. Maybe when Dr. Hebert didn't work out, I could've found somebody else. Somebody better. Somebody who could have fixed him.

Or I could've done what Jessica Martinson suggested. I could have had him locked up and then walked away.

But that wouldn't have solved the problem. You can't lock somebody up for their thoughts. I could have sent him away to school, but when he turned eighteen, there was nothing I could've done.

At half past six, my phone rings and I flinch automatically. I'm lying on the bed, watching the clock until Jason gets home—he was supposed to be home ten minutes ago. I had been unwilling to move from my safe cocoon on the bed until I heard him come in downstairs. But then I glance at the screen and see Jason's name.

"Erika?" He sounds tired on the other line. "Hey. Listen…"

"Please don't tell me you're running late…"

"I'm really sorry." He lets out a long sigh. "I've been putting out fires all day—everybody knows about Liam. I've had two investors back out today."

My stomach sinks. I didn't think this could get any worse, but here it is. We can't afford to lose Jason's income. We've got a huge mortgage and now Liam's legal bills.

I grip the phone tighter. "How long till you can come home?"

"I've got a dinner meeting now, then I need to sit down with my staff to discuss the situation. I'm not going to be able to head home for at least two hours."

"Two *hours*?" I'm going to burst into tears. I was barely holding it together, knowing Jason would be home soon. Two hours till he gets on the road means at least three till he's home. And that's if traffic has died down by then.

"I'm really sorry, Erika," he says again.

I don't want to be alone right now. I'm scared somebody else will throw a rock through our window. Or set the whole place on fire. Now that the sun has gone down, I feel especially uneasy.

"If you want," he finally says, "I'll cancel the meetings. If you really need me…"

I'm tempted to say yes. I do need him. But we also can't afford to lose his income. I've got to suck it up. After all, it's just three hours. What could happen in three hours? "It's fine. I'll be fine."

"If you're sure…"

"I'm sure."

He lets out a breath. "Okay, thanks, Erika. I'll be home as soon as I can."

I swallow hard. "I love you."

"Love you too."

Three hours. He'll be home in three hours. It's not that long.

I try to take my mind off of it by watching television. Anything but the news. I stream a movie on Netflix just so there's no chance of hearing any news reports. The only news report I want to hear is that Olivia Mercer was found and somehow my son had nothing to do with it. Fat chance.

It's around eight-thirty when I hear the knock on my bedroom door.

"Come in!" I call out.

The door swings open and Liam is standing there in the entrance. He's wearing the same T-shirt and jeans he had on yesterday— I wonder if he slept in them. He looks up at me, and his eyes are red-rimmed. It's something I've never seen before.

"Liam?"

"Mom," he says, and his voice breaks.

And then he's sobbing. My sixteen-year-old son— almost a man—is crying his heart out. His shoulders are shaking, and he buries his bruised face in his hands. I leap off the bed and throw my arms around him, and he clings to me. I've never seen him like this. Even as a child.

"Liam," I say. "Honey, what's wrong?"

It's a stupid question. What *isn't* wrong? But specifically, there's obviously something bothering him. Maybe he's frightened by the prospect of spending the rest of his life in prison. I couldn't blame him for that one.

"There's something…" He gulps, trying to catch his breath. "There's something I have to tell you."

I suck in a breath. "About Olivia?"

He nods and wipes his eyes.

"Do you… do you know where she is?"

He nods again.

It's true. Everything that I feared is true. "Is she alive?"

He's quiet for a moment. "I… I don't know."

You better hope she's alive. It's the difference between life in prison and a chance at maybe getting out someday. But I don't say all that. He's already crying. No need to make him feel worse.

"We should call the police," I say. "Right now. We'll tell them where she is."

He shakes his head vigorously. "No. It's… it's not a good idea."

"Liam…"

"I'll show you how to get there," he says. "We'll go together."

"We need to call the police."

"Please, Mom." His voice breaks again. "We'll call the police when we get there, okay? We need to go. *Now.*"

The urgency in his voice surprises me. After all, wherever Olivia is, she's been there for days. What is so important about going right now? But he's looking at me with his swollen eyes, and it's hard to say no. As soon as we get there though, I'm dialing 911.

"Okay," I say. "Let's go."

Liam doesn't say much during the car ride. He keeps his eyes pinned on the road ahead of us, only speaking to give me directions. When I ask him for an address, he says he doesn't have one. But he knows how to get there.

I focus on the road. Wherever he's taking me, I have to pray that Olivia is still alive. If she's alive, then we can make this right. He has a chance.

If she's dead, then he'll spend the rest of his life in prison.

When we come to a stop at a red light, I reach for my phone. "Let me just text your father to tell him where we're going."

"No," he says sharply. "Don't do that."

He says it so harshly, it gives me an uneasy feeling. It occurs to me that Liam is leading me into the woods all alone and won't tell me where we're going or let me tell anyone else. My son may have done some bad things in his life, but he's never laid a finger on me. Ever.

But now, for the first time in my life, I'm scared for my own safety. What if he isn't leading me to Olivia? What if he's bringing me out into the woods to kill me?

No. He wouldn't. Not my son. My baby. My favorite.

"Turn right here," Liam says.

I squint at where he's pointing. I see only trees, with a narrow clearing between them. "That's not even a road."

"Turn right," he says stubbornly.

I'm about to protest when I see a wheel spinning against a tree. I squint into the black woods. "Is that Hannah's bicycle?"

I look at Liam. He's staring at the bicycle too, an unreadable expression on his face. "Let's go."

"Maybe we should call the police," I say for the millionth time.

"Mom…"

But I take out my phone. I'm done with these games. I'm not driving my car down this tiny road to God knows where. And the fact that Hannah is here too is incredibly unsettling. This is time for the police to take over. I know when I'm out of my depth. And frankly, Liam is beginning to scare me. He keeps staring straight ahead, squinting into the woods.

I'm calling the police. I'm telling them everything. As soon as I…

Oh God. No signal.

"Let's go, Mom." Liam puts one hand on the steering wheel, and I can only barely make out his face in the shadows. "If you won't drive, I will."

Chapter 57

OLIVIA

The piece of bread and bottle of water are long gone.

The lack of water is much harder than the lack of food. My mouth feels so dry, I can barely get it open. It feels like my lips are sealed together with glue. And whenever I try to stand up, I feel dizzy. My head is spinning. When I doze off, I dream about water. I dream about finding a puddle and lapping it up like a dog. I'm not picky. I would drink out of the toilet bowl if I could.

Speaking of toilet bowls, I can't remember the last time I peed. I don't think I'm making pee anymore.

He's killing me. He's going to let me die a terrible death of dehydration. He's not even going to let it get to the point where I starve to death, although that would be awful too.

The only positive thing I can say is that my left ankle doesn't throb the way it used to. I hardly even notice it, except when I run my fingers along my calf, the skin is tight and swollen. I can't wiggle my toes anymore or move my ankle. I'm sure if I tried to put weight on it, it would hurt, but I don't have the strength to stand.

It's nighttime now. That tiny slice of light is gone. I have gotten used to the pitch blackness of this hole. Whether I open or close my eyes, it's the same. This must be what it's like to be blind. It just shows that you can get used to anything. It seems normal now to feel my way around.

The footsteps over my head startle me out of my daze. Is he back? Already? It hasn't been long enough yet, has it?

Maybe he brought food or water for me. I'm willing to do anything he wants if he'll give it to me. *Anything.* I have no pride left. I just want a drink.

"Hello?"

My head jerks up. That's not his voice. That's a female voice. A young female voice.

Is it someone here to find me?

I muster up all my strength, take a deep breath and try to yell out for help. But when I open my mouth, no words come out. My throat is too dry. I clear my throat best I can. "Help! Help me! I'm down here!"

There is a long pause and scuffling of feet. "Hello? Are you in there?"

"Yes!" My chest fills with relief. "I'm down here! My

name is Olivia Mercer! People are looking for me!"

"Hang on," the female voice says. "There's a key on the wall."

I try to get to my feet, but it's very hard. My left leg can't bear any weight, and my right leg feels like Jell-O. I've got to stand up though. I don't know how else I'll get out of here.

I hear the sound of a key turning in a lock. Metal clangs against metal, and something drops to the floor. Before I know it, that flashlight turns on me, so bright that it feels like a knife is jabbing me in my eyes. I squeeze them shut, but it's still too bright.

"Turn the light away!" I gasp.

"I'm sorry," the girl says.

And now that the light isn't blinding me, I can see that she really is a girl—even younger than me. I take in her reddish brown hair and round face. She looks familiar. In my confused state, it takes me a minute to place who she is.

Hannah Cass.

"Hannah," I gasp. "Your—"

"I know." Her voice is sad. "I followed him here last night. I didn't... I really didn't want to believe it."

She looks like she's going to cry, and I can't blame her. As horrible as this has been for me, it will be really bad for her too. Her life will never be the same after this.

"I think he's going to find a way to come tonight," she says. "We've got to get out of here."

"Did you call the police?"

Hannah shakes her head. "I didn't want to call until I was sure that… Anyway, there's no reception out here. We'll have to make a run for it. I've got my bike."

Run for it? That isn't going to be possible, given the state of my ankle. But first things first. I need to get out of this goddamn hole.

"I don't suppose you can climb out," Hannah says.

"My ankle is injured," I admit. "That's going to make it difficult."

She scrunches her eyebrows together. "If I give you my hand, do you think you could…?"

I try to stand up again. My right leg is really rubbery. I make it almost to standing, then I accidentally put a tiny bit of weight on my left ankle. The pain is like white hot coals. I scream and collapse on the floor.

"Olivia?"

"I can't stand up," I gasp. "I can't do it. You'll have to… go get help…"

The thought of sending Hannah away is nothing short of horrifying. It was an eternity waiting for somebody to come here, and I don't want her to leave. But there's no way I can climb out of this hole, even with her help. We need somebody bigger and stronger, and possibly a ladder.

I look up at Hannah, who is frowning. "What's wrong?" I ask her.

"I think I hear something."

We're both quiet. I hear my heart pounding in my ears, but nothing else. At first. But then I hear it.

Rustling of leaves. Followed by footsteps. The sound of hinges creaking.

"He's here," Hannah whispers.

Oh my God. He's here. And he'll kill us both. Well, maybe not Hannah. Maybe he'll let her live—she's family. But I'm gone. At this point, I've clearly become a liability. It's probably not worth it to him to watch me starve to death.

"Hello, Hannah." His voice fills the room above me. I cringe at the familiar sound of it. "I thought I might find you here."

She's silent for a moment. When she speaks again, her voice is shaking. "Hi, Daddy."

Chapter 58

JASON

Is it finally my turn? Has Erika finished talking? Or will it go on for another hour or two?

That's Erika. Never shuts up. Always worried about every little thing. Obsessed. Especially about Liam. Anytime he opens his mouth, she has to analyze it to death. Half the time, I'm just staring at her, waiting for her to stop talking. Hannah is the same way. The two of them might not look alike, but they are two peas in a pod. Like mother, like daughter.

Liam, on the other hand. Well, you can guess who *he* takes after.

You're probably wondering why I married Erika, considering she's certainly far from my favorite person. There is no simple answer for that, but I suppose that some part of me wanted a normal life. When I first met Erika, she was beautiful. That long black hair and dark eyes. She was wearing a fitted white blouse and a skirt that left just enough to the imagination. I wanted her. And not just for that one night and then dispose of the body. I wanted her a second night, which turned into a third, and then a year.

And for the first time, I could imagine a normal life for myself. Well, as normal as I was capable of. A wife—a family. It didn't seem like a bad idea, and before I really thought it through, Erika and I were getting married. In retrospect, it was a mistake. But by the time I realized that, it was too late. We already had a baby on the way.

The easiest thing to do was stash the family away on Long Island. I work long hours. No, not really. I don't work much at all. I come up with ideas that are great ideas and make me money without having to do much. The truth is I have a lot of free time on my hands, which I do manage to fill with various activities.

And the best part is Erika never suspected a thing. Not even a little bit. It just goes to show how brilliant I am at acting the part. Liam, on the other hand, leaves a lot to be desired. I suppose I can't blame him. I was equally careless when I was his age. My parents were not as understanding as Erika and I have been either. My mother was a deeply religious Catholic, and she believed I was punishment for one of her past sins.

My mother was terrified of me. It probably had something to do with me murdering her cat when I was five. She loved that cat, for reasons I could never understand. It was a cat, after all. It didn't have real emotions, although it did struggle quite a bit when I held that pillow over its head until it stopped moving. That was part of the fun.

Erika took Liam to a shrink, but my parents had different ways of dealing with me. After I killed that cat, my mother locked me in the closet under the staircase. She left me there for six hours and ignored me when I banged my fists on the doors and screamed until my voice was hoarse. It didn't "cure" me. After the next incident, my father beat me with his belt until I cried. Back in those days, nobody at school cared about the welts all over my back. Beating your kids used to be more acceptable. He did it frequently.

And then when I was fourteen, there was that girl. Michelle. My first. I don't remember all of their names, but you always remember your first.

I didn't get caught by the police. I was too smart for that. But my parents knew. They had no information that could have stood up in a court of law, but it was enough for them. Unfortunately for them, I was too big to be locked in the closet anymore—as tall as my father by then. And stronger.

That was when my mother hired the exorcist.

He was a priest—or at least, he had the collar. A

middle-aged man with a round, red face. They surprised me when I came home from school one day, and my father, the priest, and his assistant worked together to hold me down and tie me to my bed while they drew the shades. For hours, they shouted prayers in my face and threw holy water at me. The priest demanded I repeat the prayers, and for the first hour, I refused.

By the second hour, I was willing to say whatever he wanted to let me go free.

When they finally untied me from that bed, I was the angriest I had ever been in my entire life. There were bruises on my wrists where I had been bound to the bed, and I was soaked in a combination of holy water and my own sweat. I wanted to lunge at that priest and scratch his eyes out, but I was outnumbered. I had to wait.

That night, I removed the batteries from the smoke detectors in the house. I turned on the gas stove. That night, my parents unfortunately died in a tragic fire that their only son managed to survive. I told Erika my mother died of cancer and my father had a heart attack, but there was really no way for her to know that was a lie.

And that priest—well, he was mugged a few days later in a dark alley. Poor guy—the police report indicated he suffered quite a bit in the hour before his throat was finally slashed.

After I buried my parents, I went to live with my

grandmother. Nana was eighty years old, demented and half blind. She couldn't care less what I did with myself. We got along very well.

Everybody says Liam is a smart kid, but he's not as smart as me. I made two million dollars selling my first startup company when I was only twenty-five. No college diploma. Just brains. I made a lot more on the second one. So I've got plenty of money. Money that Erika has no idea about. She worries about the income from her stupid little newspaper job, and it's hard not to laugh.

Yes, I could do without the family. But it's not so bad. I take a lot of business trips, when I get to have some fun, then I go back home before the police arrive. I'm much more careful when I'm near home. That girl sharing the hole with Olivia was named Hallie Barton—that's what her driver's license said. She ran away from home because her mother was a drunk and her stepfather beat her up, and she was hitchhiking when I picked her up. Don't these young girls know how dangerous it is to hitchhike? I mean, look what happened to Hallie.

In any case, nobody is looking for Hallie.

I could have been happy this way my whole life. I could've continued doing my own activities on the side, and nobody would have been the wiser. But then there was Liam.

He did stupid things to attract attention. What was he

thinking, duct-taping that girl in the closet? I know he was only five, but it made me sick when I heard about it. They threw him out of the school. And Erika later ended up taking him to a shrink. As many times as I told her that it wasn't a big deal, she knew it was.

Liam was a reflection on me. And I knew it was just a matter of time before people figured it out. Before Erika realized Liam didn't get his personality from her loser, jailbird father.

Years ago, I saw Liam skulking around the house of that English teacher of his. I had gone to parent-teacher night that year, and I could tell the guy hated Liam. Saw right through him the way my parents saw through me. And now Liam was going to do something stupid and obvious, and probably get himself in just enough trouble that Erika would want to take him back to a shrink.

So I gave Liam a hand. Broke the radiator to cause the leak in a carbon monoxide. I shorted out the detector. Liam never would have been clever enough to do it himself. They were supposed to be dead by morning. A neighbor would have noticed Liam sneaking around the house, and he would've taken the fall. But the teacher didn't even die, and the police were too incompetent to arrest my son. So that was a bust.

And now this opportunity came up.

Sometimes I do listen to Hannah when she babbles

on. She mentioned this girl that Liam liked, Olivia Mercer. I wonder if he really likes women or if he's like me. I am attracted to women, but only in the most superficial way—as a sexual release, nothing more. I wonder if Liam is the same. I would have said he was, but on the night he came back from seeing Olivia, he was grinning to himself like any love-struck teenager. He's like me in many ways, but he's also different. The way he's close with Hannah, for example. The way he's protective of her. I was never close with anyone that way. Even Erika.

Although there was a time when I liked Erika quite a bit. Maybe even loved her. I don't know.

On the night Liam snuck out to see Olivia, I knew this was my chance. Especially when I saw him pull back into the driveway in Erika's Toyota. I sent him to bed, then went out myself, following the directions in the GPS. I had been wondering how I would get Olivia to come back downstairs, but it turned out she was already on her porch. Looking up at the stars. Probably fantasizing about my son.

She recognized me when I waved to her and came over to the car. She flashed me a big smile. I should have lost that extra weight years ago, because it makes a big difference with women. Women trust you more if you're good looking. Of course, Liam takes after his mother and is more attractive than I could ever be. And that makes him more dangerous.

But to be fair, I'm extremely dangerous.

"Liam told us he was heading home," I explained to Olivia. I pasted that worried expression on my face that I've noticed parents get when their children don't come home when they're supposed to. "But he isn't back yet. I'm worried."

She frowned, like she was worried too. "Oh my God, I hope he's okay."

"Do you think you could get in the car and help me look for a few minutes? It's hard to keep an eye out when I'm driving."

"Of course!"

Olivia got into the car without a second thought. I had the chloroform ready. She was out like a light. And before any nosy neighbors could realize it was me driving this time and not my son, I took off.

Liam's relationship with Olivia. The neighbor who saw him with her at two in the morning. The hair and blood I planted in the trunk. And then after Olivia died, I was going to make her body re-surface, because it's harder to get a conviction when there's no body. I had been trying to think of what else I could plant on her that would be the final nail in my son's coffin.

And now here is Hannah, messing everything up.

Well, that's what she's *trying* to do. And yes, she's

messing up the original plan. The original plan was to have a little fun with Olivia and get Liam locked away for good. I didn't have any other ambitions besides that. But now that Hannah is here, I realize this plan could be even better than I originally thought.

Here's what the police will discover:

Liam kidnapped Olivia, and when Hannah discovered her brother's plan, Liam sadly had to kill both of them. And then Erika was so distressed, she took an overdose off the Xanax she keeps in her nightstand. Except they're not Xanax, but something much stronger than Xanax that I swapped for the Xanax several months ago.

Or maybe Liam kills Erika as well. I haven't decided that part yet.

And I, of course, will play the part of the grieving widower. Who no longer has to deal with a nagging wife, a whiny daughter, and a sociopath son. It will be even easier than when I was fourteen and played the grieving son.

It's an excellent plan. I can't wait to see how it all plays out.

That's the fun part.

Chapter 59

OLIVIA

I still can't wrap my head around it entirely. Mr. Cass. Liam's dad. I had seen him once before when he was picking Liam up early from school, and he seemed really nice. And for a dad... well, he's pretty hot. *Really* hot. He looks so athletic and muscular and has a nice smile, whereas my dad is balding and has a potbelly.

So when he told me to get into the car, of course I did it. I was worried about Liam. And there was no reason to suspect Mr. Cass wanted to harm me. He was Liam's dad, after all.

If people are wondering what happened to me, they must be blaming Liam. He's the one I had a date with that night. I bet anything my nosy neighbor Mrs. Levy saw us kissing that night. If I never reappear, he's the one who will get blamed. If anyone goes to jail for this, it will be Liam.

"Dad," Hannah says in a choked voice. "Please don't

do this."

Do what? Does he have a gun? A knife? I wish I could see what's going on out there.

"Hannah." He speaks in that bland, calm voice that he used when he was asking me what it was like to starve to death. "Do you know what you're doing? You're ripping apart our family."

"I swear to God, don't come any closer."

"Hannah. Come on. I'm your father. She's nobody."

"Dad..." Hannah is sobbing now. "Please..."

"I'm going to make this so simple for you, Hannah. She's not getting out of here alive. There's no chance. The only one who has a chance is you."

My heart is beating so quickly, my chest is starting to hurt. "Hannah," I say. "Don't listen to him. He's evil."

"Would you like to finish her off, Hannah? I'll pull her up and let you do it."

"Please, Daddy, don't..."

He laughs. It's a sound I've come to despise over the last several days. "I'm just kidding. I know you can't do it. You're not like me. You're so much like your mother, it's disgusting."

I can barely make out Hannah's face in the shadows. Her cheeks are streaked with tears.

"I'm afraid this all has to end tonight," Mr. Cass says. "For both of you."

And Hannah screams.

Chapter 60

ERIKA

"Mom." Liam shakes my arm, growing urgency in his voice. "Please. Just drive."

I have no reception out here. Every bone in my body is screaming that I should call the police. But then what? My son is here. My daughter is apparently here. Something terrible is going on, and I can't imagine sitting here in this car and twiddling my thumbs until the cop show up.

Liam is not going to kill me. Sometimes I'm not sure what he's thinking, but I know that much. He would never hurt me. And the only thing I can hear in his voice right now is fear. He's scared of something.

But what?

And why on earth is Hannah's bicycle out here? I can't figure it out.

So I push on, into the woods, following his directions. I drive another five minutes on this dirt path, and finally a cabin comes into view. The cabin is dilapidated—the wood is splintered and dirty, falling apart in places. The front door is hanging by only one of its hinges. It looks like it's been abandoned for years. Except for two things:

The dim light coming from inside.

And the Prius parked right outside.

I don't know why Hannah's bicycle is out here. But I can't even *begin* to imagine why my husband's car is parked here when he's supposed to be at work.

"Liam," I say slowly. "What is going on? No more games. Tell me right now."

He takes a deep breath. "Dad went out last night and Hannah followed him. She said he came here— she showed me directions she wrote down. She told me she was going back tonight and I wanted to come, but she was worried I'd get in trouble if... well, if she found something really bad. But I was sitting in my room and thinking about Hannah and... I thought Dad might..."

I stare at him. "Might what?"

He frowns at me. "You know Dad is crazy, right?"

I get a horrible sinking feeling in my chest, like my whole world is collapsing on itself. "What are you talking about? Your father is the most normal man I've ever met."

He snorts. "You don't see it, I guess. I do. I always have. That's why it scares him so much when I... well, you know. He sees himself in me. But I'm not like him. Not as much as he thinks, anyway."

"This is crazy," I whisper. "Why are you telling me this?"

"I thought you knew." Liam blinks at me. "All those years. You didn't even... I mean, I don't know what he's doing all day, but he's *not* at work. I called his company once when I needed to reach him, and they told me he's never there. You never suspected...?"

No, I never suspected anything. *Ever.*

But there were all those late nights. All those "business trips" he always had to take. I always accepted it blindly. There was that time I worried he was having an affair, but maybe it was something much worse than that.

What if I was smelling the perfume of a dead woman?

No, that's not possible. This is crazy. Why am I thinking this way? Jason is my husband of twenty years. He's not a murderer. I don't know what his car is doing out here, but there's got to be a reasonable explanation.

"I think Olivia is in there," Liam says. "Mom, I'm really scared he might kill them both."

"He wouldn't do that," I say. Although it's pretty clear I'm no expert on what Jason would or would not do.

Liam hesitates for only a split second before he darts out of my car. I call to him, not wanting him to go inside and face whatever is in there. What if it really is Jason? Could he have done something like this? He couldn't have.

Never. I don't care what Liam says. I know my husband. A guy who can make that many puns about eggs is *not* going around murdering people. He just isn't.

I pick my way through the dirt on the ground, littered with leaves and branches, until I've reached the cabin ten paces after Liam. He's taller than me so his strides are longer, and he's more surefooted on the uneven ground. We get there just in time to see Jason stumble through the broken door.

Liam stops short, staring at his father. "Where is Hannah? Where is Olivia?"

Jason's face darkens in a way I've never seen before. At that moment, it seems entirely possible that everything Liam just told me is true. That Jason is somebody I don't know at all. Someone who could've done horrible things.

But then he catches sight of me and the dark look fades from his face like it was never there. "Erika! Thank God you're here. You've got to call the police right now!"

"Where are they?" Liam shouts at him.

Jason gazes at him with venom in his eyes. "They're both in there—dead. You should know since you're the one who killed them. You monster."

I feel like somebody punched me in the gut. "Dead?"

"I'm so sorry, Erika." Jason's eyes fill with tears as he rushes to my side. His hand is on my back. "I tried to save Hannah…"

"You liar!" Liam's face is purple. "You hate Hannah! You hate all of us!"

My legs feel like they're going to collapse under me. No, not Hannah. She can't be... No...

Jason's arms encircle me, barely catching me before I collapse. "We're going to call the police," he says in a soft, soothing voice. "They're going to punish Liam for what he did to our baby." He glares at Liam. "Don't even try to run. They're going to catch you."

Liam stares at us, his face still scarlet. But then something changes in his eyes. They grow wide, like he's seen something terrible. "Mom," he gasps.

And then instead of running, he lunges at Jason. I see the glint of a knife in Jason's hand. He hadn't been holding it when he came out of the cabin. He took it out as he was comforting me.

Oh my God. Was he going to stab me?

Jason is still heavier than Liam, but Liam is younger and quicker. The knife clatters out of Jason's hands, and Liam grapples him to the ground. For a moment, it looks like Jason might manage to get free, but then Liam takes a swing at him, and I hear a sick crunch. When I look at Jason's face, there's blood pouring out of his nose.

"You little asshole!" Jason howls. "I'm going to kill you."

"Mom, the knife," Liam manages.

The knife is lying in the grass. The knife doesn't look familiar to me—it's not one of the dull blades from our kitchen. I snatch it off the ground so Jason can't get it. My fingers close around the handle, but I'm not sure what to do with the sharp end. I point it in Jason's direction, but who am I kidding? I'd never be able to stab him.

He knows it too.

"Mom." Liam's voice is breathless. "Give me the knife."

Jason's eyes widen as he struggles against our son, who has him pinned down tightly. I'm impressed with how easily Liam is restraining him. Liam has become stronger than his father. "Erika, don't give it to him," Jason manages.

I stare at my husband. "Why shouldn't I?"

Jason shakes his head, his face pale. "You know what Liam is like. You've always known. He's *crazy*, Erika."

Well, that's not untrue.

Jason sees my hesitation, and he pushes on. "Erika," he says urgently. "You do *not* want him to have that knife. You know that. He'll kill us both."

Will he?

Liam looks at me with his brown eyes that are so much like what I see when I stare into the mirror. I'm not sure what to believe anymore, but between Jason and Liam, I know which one I want to have the knife.

I turn the blade around and offer Liam the handle.

My son smiles at me with those perfect, straight teeth—a smile I know is one-hundred percent genuine. "Thanks, Mom." His fingers close around the handle. "And you were half right, Dad."

I watch as Liam plunges the knife into his father's chest.

Chapter 61

ERIKA

Liam knew exactly where to put the knife. With that one stab wound, all the blood drains out of my husband's face, and seconds later, he's coughing it out. He's dying. He's dying quickly. So quickly that even if we called for an ambulance now, if that were possible, it would be too late.

"Erika," Jason manages, choking on his own blood. "You…"

I stare down at him, waiting for his final words to me. Is he going to tell me he loves me one last time? I don't think I could handle it if he did. I already feel like I can barely stand up.

"You *bitch*," he finishes. "After all I did for you…"

I flinch as if he hit me. Liam was right. Jason is not the man I thought he was. He's sick. He's crazy. And he's done something horrible. He was planning to kill me, and the only reason I'm alive right now is because my son saved me.

Jason deserves this death.

I take a step forward, standing over him. I draw back my foot, and with all my strength, I kick him right in the ribs. It's the last thing he feels before he loses consciousness.

I bury my face in my hands, wanting to cry but too stunned. Jason. Hannah. Gone. Is this really happening? I think I'm going to be sick.

"Mom." That urgency is back in Liam's voice, bursting into my haze. "Let's go into the cabin. Maybe we can still save them."

He tugs at my arm and I follow him without thinking. My legs move automatically, but my head won't stop spinning. I'm terrified to see what's inside there. If my daughter is lying dead on the ground in that cabin, I'm not sure I could go on after seeing that. It would destroy me.

We get inside the cabin, which is dark except for a flashlight lying on the ground. The flashlight provides just enough illumination to know there's no one in here. But I hear voices. Muffled female voices.

"Hannah!" Liam yells. He drops to his knees and plants his palms on the ground. "Where are you?"

This time I hear the words more distinctly in my daughter's voice: "Down here!"

There is apparently a trap door. There's a ring of keys

lying on the ground and Liam tries each one until the lock pops open. His hands are so steady—I'm amazed. How could he be so calm after what just happened? I don't think I could hold a key, much less fit one into the lock. He swings the trap door open and shines the flashlight inside.

There they are. Hannah, her face tear-streaked, but completely alive. And Olivia. Also alive.

The relief I feel almost knocks me off my feet. Hannah is okay. My daughter is alive.

Thank God.

Chapter 62

OLIVIA

"Hannah! Where are you?"

Hannah's disembodied voice floats through the air: "Down here!"

I reach into the darkness until my hand makes contact with Hannah's arm. "Shush! What are you *doing*?"

"It's okay. That's Liam. He'll help us out."

"Are you sure about that?"

"Of course I'm sure. He's my brother."

I don't point out the fact that her father is the one who trapped me here for four days with plans to let me starve to death. So somebody being in her family doesn't exactly make me feel good. But at this point, there's nothing more I can do.

The trap door swings open, and there he is. Liam Cass. The boy I'd been crushing on for nearly three months, who I used to think was the cutest guy in the whole dang school. He's holding a flashlight, but not pointing it at our eyes like his father did. I can just barely make out his face, and he scrunches his eyebrows together. "Can you get out?" he asks.

Hannah shakes her head. "No," she says. "I hurt my wrist when Dad pushed me down here. And Olivia's ankle is really bad."

Liam listens to this, nodding thoughtfully. "I can come down there. I'll help you get out."

Before I can suggest this might not be a great idea, Liam has climbed down into the hole. He's very nimble, and he gets in easily without hurting himself. Now that I can see him up close, I realize there's blood all over him. It's everywhere. It's staining his T-shirt and splattered all over his face. Hannah clasps her hand over her mouth.

"Liam!" she exclaims. "Are you... I mean, did he...?"

"I'm fine." Liam shakes his head and makes a face. "It's *his* blood."

Hannah's mouth falls open. "Is he... dead?"

Liam nods slowly. He doesn't give any other details and I'm glad.

"I told you not to come," she whispers, her eyes filling up with tears again. "You're going to get in trouble now."

"You've got to be kidding me, Hannah. He would've killed you. How could I let that happen?"

Then she throws her arms around him, and she hugs

him so tightly that when she pulls away, her father's blood is all over her shirt too. She wipes her eyes as he crouches down next to me on the floor, where I'm clutching my ankle. In the light of the flashlight, his eyes look black. "What's hurting?" he asks.

I show him my ankle. He shines a flashlight on it, and we both gasp simultaneously. It looks *terrible*. It's swollen to twice the size it should be, the skin is shiny and red, and yellow pus is coming out of a break in the skin. I had no idea it was that bad.

"Don't worry," Liam says. "We're going to get you out of here. I promise."

One corner of his lips moves up in a crooked smile, and I remember how much I used to like him. How he used to make my heart speed up in my chest when I watched him race around the track after school. It seems like an eternity ago.

Liam is tall enough to see over the trap door when he stands on the mound of dirt I made. He calls to someone else to come help him. For a moment, I'm paralyzed with fear that his father is there, but then I hear his mother's shaky voice.

"I'm going to lift them out through the trap door," he tells his mother. "You have to help them out."

Liam is very gentle with me. He takes his time putting his left arm under my knees so he won't hurt me when he lifts me up. I cling to his neck as he steps up on the mound and carefully raises me up to his mother. She is shaking like a leaf as she helps me get onto the wood floor of the cabin. My ankle gets twisted in the process, because she's not as careful as Liam was, and it hurts so bad, my eyes water.

After Liam lifts Hannah out of the hole, Mrs. Cass won't stop hugging her. She throws her arms around Hannah's shoulders, sobbing that she thought she was dead. Hannah clings to her just as hard. Watching them makes me want my mother so much, it's painful. At least now I know I'm going to see her soon. It wasn't like when I was trapped in the hole. This is almost over.

"He told us he was going to come back and kill us as soon as he was done with the two of you," Hannah sobs. "He meant it. You could see it in his eyes."

I still can't manage to stand up. My ankle hurts more than I would have thought possible. It's not just broken—there's something really wrong with it. Liam looks at me, writhing on the ground, and bends down beside me. "I'm going to pick you up, okay?"

I flinch, not wanting anyone to get within two feet of my ankle. "It hurts a lot."

"I'll be really careful. I promise."

What choice do I have? "Okay."

He does what he did before, gently scooping me up in

his arms. He doesn't even grunt when he lifts me. I had no idea he was that strong. In spite of everything that's happened, a sense of calm comes over me as he holds me, and I rest my head against his chest. I feel safe here.

Liam carries me out of the cabin with his mother and Hannah leading the way. After about ten paces, he stops short and looks at something on the ground.

It takes me a moment to realize he's looking down at his father.

Mr. Cass is lying face up on the dirt. His shirt is soaked with blood, far more than what's on Liam's shirt. There's blood on his chin too, his eyes are staring up at the sky, and his mouth is hanging open.

He's dead. He's definitely dead.

It's over.

Chapter 63

Transcript of police interview with Erika Cass:

"Mrs. Cass, can you repeat for me one more time exactly what happened when you reached the cabin?"

"After we parked, I saw Jason coming out of the cabin. He had a knife and he told me that Hannah and Olivia were both dead. He admitted he was the one who killed them, although I didn't realize at the time he was lying."

"Did you believe him?"

"I didn't know what to believe, Detective. Jason and I were married for twenty years. I never imagined he could do something like that. But you didn't see the look in his eyes…"

"And then what happened?"

"He lunged at me with the knife. Thank God Liam was there with me—otherwise I'd be dead. Liam ran at him and tackled him, and he dropped the knife. That's when I picked it up and…"

"Mrs. Cass?"

"I'm sorry. This is so hard…"

"Please take your time."

"He got away from Liam. He's bigger than Liam. And then he came at me again and…"

"And…?"

"I still had the knife. So I did the only thing I could do: I stabbed him with it when he came at me."

"So you were the one who stabbed him?"

"That's right."

"It wasn't Liam?"

"No."

"So here's the thing, Mrs. Cass. The blood splatter pattern on Liam's clothes makes it look like he was the one in front of Jason when he was stabbed. You have almost no blood on your clothes at all."

"I don't know what to tell you. Liam was right next to me. And he bent over Jason after I stabbed him, which I guess is how all that blood ended up on him. He tried to resuscitate him, but it didn't work. Obviously."

"I see."

"Am I… am I under arrest?"

"Given the circumstances and Olivia's corroboration of your story, we are not planning to pursue charges at this time."

" … "

"But our investigation is not complete. There will be an autopsy."

"Yes. Yes, of course."

"I have one other question, Mrs. Cass."

"Yes?"

"Why are you protecting Liam?"

"I have no idea what you're talking about. Detective, my husband just tried to kill me."

"But Liam is the one who stabbed him, wasn't he?"

"Detective, my husband of twenty years is dead. This is been a really hard day. I don't… I can't even think straight. I told you what happened. I have nothing else to say."

Chapter 64

ERIKA

Detective Rivera doesn't believe my story.

She thinks Liam is the one who stabbed Jason. To be fair, he *is* covered in blood. But I couldn't take a risk of him going to jail for this. If anyone should take the fall for it, it should be me. I'm the idiot who married the guy. I am the fool who believed his lies for twenty years of marriage.

Detective Rivera met us at the emergency room and was plainly surprised to find that Olivia was not only alive, but clinging to Liam as he carries her into the emergency room. He mostly kept his mouth shut as I told the detective my story about how I stabbed Jason in self-defense. He and I are the only ones who know the truth.

With Hannah's help, I gave her directions to the cabin where they found my husband's body.

"I can't believe it," Rivera kept saying. "I really thought…"

I couldn't blame her. I thought the same thing.

While Hannah is off getting her wrist X-rayed, I'm left with Liam in Hannah's room in the ER. It's the first moment we've had alone since we rescued Hannah and Olivia. Well, I should say *he* rescued them. I helped. A little.

There's so much I feel like I need to say to him. I thought the worst of him, and he knew it. That's not the way a mother should behave. I'm ashamed of myself. I'm ashamed of the fact that I had no idea what Jason was up to.

My own husband. I can't believe it.

"You didn't have to tell the detective you killed him," Liam says quietly. "We could have told her the truth."

"It's better this way."

"Why?"

"You know why." I look down at my hands, which have finally stopped shaking. "I'm not letting them put you in jail again. Not for that."

"It was self-defense."

"No, it wasn't. And you know it."

Liam stares down at his sneakers, which are caked in a combination of mud and blood. He doesn't contradict me, and I'm glad, because we both know it would be a lie. I'm sick of the lies.

I squeeze my knees with my fingers. "But I'm sorry I

accused you of… well, you know. I was wrong. Obviously."

He doesn't look up. "Well, it's not like you were the only one who thought so. The whole town thought I killed her."

"Yes, but I'm your mother. I should have believed you."

He chews on his lip, his eyes still downcast. "Yeah, but… let's face it—over the years, I gave you plenty of reasons to believe I'd do something like this."

It's true, but it's a shock to hear him admit it. We always pretended like Liam was the perfect son, and he played the role to a tee. "But you didn't do it."

"No. I didn't."

"Also," I add, "I want to thank you."

Liam finally looks up at me. The bruise on his cheek has faded slightly, but it's still there. "For what?"

"You saved my life. You saved Hannah's life. Even though…"

He frowns. "Even though what?"

"Even though…" I clear my throat. "Nothing. Never mind."

He cocks his head to the side. "What?"

I bite my lip, afraid to say the words that have been circling around my brain for the last decade. *Your son doesn't love you. He's not capable of it.* "I know you don't feel… you know…"

Liam is quiet for a moment. "Feel *what*?"

"Dr. Hebert explained it to me," I say quickly. "I know you have trouble with… you know, emotions."

"Emotions?"

"You know, like… love."

"*What*?" Liam blinks at me. "Um, that's bullshit. You really don't think that I love you and Hannah?"

I don't know what to say to that. "It's okay if you don't. It's just who you are."

"Jesus, Mom." He rakes a hand through his dark hair. "I can't believe you're saying that. Of course I love you. You're my mom."

"But Dr. Hebert said—"

"Oh, well, if the quack psychiatrist said it, then it must be true, right?" He snorts. "I just risked my *life* for you. I love you, Mom. If anything happened to you or Hannah…"

He's quiet then, looking down at his hands. "It would be awful," he finally says.

I don't always know if Liam is telling the truth, but at this moment, I know for sure that he is. My son loves me. I always thought he was incapable of it. But I was wrong.

Chapter 65

OLIVIA

I've been in the hospital for five days now and my parents have barely left my side. My mother has been sleeping in my room in a recliner, because she's scared to leave me. I would complain, but the truth is, I'm glad she's here. The last thing I want is to be alone in this hospital room.

I had to have surgery on my ankle. It was broken in two places, and then it got infected on top of that. I needed antibiotics through an IV, and I was also really dehydrated when I came in. My ankle is in a cast now, and the doctor told me it's going to be a while before I can put weight on it again. So I guess I better get used to crutches.

As of yesterday, I finally started feeling up to having visitors besides my parents. The first person who came to see me was Madison, of course. She gave me a huge hug and we both cried and it was like our fight never happened. She told me she never gave up hope that I was okay.

She's back again today. She's sitting at my bedside while my mother is downstairs in the cafeteria, and she's drawing a doodle on my cast. I've never had a cast before, and I'm actually excited for people to sign it. I remember being so jealous of the kids in my class who had a cast and got to have people sign it.

Other than that, it sucks having a cast. The damn thing gets so itchy. I stuck a pencil in there this morning to try to reach an itch on the side of my calf, and the next thing I knew, the pencil was gone! When I take this cast off, half the contents of my desk drawer are going to fall out.

"Leave some room for other people," I say to Madison, whose drawing is getting a little out of control. She's going to be like the John Hancock of my cast.

"Hey, I'm giving your cast an artistic flair." She's not joking around. She actually brought different color markers for just this reason. "You'll thank me later."

As she gets back to work with her design, my nurse comes into the room. "Olivia," she says in a singsong voice. "You've got another visitor."

I must be feeling a lot better, because the thought of having two people with me in this room doesn't fill me with dread. "Who is it?"

"It's a boy. And he's *very* cute." The nurse winks at

me. "He says his name is Liam. Is he your boyfriend?"

Madison freezes, mid doodle. "You're not going to see him, are you?"

"Mad, he saved my life," I murmur.

"Yeah, but if it wasn't for his dad, he wouldn't have had to."

I don't want to admit that I share her hesitation. Liam came to see me yesterday too, and my mother quickly turned him away. I was upset at her, but also a little relieved.

But at the same time, Liam did save my life. When he saw I was trapped, he jumped into that hole without hesitation and picked me up. He carried me into the hospital. He was my hero.

"Send him in," I say.

Madison gives me a look. "Are you sure this is a good idea?"

"It will be fine, but… can you give us a minute alone?"

She holds up one finger. "*One* minute. That's all you're getting, girlie."

Liam steps into my hospital room tentatively, holding a small bouquet of multicolored flowers. Madison shoots him a dirty look, but she steps aside to let him in. He steps towards my bed, holding out the flowers. "Hey. These are for you. The florist said it was, um, a summer assortment."

"Thank you," I say stiffly. "You can put them on the

windowsill."

As he places the assortment next to all the others, I flash back to the last time I saw him. He was crouched in front of his mother's car, his shirt caked in drying blood, and he was coaxing me out of the car to take me into the hospital. He was so gentle with me. It was exactly what I needed.

He drops his eyes. "I'm really glad you're okay," he says.

I study Liam's features. I noticed five days ago that he had a black eye, and it's mostly faded by now, but I can still see slight bruising. "What happened to your face?"

He laughs and touches his cheekbone. "That? Oh, it's nothing."

"So tell me."

"Um, Tyler punched me when he thought I was the one who…"

"Oh."

I only heard a little bit about what happened while I was missing. It sounds like the whole town believed Liam was the one who kidnapped me. The police actually arrested him and took him to jail. While I was locked up, so was he.

"How is your family doing?" I ask.

The smile disappears from Liam's face. "Shitty. My mother cries a lot."

"Do you miss him?"

I hold my breath, waiting for an answer. During the days Jason Cass had me trapped in that hole, I grew to despise him. But I can't forget he's Liam's dad. If I found out my dad were a murderer, would I hate him? It's hard to imagine.

"I don't know, Olivia," he says. "He lied to all of us. There were other women, you know. A lot of others. The police aren't even sure how many… honestly, it makes me sick to think about it."

I suck in a breath, realizing that if Hannah hadn't followed her father that night, I would have joined his long list of victims. And Jason Cass probably would've gotten away with it. Liam may very well have taken the fall.

"I didn't even know him," Liam says. "How can I miss him if I didn't know who he was? None of us knew."

I nod. "I know what you mean."

He smiles crookedly. "Anyway, I'm sure Madison will burst in here any minute to throw me out. And I know for a fact your mom will kill me if she finds me here. So… I just wanted to make sure you're okay. And now I better go."

I look up at him. I keep remembering that moment when he jumped into the hole to save me. Nobody has ever done anything like that for me before. I don't care what kind of person his father was, Liam is very different. He's a good person. He's a hero.

And also, that nurse was right. He *is* very cute. And I still get a little tingle in my lips, remembering how it felt when he kissed me.

"Hey," I say.

He lifts an eyebrow at me. "Yes?"

"When I get out of here," I say, "maybe you'll let me take you out for vanilla milkshakes."

His eyes widen. "Really?"

"Well," I say, "I want to thank you for saving my life."

A slow grin spreads across his face. "I'd be okay with that."

I shrug, but I'm grinning too. "So it's a date?"

"Okay." He nods vigorously. "It's a date."

And we can't stop smiling at each other.

Epilogue

One year later

ERIKA

I've got two eggs in the frying pan that I'm cooking up for breakfast. Low and slow. That's the trick.

I set up a radio on the counter in the kitchen. Liam and Hannah both listen to music on their phones using some crazy app, but I'm old school and like listening to the radio. I like hearing the new pop songs, the insipid DJ banter, and even the commercials. Right now, there's a Bruno Mars song on the radio, and I'm singing along to myself.

"Mo-om," Hannah groans as she looks up from her bowl of Cheerios. "You're getting all the words wrong. If you're going to sing along, don't say all the wrong words."

"I'm getting some of them right."

"You think you are, but you're not."

"Yes, I am."

"You're not. It's *really* cringe-y."

"Well, I don't care." And just to make a point, I belt out the wrong lyrics on purpose: "I'll slap a grenade in ya!"

"Oh my *God*, Mom."

Hannah stands up with her bowl of cereal, unable to tolerate another moment of my singing. She plunks the bowl down on the counter and lets out one more monstrous sigh before she heads upstairs.

I smile to myself as I stir the eggs. One year ago, I never would have imagined we'd be in this same kitchen, making eggs like everything was normal again. Hannah has improved her grades in school, and Liam just got back last night from the state-wide debate competition in Albany, which his team won. Things are back to normal and going as well as they could be, given all the revelations that have come out in the last year.

For example, that my husband was a serial killer.

Yes, that one came as a huge shock. It was bad enough finding out he was responsible for taking Olivia. But Detective Rivera has kept me in the loop, and Jason Cass has now been linked by DNA evidence to twelve murders over the last twenty-five years. And those are only the ones where he left evidence behind. God only knows how many others there were. But because he's dead, we'll never know for sure.

The animosity we experienced when the truth first emerged was overwhelming. I thought we were going to have to leave town and change our names to escape the death threats. But then I was offered a spot on a national news show to tell my story. When I shared the tale of how I discovered my husband's secret, killed him in self-defense, and rescued the girl he kidnapped, I became a national hero. Brian offered me back my spot at the *Nassau Nutshell*, but I turned it down because I got a book deal for quite a lot of money.

Wife of a Serial Killer. Has a ring to it, doesn't it?

As I stir the eggs, Liam sprints through the back door, wearing a damp T-shirt and gym shorts. He was out running early this morning. I don't know how he has the energy after getting back from Albany with the rest of the team late last night. His face is pink and he's grinning ear to ear. "Eggs!" he exclaims when he sees what I've got in the frying pan. "You're making me some, right?"

"Of course."

"They smell amazing," he says. "I'm starving."

He's still smiling as he takes his phone out of his pocket. He's in a *really* good mood this morning, but he's been in a good mood a lot lately. He types a message into his phone with his thumbs, then grins wider when his phone buzzes in response. He's probably texting Olivia.

Amazingly, Liam and Olivia are still together. He's

crazy about her. They go out several nights a week and talk on the phone every night. She's at his track team practice cheering him on every time he runs. They're coordinating which colleges they're applying to, so they can stay together after graduation in June. I'm not sure if it's a great idea— they're only seventeen and have so many new experiences ahead of them. And to be completely frank, Liam is a much more competitive college applicant than Olivia. I don't want him to give up an opportunity on her behalf.

But I can't deny she's good for him. And I certainly can't deny that he loves her. I can tell by the way he looks at her and wants to spend every minute with her.

As for me, I doubt I'll ever date again.

"I'm going to go take a shower now." Liam wipes sweat from his forehead with the back of his arm. "But when I get out, you're going to have eggs for me, right, Mom? Five eggs." He holds up one hand and wiggles his fingers. "*Five*. I'm hungry."

"You got it, kid."

"You're the best, Mom." He kisses me quickly on the cheek and dashes up the stairs to his bedroom, whistling in the hallway. He's in an exceptionally good mood. He must be happy about winning the debate yesterday.

The Bruno Mars song has ended, and the DJ is reading off news stories. I listen idly when I cook the eggs.

JLo is dating somebody new. New York City was determined to be the most expensive city in the country to live. And a girl was reported missing in a town called Troy in upstate New York.

Troy in upstate New York…

I wonder if that's anywhere near Albany.

I lay down my spatula and turn up the volume on the radio. The DJs voice fills the room: "Eighteen-year-old Kayla Rogers went out with her friends on Saturday night. Her friends stayed at a bar, but Kayla left alone. Police say she never returned to the apartment she shared with two other girls…"

My hands won't stop shaking as I pick up my phone from the kitchen counter. I type Troy, NY into the map app. Then I calculate the time it would take for someone to get from Albany to Troy by car.

Sixteen minutes.

My eyes raise upward to the ceiling. I hear the shower running, and even over the droplets of water, I can hear Liam singing to himself.

It couldn't be.

He wouldn't. He's not like that. He's not like Jason. Not really.

It's a coincidence. It's got to be a coincidence.

I lean against the counter, my knees weak. I can still hear Liam singing in the bathroom above us, as the stench of burning eggs fills the kitchen.

THE END

Acknowledgments

Those who know me know that I write my books quick but I edit slowly. I'm very grateful for all the supportive people in my life who help me through the painful editing process. It is incredible how much help I get from the point I finish my first draft to the final version. There are times when things happen in my life to make me realize how lucky I am to have the support I have—friends and family who are always there to give me an opinion or more.

Thank you to Kate, for the positive supportive as well as the awesome and thorough editing job. Thank you to my mother, for the advice on the beginning of the book. Thanks again to Rhona for cover and blurb advice—how many times did I text you??

Thank you to new friends. Thanks to Rebecca, for your great advice. Thanks to Jen, for the thorough critique. Thanks to my new writing group. It's incredible to have that support in my life.

And thank you to the rest of my family. Without your encouragement, none of this would be possible.